ANTIVIRUS

MICHAEL KOOGLER

Antivirus
By Michael Koogler

Copyright © 2015 Michael Koogler

ISBN: 978-0-9961537-3-7

Book editing by Elizabeth Humphrey
Bookworm Editing, Littleton, Colorado USA

Book cover art, packaging and design by
Kreative Storm Press, Coralville, Iowa USA

Other works by Michael Koogler:

Novels

Hade's Gambit

The Rise of Cain

Short Stories

"Jigsaw", **Sadistic Shorts**

"The Summoning", **Sadistic Shorts**

"The Agent", **Never Fear**

And Coming Soon!

Convergence

Antivirus 2, The Awakening

For Bryanna…

…with slobbering wolf kisses

from a **Canus Lupus** *named Dakota*

and cuddly hugs

from a **Chinchilla Lanigera** *named Koda*

Prologue

The worm continued working, effortlessly traversing the global pathways of the internet at speeds incapable of being tracked. It went where it would, seeking the unlimited lines and threads of computer code. It assimilated, rewrote, and reprogrammed a thousand times a second, and every time that it did, it grew in strength, in size, and in intelligence. Already far beyond the initial parameters of its creation, it had recently added a new phase to its structure. It was capturing voice and video streams. It had not yet figured out what the significance of the new data was or how much of a threat the source was, but it was learning. In time, it would understand. Once it did, it would know whether to assimilate the source…or destroy it.

Chapter 1

Sherrard Residence, Helena, Montana: Jennifer Sherrard leaned back in her chair and drew her long legs underneath herself. She let her hand dangle over the arm of the recliner, absentmindedly tangling her fingers in the thick fur of Dakota, their grey wolf family member, who reclined lazily beside her. The regal-looking canus lupus was more black than grey, but whatever his true color, he reigned supreme in the Sherrard household. Raised from an orphaned pup when a rancher killed his mother—on Sherrard land, no less—Dakota had filled the childless void in the Sherrard's lives for nearly six years. Tonight, he was doing duty as Jen's confidant, lying within easy reach of her as she continued to debate her husband's announcement.

"Come on, Jen," Jon Sherrard went on, continuing an argument that had been going on for some time. "It's not like I haven't done this before."

"And I've never liked you doing it, either," she replied evenly. "Why you?"

"I'm a test pilot. I'm *their* test pilot," he answered in exasperation.

"There are others."

"Not for this and you know it."

She sighed and lowered her head, letting her long raven-colored hair fall over her face. For her husband Jon, that signified the end of the discussion and a hard-fought victory for him. He knelt beside her then, reaching out and running his hand tenderly along her cheek, before gently lifting her chin so that he could look into her deep blue eyes.

"Look," he said softly, mindful of her feelings, but wishing to make the obvious point he had been working on the entire argument. "You spent ten years in the agency and I never said a word. You've been involved in assignments that should have been the death of you, and several times, nearly were. I spent ten years wondering if your current mission was finally going to be the one that delivered you back to me in a box."

"That's not fair, Jon," Jen replied, her eyes glistening.

"It's not supposed to hurt, hon," he soothed, leaning forward and kissing her gently on the forehead. "It's just...well, you have to trust me," he switched tactics, trying to downplay what he was actually going to be doing in that pilot's chair. "Remember, you were out hunting down bad guys for a decade. I'm only playing with computers with a bunch of genius-level nerds."

"*In* computers," she corrected, giving him a hard look.

"What's the difference?"

"Everything."

"Look, I'll be fine."

"Said the dumb jock before telling his friends, 'Ya'll watch this!'" She forced a smile, but the worry and concern never left her face.

"It's just a bunch of computers, babe."

"You were safer in the air," she dead-panned.

Jon Sherrard smiled and sat down on the floor, pausing to scratch behind Dakota's ears, which elicited a low growl—the wolf's way of saying, *"If you stop now, I'll tear your arm off."* "I could always go back," he teased, referring to his past career as an actual fighter jet test pilot. "There's a lot of next generation equipment needing someone to run it through the grinder."

"Over my dead body," she quipped.

"Would you rather I just tie on an apron and confine myself to the kitchen?" he asked. "Would that better place me in the realm of acceptable house-husband for Jen Sherrard, Super Spy?"

"At least you'd be safe," she replied. "And I'd get an occasional good meal out of it."

With a chuckle, he leaned forward and kissed her knee and she dropped her head down to rest her forehead against his. It would have been an intimate moment between husband and wife had Dakota not stuck his own huge head up between them, immediately bathing them both with slobbering wolf kisses. Always in tune with his human companions, he had been uneasy during their argument. Now that it was over, he had no problem letting them know he was relieved.

"You better do something about your *dog*," Jon said, playfully pushing the big wolf away.

"Me? You were the one that saved him."

"Oh yeah, that's right," he replied, grabbing Dakota's ears as the big animal barreled back into him, growling playfully. "Beat it, doofus!" he lamented, before getting completely bowled over and managing to pull his wife off the chair at the same time. Laughter and happy wolf barks and howls filled the Sherrard household for some time after that.

It was nearly three in the morning when Jen Sherrard came awake, still lying naked in her husband's arms after a passionate night of lovemaking, their way of telling each other everything was going to be all right. She managed a smile as she listened to Jon and Dakota, who was sleeping peacefully across the lower half of their bed, competing against each other for the loudest snore.

She lay awake for nearly an hour, once again seriously contemplating what her husband was about to do. Taking risks was something that both of them had done plenty of times in the past; he with his flying and she with her gun. But this? This was more than she felt she was willing to accept. And now, with more to lose than ever, she was frightened.

She paused to remind herself that Jon's employer, FutureTek, was a good company with good people, and Kat Hale was one of their dearest friends. Kat would never put Jon's life in danger and she knew that. But how could Kat be sure? How could any of them be certain? Where Jon was planning on going was a place no one in history had ever visited before. How could anyone know what he would find? How could anyone know that he would truly be safe?

She placed her hand gently on her belly, thinking of the tiny life growing within her, wondering if the miracle would finally hold— desperate that it would. It was nearly dawn before she fell back into a fitful sleep.

Chapter 2

FutureTek Headquarters, Helena, Montana: Jon Sherrard yawned deeply while listening to the music of Fireflight's newest release humming in his ear piece. He was far from tired, but as calm as he could get. Relaxation, of course, was standard protocol for someone getting ready to make the journey he would be making within the hour. Getting wound up was not only pointless, it could be extremely dangerous. He thought back to his discussion with Jen the previous night and allowed himself to smile. He loved his wife deeply and he understood her concern for him. After all, he had experienced the same apprehension for her safety before she retired, hadn't he? So, her worry was not misplaced and this was admittedly not just any test flight, either. But it was an opportunity to do something no one had ever done before and make him a pioneer in a field that did not even exist on a public level yet. He could not pass that up.

"You scared?" a voice spoke quietly from the doorway.

Sherrard didn't turn as his friend stepped into the room and shut the door. "You're not supposed to be in here, Perry," he admonished, but grinning nonetheless.

Perry Edwards took a seat near Jon's reclining lounger. He was middle-aged, a couple years younger than Jon, but worry lines creased his forehead deeply and made him look far older. He had been friends with Jon for years, having struck up the relationship during their days in the military sector when Perry was designing aircraft and Jon was testing them high above the ground. "You didn't answer my question," he pressed.

"A little," Sherrard admitted. "We're flying free this morning, Perry. First time jitters, I guess."

"You've done it before."

"True, but that was a closed environment," he replied. "Today we're opening the gates to a world no one has ever seen."

"You know we should have waited and done open world tests before a big presentation like this," Perry said tiredly, rubbing his eyes and falling silent. He hadn't slept in more than twenty-four hours, preparing for this day for longer even than Jon.

"You know what they say," Sherrard responded. "No better time than the present."

"But would it have hurt to wait it out for a bit, do some testing while no one was watching? Then do a bigger presentation? Imagine doing this at a consumer electronics show!"

"You know how Drew is," Jon sighed. "He's always looking over his shoulder, thinking someone else is going to score before we do. We come out first, we control the game."

"Or at least the money."

"There's that, yeah. But we're ready, Perry. You know that. Drew would never let us wait."

Perry was silent, fighting the fatigue. He had been working his own magic on the project as a developer and knew Jon was right, probably more than Jon actually did. If they waited and someone hit it before they did, they would lose everything, and he would lose even more. As it was, Systemtech controlled the market and had the wallet to bankroll the new technology and right now, they had Systemtech's attention. That allowed him the lateral movement to complete his own personal agenda in the release. He had to keep telling himself that he was almost there. He simply had to time things right.

"Have you ever thought about what's really out there?" Jon said after the silence had stretched for a couple of minutes, drawing Perry back to the present. "Or in there," he amended.

"Data, I suppose," Perry shrugged, feigning boredom. "Endless streams of data for you to play with, no different than the sandbox you've been playing in for the past few months."

"There's life beyond any sandbox, my friend. Don't you ever wonder what it might be? What hidden place we might uncover?"

"Well, I'm pretty sure it isn't going to turn into some Tron universe," Perry chuckled. "Sorry, pal, no light cycles for you."

Sherrard smiled and settled a little deeper into his chair. He still had an hour or so to go before they fetched him for the run. Plenty of time to stay relaxed and maybe even nap a little. "What are you going to do if we sell, Perry?" he asked.

"If you make a clean run and this Systemtech fat-cat is satisfied, they're going to drop a high nine digits in our lap, possibly ten," Edwards replied. "I can't even imagine that much money, but I can tell you that I'm definitely going to spend my share of it. I think I've earned the chance at a good life."

"Didn't your mom ever teach you to save your money for a rainy day?" Sherrard chuckled.

"I've never had it to save," was the truthful reply, and Sherrard caught the barest hint of anger in his friend's voice. "I've scratched all my life and I'm done scratching, Jon. We're going to nail this and then

I'm gone. I figure I've got half a lifetime still to live and I intend on living it in style."

"Whatever floats your boat," Jon said with a smile, closing his eyes again. "I guess you've earned it."

"Perry!" a new voice called out as the door to the quiet room opened again. "What on earth are you doing in here?"

"Just leaving, doc," Perry said as he quickly stood up. He glanced at the angry woman in the white coat and couldn't help but chuckle. Doctor Diane Faust was every bit the strict physician disciplinarian that she looked—white lab coat, black-rimmed glasses, perpetual angry scowl. Only her angry scowl at the moment said that she was truly pissed off.

"It's okay, Diane," Jon spoke up, coming to his friend's defense. "We were just having a nice relaxing chat, nothing more."

"I don't care. Protocol states that you are to be left alone before engaging in the process," she said quietly to him. Turning back to Edwards, she continued, her voice regaining its hard edge. "You should know that better than anyone, Mister Edwards," she said. "Now get out of here."

"I'm leaving, doc," Perry said, clearly amused. Reaching out, he patted his friend on the shoulder. "Knock 'em dead, Jon. I'm going home, so get this baby landed for me, will ya?"

"Not going to wait around for any fireworks?"

"Are you kidding? I have all the faith in the world in you, but if this does go south, I don't even want to be here to see it."

"We'll be fine."

"Oh, I'm sure you will be, Jon," Edwards said. "Which is why I am going to go home and sleep while dreaming happy money-filled dreams." With that, he walked out of the room, pausing long enough to throw an exaggerated wink toward the irate doctor.

"How are your vitals?" Faust asked Sherrard as Perry swept past her and left. She shot him a final angry glance and then turned back to the man in the chair.

"Everything is nominal," he replied, looking at a bracelet on his left wrist that was cycling through his physical readings. "Heart rate, breathing, blood pressure—all green. I'm about as relaxed as I'm going to get."

"Good," she said, her demeanor softening. "You have about an hour, so I'll leave you be. And I'll make sure you're not bothered by anyone else," she added.

Without waiting for a reply, she ducked out of the room, shutting the door softly behind her. Jon Sherrard sighed and closed his eyes, taking in the music again and thinking positive thoughts. He focused on happy memories, time spent with his wife and their adopted pseudo-son, Dakota. It wouldn't do to focus on the task at hand and whether it would or would not be dangerous. He was committed now and was going to do it no matter what, so he might as well simply let his mind wander for the time being.

He had no idea just how literal that thought would become.

Chapter 3

FutureTek Headquarters, Helena, Montana: "Kat," David Rivers said as he stuck his head inside her office, beaming broadly. "They're here."

Kathryn "Kat" Hale allowed herself to smile with him. After all, they had been working toward this day for nearly four years now, and with a successful demonstration of the new technology, not only would they all be rich beyond their wildest imaginations, but FutureTek would suddenly be on the map, a new giant among giants.

"Where's Jon?" she asked as she stood up and pulled out a small compact. She surveyed herself critically in the small mirror, looking for anything that might detract from the long-awaited meeting with the technology world's super power. She needn't have worried, though. Kat Hale could have taken a four-wheel ATV through a mud bog and still come out looking just fine. She was tall and willowy, her slender figure filling out her one and only navy blue business suit quite nicely. She wore little makeup, but then she really didn't need to. Her features were smooth and flawless, almost waifish, and her long auburn hair was pulled back into a tight ponytail, giving her appearance a somewhat maverick-looking flair. She quickly smoothed her skirt and looked back at David, her ice-blue eyes flashing.

"Getting ready himself," David said, stepping fully into the office. "And you look just fine, Kat."

"Thanks," she replied. "I'd better. There's a lot riding on this."

"Well, to be honest with you, you could look like the Wicked

Witch of the West and the product will still sell itself."

Kat shot him a withering look. "I appreciate the vote of confidence."

"Hey, I was just kidding," Rivers said, throwing up his hands in mock surrender.

"Well, don't," she replied sternly and moved around the desk toward the door. "At least wait until after the presentation. Then I can get out of this morgue attire and we can all suitably cut loose and celebrate."

"Nervous?"

"Are you kidding?" she answered, feigning shock. "I'm absolutely petrified."

"Well, stop worrying, will you? This is our tech. We know it works and Jon is the bomb. He'll put on a great show."

"Yeah, but this is live. We're out of the box today, Dave."

"We've done this lots of times, Kat."

"But never with a billion dollars in the swing," she answered, "and never with an open gate."

"Would you relax?" he cut in, exasperated. "We're fine, Kat. Everything will work out perfectly. I promise."

She gave him an appreciative look and then walked past him and into the hall. David Rivers, head lab technician for FutureTek, fell in behind her.

"Are the honeypots ready?" she asked as they walked.

"Online and infested," he answered happily. "I put out the first one last night and the other two went online this morning. All three are showing various worm hits. Jon will have his pick of the litter."

"We need to make sure the virus infestations are verified by Systemtech's people," she cautioned.

"Already taking care of it, Kat."

"Where's Drew?"

"Schmoozing as we speak," Rivers replied. "You don't think he would be doing anything else at this point, do you?"

"Sounds like we're about as ready as we're going to get, David," she answered and then pushed through a set of double doors into the largest room in the building that was home to FutureTek, the tiny technology firm that was about to become front page news all over the world.

The room was little more than a large working lab with numerous computer work-stations around the perimeter and enough wiring and cabling to stretch several miles. In the center of the room was a large barbershop chair, its armrests bristling with unattached electrodes, wires, and finger pads. The wires led to a bulky looking machine sitting next to it that resembled several desktop PCs cobbled together into the most bizarre-looking apparatus. From that machine, additional wires snaked across a table into three separate, normal-looking computers.

At the computer terminals, a sandy-haired young man named Alex Jordan was walking three black-suited men through a virus check using their own software. Jordan was one of FutureTek's young wiz kids and was an absolute genius when it came to viruses and trojans and what made them tick. Kat could hear him reciting off the names of several viruses that had apparently infected the three PCs, known as honeypots for the particular configuration they used to attract the various worms and viruses that were always crawling about the internet. A fifth man, also wearing a business suit, stood nearby, nervously folding and refolding his hands as he watched.

As Kat walked in, the anxious man, Andrew Jackson—Drew, as he was known to his employees—looked toward her. He was the president of the little tech firm and brightened immediately when he saw her. "Kat!" he exclaimed, obviously relieved to have something to occupy his time while Jordan worked. He motioned to the three business men who had all straightened and turned around. "Come and meet our distinguished guests."

Kat put on her best smile and extended her hand as she walked up to them. "Kat Hale, lead program designer," she introduced herself smartly, firmly clasping the first hand extended to her.

"Michael Monroe," the man intoned with a smile. "Chief operations officer of Systemtech. And may I introduce you to Allen Turner, lead programmer, and Dan Hyde, our top security specialist."

"It's a pleasure," the young woman answered, flashing a brilliant smile and turning to indicate the man that had accompanied her. "This is David Rivers, FutureTek's lead lab technician and resident technology wizard."

Handshakes and polite greetings were exchanged all around and then Michael Monroe spoke up, taking the conversational lead and getting right down to the business at hand. "This is some pretty amazing technology you're dealing with, Miss Hale," he said, giving Kat a knowing smile.

"We believe it is, Mister Monroe," she agreed. "In this high-tech world, we believe the only way to succeed is by breaking down the barriers and forging ahead into new frontiers."

"Well, you've certainly done that," the man replied. "If the presentation videos we have seen are to be believed, then you are breaking ground never before seen."

"That's been our goal."

"Break it down for me once again, Miss Hale," he went on, just the slightest trace of condescension in his voice, as if he did not quite believe what he had heard about FutureTek's new toy. "I understand that, to date, your testing has been done on closed systems. Is that correct?"

"Precisely," Kat answered, ignoring the hint of skepticism. Moving to the large machine that was the central hub of FutureTek's new technology, she continued. "All of our testing has been done on closed systems simply for the sheer unpredictability of the internet."

"But the technology is not viable as a closed machine entity," Dan Hyde broke in, his voice almost bitter with undisguised contempt. He was certainly not afraid to show it, either. "It becomes nothing more than a novelty."

"Agreed," said Kat, maintaining her composure in the face of the early challenge and doing her best to ignore the man's contempt. "But for the past two weeks, we have been conducting extended testing on linked machines, and the success has been excellent. We believe that the transition to the open world of cyberspace will be seamless."

"You're taking quite a gamble then," Monroe added. "Is it the rational approach or a touch of desperation?"

"Maybe a little bit of both, if you don't mind me saying," she answered without elaborating. "But all things considered, if you're present for the first live run through, the result is a little more genuine."

"Point taken," Monroe replied with a nod.

"How are you doing it?" This time it was Allen Turner who asked and he made no attempt to hide his amazement, which was in stark contrast to the attitude displayed by the company's security specialist.

"With this," Kat answered proudly, laying a hand on the large machine. "This is the hub, as we call it. It's not pretty, but it does the job. This is what drives the process."

"You must use an enormous amount of memory to pre-program counters and fixes," Turner went on. "How do you know you can even cover it all? The maintenance uploads would have to be almost continuous."

Kat smiled broadly, silently grateful for the perfect question. "That's the beauty of the system," she explained. "We don't require any memory at all."

"Impossible," Hyde scoffed, and there was no mistaking that the man thought very little of what FutureTek was hoping to accomplish.

"No, it's not impossible," she countered quickly, remaining calm. "The hub is simply the vehicle. The brains behind the machine come from whoever sits in the chair," she finished, indicating the empty barber chair next to the table. "The driver is what makes this all work."

"So, you're telling me that the person operating this system is doing so on his own memory and not simply manipulating preprogrammed memory packets?" Monroe asked, holding up a hand and cutting off his security specialist before he could disagree again.

"Exactly," Kat said, her smile never wavering. "This technology is only limited by the mind behind it, and the particular mind we are talking about today is Jon Sherrard. He's been with FutureTek since its inception and he's a crack computer expert, among other things."

"So memory is not an issue?"

"No, sir," she shook her head.

"And you rely on the intelligence of the operator then?"

"We do. But to be honest, we originally approached this project from the direction you initially indicated," she explained. "The idea was to have a driver manipulate pre-determined codes and instructions to eliminate a virus. In effect, we were simply making a human copy of an antivirus program and we quickly realized that took the intuition out of the equation and ultimately did nothing to advance or improve our ability to deal with malicious coding or damaged software."

"But today's worms adapt and change to given situations," Turner put in, understanding better than the other two where the young woman was going with her explanation.

"Exactly," Kat agreed. "Doing it the old way quickly brought into play the limitations of the technology. A cyberspace toolbox for our driver could be outdated and obsolete before he even made contact with a worm or a virus. So, we altered our direction, instead deciding to rely on the intelligence and ingenuity of the human mind. A computer virus may be smart, but its actions are still based on its programming. So its intelligence is limited to the finite area of its programming. A human mind, however, has no such limitations."

"So the person using the technology would have to be up-to-date on the latest virus info."

"Somewhat," she answered, "but nothing like us having to update virus programs as we do today. You see, because the driver has the ability to think, he might find half a dozen different ways to defeat or deconstruct a virus or a worm when he's looking directly at it. While today's viruses are smart, they are still only so much coding, and it's the coding that the driver repairs or manipulates."

"How?" the security specialist snapped.

"Any number of different ways," Kat said, standing him down. "The driver might be in the virus's domain, but that also affords him the ability to easily see the coding, almost like it was a tangible object right before his eyes. He can then reform the malicious coding, simply delete it, or even rewrite or reformat the virus to act out a non-malicious result. The possibilities are endless."

"That is absolutely fascinating," Michael Monroe said, allowing a broad smile to grace his handsome face. "And all this time, we were under the impression that your driver was simply maneuvering the required programs within the system. You have taken this technology to a potential that we had only briefly considered."

"You are impressed then?" Drew Jackson asked, beaming himself as he leaned into the conversation.

"Indeed, we are," Monroe answered. "But obviously, we're here to see it first-hand. Whether we remain impressed is going to rely heavily on what we see here today."

"Then let's not waste any time," Jackson said enthusiastically. "Kat, how's Jon?"

"He's in prep," David Rivers answered for her. "He ought to be ready to go shortly."

"What kind of prep-work are you talking about?" Hyde asked, his perpetual scowl of suspicion still locked on his face.

"Standard medical safeguards," Kat explained. "As successful as we have been to date, we're still dealing with a brand new and relatively untested field. We don't know if there's any long-term side effects yet, and probably won't until after years of testing. But we've found that the best success is attained when the human brain is relaxed and focused. So, we put our driver under a minimum of an hour's observation before he goes and, if he's not sufficiently calm, we scrub the run."

"What about drugs?" Hyde pressed.

"We've never used them, nor do we intend to and it's certainly not something I would recommend," Kat replied. "There are just too many unknowns. We want the driver in complete control of his mind."

"Understandable," Monroe agreed. "Have you had any side effects whatsoever?"

"Nothing really," she answered. "Our records are open for you to check, complete with video. But outside of minor anomalies or a glitch here and there with such a new technology, it's been pretty smooth sailing."

"What kind of anomalies?" Hyde asked quickly.

"Well," Kat said, clearing her throat. "We actually communicate directly with our driver while he's in the machine. It's a simple speech program that projects through the system speakers. There have been a few instances where we've lost communication for brief moments, but we have attributed it to simple lag spikes, nothing more. Jon has done countless closed box test runs and has never experienced any physical or mental complications of any kind."

"What about with the linked machines?" Hyde continued to press.

"No anomalies," she answered easily. "Jon is healthy and exhibits no side-effects from the disassociation, other than a short period of re-adjustment after ending a session and returning to his body. But that's normal."

"So when do we get to see him in action?" Monroe asked with a broad smile. "I am truly excited to see your demonstration." Apparently he did not share his security specialist's cynicism.

"Right now," a new voice answered and all heads turned toward the door as Jon Sherrard entered the room.

Chapter 4

FutureTek Headquarters, Helena, Montana: Jon was a tall, rangy man with tousled black hair and warm brown eyes. He was flanked by a woman who was quite obviously a physician, complete with clipboard and stethoscope draped around her neck. He stuck out his hand as he strode forward and clasped Michael Monroe's hand firmly. "Jon Sherrard," he greeted.

"Michael Monroe," answered the COO of Systemtech who then introduced his two employees.

"A pleasure to meet everybody," Sherrard said easily, "and this here is our good doctor, Diane Faust."

Faust merely nodded with the introduction, her look unemotional.

"You ready for this, Jon?" Jackson asked, looking at the man with more than hopeful eyes.

"As long as Doc has me cleared, I'm all set," he answered.

"He's cleared," Faust said softly, offering her clipboard to Monroe. "You may look at his vitals if you wish."

The head of Systemtech took it, scanned it quickly, and then shrugged and handed it back to the physician. "Looks fine to me," he said with a smile, hardly caring what the numbers said. He just wanted to see if the technology he was getting ready to spend a billion dollars on was going to be the next frontier for mankind.

"Then let's get started," Jackson said, rubbing his hands together.

Jon Sherrard seated himself in the central chair and leaned back and relaxed as Rivers and Faust began attaching electrodes to his arms, temples, and forehead.

As they worked, Monroe asked with extreme interest, looking directly at Sherrard, "What's it like?"

"It's a trip," Jon said with a smile. "Out-of-body about covers things, I suppose."

"What do you see when you're in there?"

"That's hard to explain, sir. I can't actually see, since I don't take my eyes into the machine with me. But I can sort of feel the images in my brain and somehow know what the coding is, kind of like a dream. It's a weird sensation and it took me a few times to get used to it. Now, it's just a walk in the park."

"How about when you come out?" Hyde asked.

"It's kind of like coming off a pretty wild amusement park ride," he answered. "It's pretty disorienting at first, but it passes quickly."

"What about when you're in the machine?" Monroe pressed. "Are you aware of physical sensations in reality?"

"We've actually run several tests on that," Kat stepped in. "As far as we can ascertain, when Jon's conscience is in the machine, there is no response to physical stimulus. His vital signs are monitored the entire time and there has never been a problem. Heart, respiration, etc. all continue normally."

"Have you tried external stimulation?"

"Yes, we have," she answered. "From temperature sensations to actual pin pricks, yet there has been no physical response to any of it. Jon can feel nothing."

"Is that true, Mister Sherrard?" Monroe asked.

"Spot on, sir. We've tried a lot of different things. Even had my wife come in one time and kiss me and try…er…other things," he stammered, suddenly embarrassed.

"And you weren't aware of anything?"

"No, sir."

"So his conscious has truly left his body, then," Monroe said, turning to address Jackson. "That is most extraordinary. You do realize there are some wonderful medical possibilities here as well? Imagine the opportunities in dealing with coma patients or someone with Alzheimer's. You have here a technology that could allow a patient to leave their damaged brain and converse with their doctors or family members. The potential is off the charts!"

"It has crossed our minds," Drew laughed a little too loudly.

"Well, then," said Monroe, clapping his hands together. "I think you have answered all of our questions for now, so let's see your demonstration. Let's see what Systemtech is considering buying," he finished with a hint of mischievousness.

"You are satisfied with the test bed then?" Kat asked, nodding her head toward the three machines.

"We are," Hyde said curtly, sounding almost disappointed that he didn't find any trickery. "All three systems check out."

"Jon?" Kat asked, turning to the seated man.

"I'm ready to go," he answered easily, flexing his fingers before placing them on the armrest keypads. As soon as he did, Rivers immediately looped small pieces of Velcro over them, securing them in place.

"What are the pads for?" Allen Turner asked, peering closer.

"This is what I use to initiate contact with the hub," Jon answered the question. "There is some mechanical manipulation involved to get me inside. It's almost like opening a gate. Once I'm in, the keypads are not used again during the session."

"What is the concept used to initiate mental contact with the hub?"

"To put it in the simplest terms, the hub reads his alpha waves through the electrodes," Kat explained. "He uses his hands to input some specific program commands to open the gate and then his conscience is able to slip right in, like any other electrical current. That's how it works in layman's terms, anyway. Full technical disclosure will happen upon completion of the business transaction," she said with a sly smile.

"Indeed," Monroe laughed.

"All right everybody," Doctor Faust spoke up. "We are ready to begin, so until he's engaged, everyone needs to be silent. This is new territory and I won't have anyone interrupting his concentration."

The silence was immediate and all eyes turned to Jon, but the man had already closed his eyes. Doctor Faust locked her gaze on a small computer screen showing his vitals. For almost a minute, nothing happened. Then Jon's fingers began moving over the keypads, making a soft tapping sound. After a few seconds, they stopped. Almost immediately, Jon's voice was the first to break the silence, only now it was originating from the hub and had a somewhat robotic sound to it. "I'm in," he said.

"Can you hear me okay, Jon?" Kat asked as she looked at the machine.

"Loud and clear, Kat," he answered.

"Remarkable," Monroe said quietly under his breath, looking from the unmoving body of Sherrard in the chair and back to the machine, where Jon's voice was sounding from. "His lips do not even move."

Kat smiled and explained. "They can't. The voice you are hearing is Jon's thoughts, being read into the hub and translated into speech. I apologize for the robotic sound, but we haven't been as concerned with aesthetics as making the actual technology work."

"Understood," Monroe said, taking it all in, his face eager.

"I'm ready when you are," Sherrard said from the machine. "Let's get this party started."

David Rivers looked up from his place at the head of the machine, keyboard on his lap, fingers poised.

Kat hesitated for only a moment, knowing this was it—the moment of no turning back. And there wasn't. They had come too far. "Proceed," she said quietly.

"Roger that," Rivers replied, his fingers flying over his keyboard. "Opening the internet gate now, Jon." A moment later: "You're free to navigate to the honeypots."

There was silence in the room as all eyes focused on Jon.

"Jon?" Kat asked tentatively.

"Still here," his voice sounded from the hub. "This is all new, so it's slow going. Bear with me. The vastness is incredible."

"What do you see?" Monroe asked breathlessly.

"Nothing. But then again, everything," came the cryptic reply. "I feel it all around me. It's like it's alive. Wow. I just…I just can't explain it."

"Never really was the poetic type," Rivers chuckled as he placed the keyboard on the table and then began manually checking connections along the hub.

"Jon, remember what your task is," Kat said, suppressing a smile. "You're not being paid to go sightseeing."

"Oh right, virus checking time." Another few moments of silence. "Okay, I'm here. Down and dirty with the hard drive."

"Everything okay?" she asked.

"Fine," he answered quickly. "Are our guests still on board?"

"Right here," Michael Monroe said.

"I'm in machine number three," Sherrard went on. "You have a listing of the active worms?"

"I see them. They're right on the screen," Monroe answered, looking at one of the monitors as Rivers pointed out the data. "There are six of them showing."

"That's what I've got," Jon agreed. "Shall we get to it?"

"Certainly, but go after the fourth virus on the list first," Monroe said slyly.

"Yes, sir," Sherrard laughed.

All eyes went to the monitor and the real-time readout of the viruses that were currently infecting it. As they all watched, the fourth one suddenly went from red to green and then disappeared. The game was on.

There was a murmur of approval from the Systemtech

representatives, and Monroe then began directing Jon Sherrard through the repairs of the other five viruses. When he had completed that, Monroe sent him into the other two machines and occasionally between the two of them, picking his targets at random. Each time he did, Sherrard cleaned it up. For nearly fifteen minutes, Sherrard performed flawlessly, and when he was done, Monroe clapped his hands. "Phenomenal work," he said with a smile. "Absolutely brilliant!"

"Aww, twarn't nothin', sir," Sherrard's voice deadpanned in its computer-generated monotone.

"Now tell me, Mister Sherrard, how exactly did you do all that?"

"Well, it's a simple matter of accessing the information directly from the hard drive or the boot sector, wherever the problem might be found. I then recode things from the hard drive on up," Jon's voice answered. "In this case, I simply deleted the malicious coding, in effect killing the worm."

"So you can affect other repairs as well, besides just dealing with viruses?"

"Sure can," Sherrard answered, knowing this would be part of their presentation. "Kat?"

Kat Hale reached out and picked up a flash drive they had prepared earlier and then handed it to Monroe. "This thumb drive has been purposefully damaged, having some of its information stuck in damaged sectors. It's not a total loss, but should provide an adequate challenge. Jon will move the data from the damaged sectors into an undamaged one, thereby recovering it. He can then isolate the damaged sectors and render them inert. That way, additional data cannot be placed in them at a later date." She turned and was almost ready to place the stick in one of the many ports on the hub when Monroe touched her hand to stop her and held out his other hand.

"May I?" he asked politely.

Kat hesitated only for a moment and then turned the drive over to him. "Certainly," she said, wondering what the man was up to. "Standby, Jon," she added.

Monroe took the disk and then turned and handed it to Dan Hyde, who immediately reached down and picked up a laptop computer that he had brought with him. With deft hands, he popped the computer open and then placed the stick in its own USB port. In a matter of seconds, he had a diagnostic running on the damaged disk. A minute later, it confirmed what Kat had said.

"You understand, Miss Hale, that it's not about trust," Monroe said easily. "I simply want to see how Mister Sherrard adapts to a curve ball."

"I understand completely," Kat answered flatly, but her nerves felt on edge. There was nothing about their presentation that was dishonest, but she was understandably nervous about any possible glitches popping up with the unknown.

"Excellent," Monroe said and motioned to Hyde, who reached into his bag and produced a linking cable. The security specialist plugged one end into his laptop and handed the other end to Rivers, who cast a questioning glance at Kat. After a moment's hesitation, she nodded and Rivers plugged the other end into one of the hub's USB ports. "Mr. Sherrard," Monroe went on, "I would like you to repair this disk, but do it on Mr. Hyde's machine. Can you do that?"

Kat started to say something, but Monroe quickly held up a hand to silence her, while waiting for Sherrard's answer.

"Well, it might take me some time to locate it, but yeah, I should be able to do that," Jon's voice finally said hesitantly after a long pause. "I think I will probably need…."

"We have hard-linked Mister Hyde's laptop to the hub this time," Monroe cut him off, a bit too smugly. "So you should be able to go right to it. Perhaps in future demonstrations, we can see how good you are at wireless hide-and-seek."

After another pause, Jon answered. "Sure," he said. A moment later, he added. "I see it." Hyde's laptop started working and they all watched in anticipation as the flash drive began to boot.

"Accessing the drive now," Sherrard's voice continued. On screen, the drive went through a number of failed boot routines, each time followed by various error messages. After several minutes, the drive rebooted and this time, the disk contents popped onto the screen. "Finished," Sherrard's voice said with his own trace of smugness.

"Remarkable," Monroe breathed in amazement.

"Would you like me to display some other files for you? There's some large files on the primary hard drive here that are likely pics or videos, if my guess is correct."

"No, that won't be necessary," Hyde interrupted and quickly lowered the laptop's lid.

"Well, I have to say, I'm truly impressed," said Monroe appreciatively, casting a sour glance at his security specialist before turning back to face Kat. "That was a most convincing demonstration. You understand, Miss Hale, that we needed to ascertain the feasibility of this new technology operating correctly under less-than-controlled circumstances."

Kat nodded, quietly breathing a sigh of relief that it had worked out as well as it had. "I understand perfectly, Mister Monroe."

Sherrard's voice came back through the hub, a note of concern in it. "Hey, Kat?"

"What is it, Jon?"

"Take a look at number two, will you? What do you guys make of that?"

Immediately, all eyes turned toward the monitor, which still showed all three machines clear of viruses.

"What am I looking for?" Kat asked, somewhat confused.

"You don't see it?"

"No," she replied. "Our board is green."

A pause. "There's something going on in here, Kat."

"Jon, I don't see anything. The read is clear. Nothing in the honeypots..." Her voice trailed off as the display suddenly blazed with colors, then went into emergency diagnostic mode. "Jon? What just happened?"

"Pull the plug!" his robotic voice suddenly screamed from the system. "Pull it! Pull it now!"

"Jon?" Kat pressed, panic rising within her.

This time, there was no answer.

"Jon!?" she asked more insistently.

Silence.

"What's going on?" Monroe demanded, his smile gone.

Kat ignored him and threw herself into the chair, her fingers flying over the keyboard. "David! Isolate the honeypots!"

Even as she was speaking, Rivers ran around the table, manually tearing out the hard lines to the three machines.

"Jon!" she nearly screamed in frustration this time.

"Honeypots are offline!" Rivers shouted, true horror in his own voice.

"Jon, talk to me!" Kat exclaimed, pulling up several diagnostic screens, her fingers flying as she scanned the readings.

"What's going on here?" Monroe demanded again.

"I don't know," Kat snapped. "Looks like something is in the system."

"What about Mister Sherrard?"

Kat ignored the question and paused for just a moment, looking at the computer screen. The changing diagnostic readings told her all she needed to know. She spun out of her chair and ripped the wires out of the back of the hub.

"What are you doing, Kat?" Drew yelled, looking at her with a wild look in his eyes.

Kat spun back to the system and quickly powered it down. Then she sat back with a devastated sigh and stared blankly at the now-dead screen.

"Kat?" Rivers asked, his voice shaking. "What just happened?"

She shook her head.

"Kat," he pushed, laying a hand on her shoulder. "Where's Jon?"

She continued to stare at the dead screen. "He's in there," she finally whispered.

"There's no power to the computer," Monroe snapped angrily. "You just killed your driver!"

She shook her head again. "No, Mister Monroe," she answered quietly. "A power outage is harmless. We've already tested it. He's still in there. We just need to think this through before we go retrieve him."

"Then what just happened?" he demanded.

She paused before answering, her voice a whisper. "It's the Horde."

Chapter 5

St. Peter's Hospital, Helena, Montana: The soft beep of the heart monitor was the only sound in the room as Jen Sherrard sat by the hospital bed where her husband lay. The official medical diagnosis was coma, but Jen knew there was more to it than that. She knew what her husband did with FutureTek and now, as he lay motionless on the hospital bed, all her arguments had come roaring back to her. She wanted to shake him, to scream at him *"See what I mean?"* But Jon would never hear her, because he wasn't there.

"How's he doing?" asked a soft voice from the doorway.

Jen turned her tear-stained face toward the door and forced herself to remain calm. The woman standing there was the obvious target for her simmering anger and frustration, but she wasn't yet ready to unleash it on her. "He's alive, Kat," she said simply, before turning back to watch her husband's unmoving face.

Kat stood in the doorway for several moments before entering the room and quietly pulling a chair over to sit next to the other woman. The two women had been friends for years, all the way back to their college days. Their paths had diverged after graduation, when Kat had thrown herself into her career and stayed single, while Jennifer had worked her way into government contract work, eventually catching on as a field agent with the Agency. Jen also married one of their college friends, the very man who lay motionless in the hospital bed in front of them, who was also a one-time flame of Kat's. It had never been a point of contention between the two of them, but Kat would be lying if she claimed she never thought about what might have been between her and Jon if she had pursued things.

"He'll be okay," Kat said quietly, though her voice wavered and she knew she was lying. She simply did not know if he would be alright or not. She studied Jon's face for any trace of movement, but she knew there would be none. Jon Sherrard wasn't in there.

Jen picked up on her apprehension right away. "How can you say he'll be okay, Kat?" she questioned, an edge coming to her voice. "You don't even know what happened in there, do you?"

"Only a hypothesis right now," Kat admitted, shaking her head helplessly.

"How could you let this happen? He was your friend."

"Look, it's not like that at all, Jen," Kat replied, trying not to be defensive, but knowing she was failing. "We've been so very careful with this project and Jon's done this numerous times with never a glitch."

"This was the first time he was out of the box, though. You had to know it would be dangerous."

"New and unexplored, yes," she countered. "But dangerous? Jen, we're talking about computer viruses in cyberspace. They're nothing but lines of code. Jon's been working with them for months."

"Except for this one."

"Except for this one," Kat agreed gloomily, thankful to have something else to vent her own anger at and hoping Jen would steer the blame away from her and FutureTek. "Everything had gone so well up to this point that maybe we were too confident in our abilities to handle viruses in general. The Horde is…well, it's different."

"But why would this one be a problem?" Jen asked. "Despite all the doom and gloom about it, it's still just lines of code, right?"

"We're still trying to figure out why this one is so different, but we think it has something to do with its makeup," Kat explained. "Most other viruses or worms are preprogrammed to do a certain thing. They have well-defined parameters, even the extremely complex ones that are designed to cause physical damage to systems and equipment. That gives our technology a considerable advantage to combating them because we understand the reason for their existence. This one, however, appears to be well beyond that."

"How so?" Jen asked. As a computer science minor in college and then wife to FutureTek's version of a test pilot, she was very familiar with technology and the makeup of viruses. She had heard a little about the Horde virus, but it had only been in passing as it was a relatively new challenge to the high-tech world and she hadn't taken the time to study up on it. It was, however, a pretty big deal to the people who had to deal with it.

"Well, for starters, it has no defined parameters. It's a free-range virus and actually learns as it goes. Some experts have floated the hypothesis that it possesses a crude form of A.I."

"Artificial intelligence? That's absurd."

"Normally, I would agree with you," Kat admitted. "Now, I'm not so sure."

"But what does all that have to do with Jon?"

"That's what we don't know yet," Kay answered after a weary sigh. "It all happened so fast and Jon simply disappeared before we even knew it was the Horde that was attacking the honeypot."

"Could he be dead then?" Jen dared to ask, her eyes going back to her husband's face. He looked so peaceful; it was hard for her to believe he was doing anything but sleeping.

Kat shook her head again. "I don't believe so," she answered truthfully. "Jon's conscious is no more than electrons in the system, able to manipulate code and software. So he doesn't actually exist on a physical or a coded level. In essence, he exists outside the effectible realm of the virus."

"So he's still out there?"

Kat nodded.

"Do you truly believe that?"

"I have no reason to believe otherwise," Kat replied, looking her friend in the eyes. "But we just don't know where. We've run tests in the past where we've shut down the test bed while Jon was plugged in and we've never had a problem. So we know that being separated from the hub isn't harmful."

"Then what happened this time?"

"We just don't know," she admitted helplessly. "We're not even sure he's in an active state. If he's dormant somewhere, we could have looked right at him a hundred times and never saw him."

"What do you mean by being dormant? Is that something he can do when he's inside?"

"We discovered it by accident, really," she explained. "During one of our closed system tests, we were playing around with external stimuli and trying to see if there was any way Jon could access his body while remaining in the system. During the test run, Jon accidentally sent himself into a dormant phase. When he did, we lost all track of him.

He was effectively invisible."

"Wow," Jen breathed as she quickly understood the ramifications of that discovery. "The military applications of that in cyber warfare could be astronomical."

"Something we considered as well."

"So you think it's possible that he's in a dormant state?"

"I think it's definitely a possibility," Kat said. "He may have seen a threat in this Horde virus that we couldn't see and he shut himself down to avoid it."

"Can he wake back up?"

"He always has in the past," Kat replied. "After the first time, and a little bit of worry on everyone's part, it was easy for him. We've tested it a number of times."

"So why hasn't he come back this time?"

"I don't know," Kat shook her head. "But I promise you, we'll find him, Jen."

"How?"

"That's what I wanted to talk to you about," Kat said carefully, looking directly into her friend's eyes. "We're kicking around an idea, but it's going to take a little bit of time to get it ready. And I won't lie to you. It could be dangerous."

Before she could explain further, there was a knock at the door and both women turned to see an ashen Drew Jackson standing in the doorway.

"What is it, Drew?" Kat asked, immediately noticing his drained appearance. The man had been deep into crisis management since the accident and it was wearing on him. His face now told her that something new had developed.

Drew cleared his throat and looked plaintively at Jen, before turning to look at Kat again. "Perhaps we should speak outside."

Kat shook her head. "No," she countered, swallowing her own fear. "Jen has as much right to know what's going on as anybody. Now tell me what happened."

Drew looked back and forth to each woman before clearing his throat again, definitely uncomfortable with what he was about to share. "It's the prototype," he finally stammered.

"What about it?" Kat demanded.

"It's gone."

"What?"

"It's gone, Kat," he repeated. "When I told Rivers to unpack it and begin setting it up for emergency use, it wasn't in the case. He thought you might have it."

"Why would I have it, Drew? It's been locked up in storage since Systemtech started showing interest in us."

"Kat, what's going on?" Jen interrupted. "What's this about?"

"It's a wireless prototype unit of the hub," she explained quickly, shaking her head in a mixture of alarm and disgust.

"Another one?"

"In a sense, yes," she answered. "But it's wireless and portable. However, we haven't worked out the bugs and there's a lot of questions about its safety. In limited testing by Jon, we know that it works, but we don't know enough about it to use it without a lot more careful thought. When Systemtech started nosing around, we suspended work on it to fine-tune the main system so we could get ready for the demonstration."

"So what does that mean for Jon?"

"Nothing concrete," Kat answered truthfully. "The idea was for someone else to use the prototype to try and locate Jon. And I stress that it is just an idea right now."

"But why not use the regular hub?"

Kat was silent for a few moments before answering. "We don't dare use it, Jen," she finally said softly. "The main hub is attuned to Jon right now and there is no telling what would happen if we put a different person in the chair. If we use it, there may be a chance we could never get Jon back, even if we did find him. Not to mention, there would be risks to someone else using the hub until the machine was cleared of Jon's settings."

"So we were going to use the prototype to go and search for him," Drew put in, still from his place at the door.

"We were thinking about using it," Kat corrected, shooting Drew a nasty look. "There's no guarantees that we would be successful and, we're scared to death that we'll end up losing someone else out there."

"That's just it, Jen," Drew added. "Jon is the only one who has been truly out in cyberspace, and the accident happened the very first time he went long. Even on the closed test beds, Perry's the only other one who has been a driver and he only did it one time. We just don't know how dangerous it would be to put someone else out there when they're not prepared for it. And with the prototype, that level of unknown goes off the charts."

"But the prototype could do it?" Jen pressed.

"In theory, yes," Kat replied. "But it's a real shot in the dark."

"So, why would someone steal it?" Jen asked, looking at both of them.

Neither had the answer and Kat could only shake her head. "I don't know, Jen," she said, putting her arm around her friend's shoulder. "I really don't know."

Chapter 6

Channel 9, 6:00 News, Video Capture: *"On the technology front tonight, our top story has much of the technological world more than a little worried, while many high-tech security firms have been left scrambling. The reason? That's right. Another virus. But this one isn't just any virus, according to experts. This one is being hailed as perhaps one of the most destructive yet. Let's take you to our own expert, Leslie O'Neil. Leslie?"*

"Thanks, Nick."

"So what are we looking at here?"

"Quite frankly, it's a tough call, Nick. They're dubbing this particular worm the Horde virus and, as yet, they know very little about it."

"Can you tell us anything?"

"Only that it's a real threat, and leading anti-virus software creator, Systemtech, has upgraded its damage potential to catastrophic."

"Another Stuxnet?"

"No, this one is different. Stuxnet went after critical infrastructure— power stations, grids, and the like. This one does not. It does resemble Stuxnet in sheer size, but the complexity of it is off the charts compared to Stuxnet."

"Explain."

"That's the hard part, Nick. The coding is so complex, Systemtech engineers have been working non-stop for the past two months and still haven't come close to cracking its real purpose, let alone what makes it tick."

"Any theories?"

"More than you can count, and none of them likely correct. Only two things are certain at this time. In the first place, its sheer size is positively

frightening. "

"What's the other?"

"It's an eater, Nick."

"Say again?"

"It absorbs code. It attacks a program, breaks it down, and adds parts of it to its own."

"Sounds like the Borg."

"Star Trek isn't real. This is. As the Horde virus progresses, it grows larger and more dangerous."

"And it can't be stopped?"

"We'd have to know its true purpose to stop it. Unfortunately, as it grows, that purpose gets buried deeper and deeper in its coding mass. Already, Systemtech believes that it's too big to discern its primary function."

"What does that mean to us?"

"We're a computer-driven society, Nick, with technical boundaries and limitations that are broken all the time by brilliant men and women around the world. Imagine what would happen should something we created begin to outpace our own ingenuity."

"Are you talking about A.I?"

"Artificial Intelligence has been a real goal, as well as a real threat, for years, but no one has ever perfected it. Under the right circumstances and, in the right hands, it could be an enormous boon to the world. However, I shudder to think what would happen if it was birthed in a computer virus."

"Turn that off," Kat snapped a little too angrily as she walked into the central room where David Rivers was hunched over the hub, feverishly working on trying to discover what had gone wrong with their presentation.

"Sorry, boss," he said sheepishly, reaching over and tapping off the video stream that was running on his tablet. "Just listening to sound bites on this worm, thinking maybe I could get a lead on what to look for."

"It's pretty new, David. First official word on it wasn't more than two weeks ago."

"Yeah, that was about when that video came out."

"Are you finding anything with the hub?" she asked, exhaustion heavy in her voice. She walked around the machine and placed her hand on the cool metal, as if she might somehow be able to sense Jon's presence inside.

Rivers looked up, his eyes hollow. "Nothing," he said with a sigh. "Two days going over these machines with a microscope. He's not in here, Kat. I swear he's not here."

"What about Perry?"

He shrugged and went back to his work. "What about him?"

"Has he had any luck?"

"What are you talking about, Kat?" Rivers snapped irritably.

"Do you mean you haven't seen him?"

"No," the tech retorted, turning back to look at her. "Why?"

Kat stared hard at Rivers. "He was supposed to be here last night and take over for you for a few hours," she snapped. "Are you saying he didn't show?"

"Nope," he answered. "I was here until nearly 3:00 in the morning and then went home on my own to catch a few hours of sleep. Come to think of it," he went on, scratching his stubble-covered chin, "I did see him around midnight for a bit. He said he came in to go over some figures, but that was it."

"So he never came in here to take over on diagnostics?"

Rivers shook his head no.

"Damn it," Kat exclaimed angrily as she hurried out of the room, ignoring Rivers' trailing questions.

Five seconds later, she was bursting through another door and into Drew Jackson's office. "When did the prototype go missing, Drew?" she blurted out as the CEO was hanging up the phone.

"What?"

"The prototype," she repeated quickly. "When did it disappear?"

"I don't know," he answered. "It was supposedly packed up in storage for a couple week's now."

"Ever since we got the call from Systemtech," she nodded.

"Yeah, that would be about right. We only discovered it missing this morning. Why?"

"It's Perry," she stated flatly.

"Perry?"

"He has it. I know he does," she went on. "Only a few of us have the security code for the storage room and he's one of them. We need to get over to his house right away, Drew. If he's using that prototype without supervision, there's no telling what might happen."

"You can't be serious."

"I'm very serious," Kat countered. "He's driven once before, so he knows the tech."

"But why would you blame him for the missing prototype? I

mean, this is Perry we're talking about, Kat. He may be a grumpy pain-in-the-ass at times, but he's been with us for years. This isn't like him at all."

"Look, he was supposed to relieve Rivers last night and he never did. Rivers said he came in around midnight for a few minutes, but left. He has it, Drew. I know he does."

"You better be wrong," Drew said in growing anger as he quickly stood up. "What happened to Jon was bad enough. We can't afford any more blows to this deal, Kat."

"I'm more interested in not losing any more lives, Drew," she said flatly, an angry scowl on her face.

"Ease up a little," he soothed, waving a hand in the air to calm her down. "I don't want to lose anyone else, either. But we don't know that Jon is dead and Systemtech is still very interested in the product."

"Systemtech?" she repeated, somewhat confused at his statement. "How do you know that?"

He indicated the phone. "That was Monroe who just called. He said they are prepared to table an offer, but they won't do it until we close the investigation into Jon's death."

"Disappearance," she corrected angrily.

"Disappearance," he agreed. "Regardless, they still feel that, despite what happened, we are still a viable acquisition," Drew finished, ignoring her mounting anger.

"That's mighty big of them," she said sarcastically. "But right now, I want to find Jon. That's all the matters, Drew. Frankly, I don't give a damn about Systemtech or their offer at the moment."

"Of course," he agreed. "And we'll find him. Now, tell me

what you know about Perry. What make you think he has the prototype?"

"I'll tell you on the way," she fumed as she turned and headed back out of his office. Drew followed close behind.

Twenty minutes later, Kat pulled her Honda Accord to the curb in front of Perry Edward's house, right behind a waiting ambulance. There was a patrol car in the driveway and two more official-looking black sedans parked on the other side of the street. She turned and flashed her boss a worried look before both of them quickly got out. They had taken two steps onto the lawn when a uniformed police officer emerged from the house and looked hard at both of them.

"Can I help you?" he asked sternly.

"Drew Jackson," Kat's boss said smoothly, stepping forward. "President of FutureTek Enterprises here in Helena."

"What is your purpose for coming here, Mister Jackson?"

"We came to check on Perry Edwards," Drew answered worriedly. "He works for me. Is everything all right here?"

The police officer stepped off the porch to stand before them. "Can I see some ID, Mister Jackson?" he asked, his tone all business.

Jackson reached into his jacket pocket and withdrew his wallet, flipping it open and offering it to the police officer. "Driver's license and business card," he said and then motioned to Kat. "This is my lead program designer, Kathryn Hale. Perry didn't come into work today and we were concerned about him."

"So you drove out here to check on him? The both of you?"

"Yes," Drew answered, looking sideways at Kat, then back to the officer. "Why? What happened?"

"What made you think something was wrong in the first place, Mr. Jackson?" the officer went on, ignoring the question.

"We're dealing with a bit of a crisis, officer," Jackson replied with a sigh. "It's a long story."

"Try me."

"Well," he began, "we've been working with a very new and relatively untested technology and we fear the Perry might have brought home a prototype model we have had locked up in storage. When he didn't show up for work today, we thought it best to come out to his home and check up on him."

The officer was silent for several moments, before nodding his head. "That's all I needed to hear," he said finally. "Come with me, please."

He walked back into the house, followed closely by Jackson and Hale, who exchanged worried glances as they did. As they walked through the entryway, Kat caught a quick glimpse of Perry's wife, Danielle, hunched over and crying at the kitchen table, flanked by a police officer and two other men in dark suits.

"What's going on here?" Kat asked the officer as he led them down the hallway and through a bedroom doorway.

"You tell me," he answered, stopping and indicating the room.

Kat looked in and immediately shuddered, stifling the anguished cry that nearly erupted from her throat. The room was filled with computer and electronic equipment, books, design guides, and stacks and stacks of papers, much of it from FutureTek's archives. A quick glance around and she knew immediately what had happened. Perry Edwards himself was sitting in his office chair, his head lolled back to the side, his eyes open but unseeing and his skin a pasty blue. The prototype was still hooked up to him and two separate computer monitors in front of him told the rest of the story.

"How much?" she asked in a horrified whisper, staring at one monitor and not wanting to believe what she was seeing.

"Solid nine figures," came a voice from behind them, and she turned around to see one of the suited men looking at her, his features not at all unkind. He was middle-aged with salt and pepper hair and smooth features. He looked friendly enough, but there was a definite air of control about him—the air of someone who knew their job and did it well. "Deposited into a series of Cayman Island accounts about four hours ago."

"Oh, this cannot be happening," Kat said desperately. "This has to be some kind of a mistake."

"Unfortunately, there's no mistake," the man said, pointing to the account listings on the right hand monitor. "My question is, what was Mister Edwards selling to an enemy of the state that was worth half a billion dollars?"

"This is outrageous!" Drew suddenly stormed, his own face a mask of shock and betrayal. "Perry? A traitor? Who was he selling our technology to?"

"Let's just say that it isn't someone we would want to be selling high-tech gizmos to," the man said and then stuck out his hand. "Rick Alders. Homeland Security." The CEO of FutureTek accepted his handshake.

"Can you tell us what's going on here?" Jackson asked, his voice wavering but holding his ground.

"Well, Mister Jackson, that's what we're trying to ascertain," Alders replied easily. "Would you mind telling me what your boy was trying to sell?"

"It's a prototype," he explained, placing a hand firmly on Kat's arm to keep her quiet. "It's a wireless version of a technology that allows the user a unique perspective on dealing with computing issues such as viruses and software failures. That's all we can tell you about it right now."

"Must be some tech," Alders said, "if it's strong enough to kill someone and worth that much money to another country."

"That's just the thing," he continued. "It shouldn't kill anyone, but it's also a prototype and untested in the field."

"But worth a lot of money?"

"You could say that," he answered. "We just demo'd the product for a major corporation two days ago. Rumored acquisition price would have been pretty substantial."

"Making everyone a lot of money."

Both Drew and Kat nodded.

"But a lot of money wasn't good enough for Mister Edwards here, it would appear," Alders added.

"Apparently not," Kat said quietly, ignoring Drew's look. She was clearly agitated. "Can you tell us what happened?"

"It's not a big secret at this point," Alder shrugged. "I'm assuming that because the equipment is still attached to Mr. Edwards, our foreign friends do not yet have what they wanted."

"Unless the deal was for technical specs only," Kat pointed out, looking around the room at the stacks of papers, much of it company classified and definitely not supposed to be in the personal home office of one of their techs. "My guess is that this was just a demonstration."

"That's probably correct," Alders agreed. "Anyway, we've been tracking the movements of this target organization for several years now, particularly since they have shown extreme interest in acquiring new technologies coming out of the States and they seem to have an unlimited bankroll."

"Who are they?" Drew asked sharply.

"I'm not at liberty to say right now," he answered. "But it seems your boy made the deal and then died demonstrating it."

"Or he was killed," Kat added thoughtfully. They were dealing with an incredibly new technology and she had no doubt that it could be put to dangerous use in the wrong hands.

"We haven't ruled that out, either," Alders said. "But I'm going to need to hear a lot more about this technology before we can make any deductions. How much can you tell me?"

"As long as we aren't giving you technical specifications, we can probably answer most of your questions," Drew replied after breathing out a long sigh. "The technology isn't a big secret, at least the general concept. Lots of companies are researching it. FutureTek simply turned out to be the first to make it work."

"Let's go outside where we can talk, then," Alders said.

"How's Danielle doing?" Kat asked.

Alders offered her a sad smile. "She just found out that her recently-dead husband was engaged in industrial espionage that would have branded him a traitor in the eyes of the United States. My guess is she's not doing well at all."

Kat shook her head and looked at her boss. "This is getting out of hand, Drew. We are in way over our heads."

"I take it there's more to this story, then?" Alders said, picking up on her inflection. "If you have additional information, I would greatly appreciate you sharing it with me."

Drew nodded. "Let's go talk, Agent Alders."

Chapter 7

FutureTek Headquarters, Helena, Montana: Kat closed the door to her office and then fell into her chair, nearly numb with fatigue. With Jon still missing and Perry dead after apparently selling them out, exhaustion was quickly beginning to catch up to her. It didn't help matters that Dan Hyde from Systemtech had smugly let Drew know in no uncertain terms that they would be pursuing a breach of first-rights suit against them because of Perry's actions. And finally, there was Agent Rick Alders who was now hip-deep into everything FutureTek and its employees had ever done. While she held out hope that Alder's involvement would help them in the end, it was still another unknown in a sea of question marks.

But at least they had the prototype back, and although Alders indicated that could be used as evidence and thus could be legally seized, he had agreed to let it return to the labs if it would help find Jon Sherrard and maybe shed some light on the whole mystery. Still, it was a small consolation since it was useless unless they knew where to look in the first place. There was also the matter of identifying a new driver; someone willing to separate their consciousness from their physical body in a prototype piece of equipment with no guarantees they would ever be able to return, and with the job of locating the proverbial needle in a haystack that was roughly the size of Canada.

Three days ago, Kat Hale and her colleagues were on the cusp of the biggest technological breakthrough in the last half century when one considered the potential inherent in being able to separate a person's conscious self from his body. Now, their world had not only fallen apart; it had been thoroughly obliterated.

She leaned forward and laid her head on her arms. She willed the tears not to come, but they wouldn't be denied, so she lay there, quietly sobbing, wondering just how things had gotten so bad, so quickly.

A tiny chime from her laptop alerted her to an incoming e-mail and she half-heartedly raised her head and glanced at the screen. One e-mail was in her box and she opened her eyes a little wider when she noticed that it had originated from her own PC. Grabbing her mouse, she clicked on it, opened it up, and read the three words on her monitor.

Kat...Hub...Jon

For a long moment, she could only stare and then suddenly it dawned on her. She nearly screamed as she jumped up, slamming her chair back against the wall. "David!" she yelled, running through her door and nearly colliding with Drew as she did so.

"Kat," he said, grabbing her by the shoulders. "What's the matter?"

"It's Jon!" she shouted. "Get to the hospital, Drew! Get Jon over here immediately!"

"What are you talking about?"

"He's back, Drew," she said. "He's here!"

"Who's here?"

"Jon!"

"Jon?" Drew repeated in shocked surprise. "Come on, Kat. We're all having a hard time here. Take a deep breath and settle..."

"Just do it!" she practically screamed and then turned as David Rivers came running down the hall. "We need to get the hub back online, David!"

"Online?" he asked incredulously. "Kat, I have that whole thing broken down! It would take weeks to get it back together and calibrated correctly! Why?"

"It's Jon," she answered. "He's made contact!"

"How the hell is that possible?" Drew asked, his brow furrowed.

"I don't know," she panted. "But he just left a message on my e-mail."

Jackson and Rivers both stared at her skeptically and she practically shoved Rivers against the wall in anger. "Look, this might be our only chance to get him back! Now do it!"

"But how?" Rivers asked helplessly, nearly cowering at her rage. "I can't get it back together unless I have some time."

Kat shook her head. "We may not have the time," she growled, before brightening suddenly and turning to Drew. "What about the prototype?"

The CEO started to reply, but stopped and looked at Rivers questioningly. "Can we?"

"Hard to say, really," Rivers said with a shrug. "Theoretically, I suppose it's possible. He went in through the hub, but I don't imagine it would be a problem having him come back out through the wireless prototype. The technology is the same. The prototype just isn't attuned to him. However, we can clear Perry's data easily enough and, with no one else in its memory matrix, it might be possible to overlay his settings onto it."

"Then let's do it," Kat exclaimed.

"Hold on a sec, Kat," Drew put in. "There are still a lot of variables to consider. We haven't worked out the bugs and we don't even know why Perry is dead. Weren't you telling me just yesterday that you thought it was too dangerous to try to use it to rescue Jon?"

"Sending someone in, yes," she snapped. "Bringing Jon out on his own is different. It's the only way."

"He's been gone for three days, Kat. How do you even know he's back?"

"I told you, he just sent me an email," she said quickly.

"But where did it come from? Can someone be screwing with you?"

"It was from my own account," she answered. "And it came in while I was sitting there."

"I don't know, Kat," Drew said doubtfully, shaking his head.

"We have to try, Drew! If it's him and this is our chance to get him back, we have to take that chance!"

Drew was silent for a minute before replying. Turning to Rivers, he finally said, "All right, David, get the prototype ready. Is it still routed through our network?"

"Yeah," Rivers answered. "Perry never changed any of the settings."

"That's fortunate. Get it together and get out to my car with it."

"Why?" Rivers asked.

"It's wireless, David," Drew said, tapping his temple with his finger to accentuate the obvious point. "The hospital might not let us check him out, so we'll simply take it to him."

"Oh, right," he answered sheepishly. "Okay, I'm on it. Give me five minutes."

"You really think he's back, Kat?" Drew asked plainly as David raced back into his lab, leaving them alone.

She nodded again. "I do."

"Well, see if you can communicate with him and tell him what we're doing. We're in new territory here."

"Will do," she said and swung back and headed into her office. She threw herself into her chair and quickly rattled out a reply to the e-mail, hoping that somehow, he would get her message.

Hub down, using prototype. Can you get there?

30 agonizing seconds later, she had a two-word reply.

Yes. Hurry.

A short time later, they were at the hospital and Kat's fingers worked feverishly, attaching the electrodes to Jon Sherrard's left arm and left temple, while David Rivers did the same on the other side of the bed. The prototype equipment lay across his chest and Alex Jordan, the other lab tech, was quickly checking and rechecking the connections.

"We're good here," Alex said.

"Is this going to work?" Jen Sherrard asked doubtfully, looking at Drew as they worked.

The CEO stood beside her, his arms folded tightly as he

watched. "I hope so," he answered quietly.

"Done on this side," Kat said, standing up.

"Here, too," Rivers added. Reaching down, he positioned Jon's fingers on the gateway pad and then pressed in the code. Looking up, he said hopefully. "Gate is open."

"So what happens now?" Jen asked.

Kat shook her head. "We wait, Jen," she said softly. "It's a long shot, but we think it can work. All we have to do is wait for Jon to make the transition."

"How long will it take?" Jen started to ask, but stopped suddenly as her husband's eyes snapped open.

For a moment, no one spoke

And then it was Jon who broke the silence, his voice little more than a dry croak. "Lord, do I have a headache," he whispered with a wince and the whole room erupted into cheers. Jen threw herself on her husband, alternating between crying into his neck and kissing his face. Kat couldn't help but cry, too, and she threw her own arms around Drew's neck and hugged him close. Rivers sat back in stunned amazement and just smiled, while Alex patted him on the shoulder and beamed.

The nightmare was over.

Or so they thought.

After a few minutes, Kat leaned down and kissed her friend on the forehead. He still had his arms wrapped tightly about his wife and was refusing to let the startled nursed pull her away so they could check his vitals and try and figure out what had just happened. "You be good now, you hear me, Jon?" she asked, wiping away a tear.

"Where's the fun in that?" he whispered, but managed a weak smile.

"Get yourself better," she added. "We'll talk when you feel like it. I'm sure you have a lot to tell us."

A dark shadow crossed Jon's face and he looked momentarily confused, before refocusing and smiling up at her. "Yeah," he finally whispered hoarsely. "A lot."

Kat straightened up and took Drew by the elbow and looked at the two lab techs. "Come on, guys," she said happily, her relief nearly overwhelming. It was over. Jon was back. And all she wanted to do now was go home and sleep. "Let's get out of here."

"Sure thing, Kat," Rivers said and paused to give Jon a quick pat on the shoulder. "Good to have you back, boss." Sherrard smiled at him and Rivers turned back to Kat. "I don't know about you guys, but I could use a drink."

"I'm buying" Drew said, casting a knowing smile at Jon, who was again busy kissing and hugging his wife. "And when he gets his lazy ass out of bed, I'll buy one for him, too."

Kat returned the smile as she watched her two friends and figured her bed could wait a little longer. A drink beforehand sounded perfect. With that, she hooked arms with Drew and the four FutureTek people walked out of the hospital room, leaving Jon and Jen to do their best to fight off the nurses and reacquaint themselves.

"All's well that ends well, right?" Drew said as they walked down the antiseptic-looking hallway.

Kat thought back to Jon's brief look of…what? Horror? Desperation? As glad as she was that he was back, she wasn't quite sure she was ready to hear what he had to say. "Yeah," she said thoughtfully in answer to Drew's question. "Let's hope it does."

Intermission

The worm continued its work, day and night, as it traveled through the endless channels and pathways as part of the system's electrical current. Here and there, its programming kicked in and it would break down and reconfigure key components, reworking hardware and rewriting software in order to reconfigure the system to better accept its own programming and meet its ultimate goal.

Normally, the Horde could reconfigure a system in time measured in nanoseconds. But two things had happened to drastically change that. In the first place, this wasn't just any system. It was one of the most complex creations on the face of the earth and it would take days to reach a satisfactory level of assimilation and reconfiguration. More importantly, the Horde had moved beyond simple artificial intelligence and had achieved consciousness. It was thinking.

And it had a plan.

Chapter 8

National Security Agency Headquarters, Fort Meade, Maryland: The man's footsteps reverberated off the plain gray walls, echoing down the long corridor as he walked quickly to his destination near the end of the hall. Were Major Thomas Bolson to continue to the end of the corridor, he would pass through a huge steel door after a retina and a palm scan, and into the heart of the United States government cyber warfare division.

However, the emergency meeting he had been called to would have a couple of high-ranking officials who did not have the same clearance for the actual lab that he and only a handful of others did. So it would be held in the conference room outside the lab, which was just fine with him. He had neither the time nor the inclination to explain the complexities of what it was he did for the country and he reveled in the fact that he never had to worry about an endless stream of bureaucratic retards bumbling through his lab and pestering him with questions that any 6th grader with an X-box could answer. They would simply have to accept the fact that he was one of the world's leading experts on cyber warfare, virus creation, and security.

What he didn't know, though, was that his secret was out.

He entered the room and was surprised to find several others already seated, as if they had been waiting for him. The meeting wasn't for fifteen more minutes, but Major Bolson was always early for meetings as he felt it gave him an edge, regardless of the meeting circumstances. This time, however, he was immediately uneasy, and for good reason.

"Close the door, major," General James Hawthorne said, his voice clipped and formal. His blue eyes, set in a craggy but stern face, were cold and bored relentlessly into the young officer.

Bolson swallowed the sudden rise of concern and did what he was commanded. He then took a seat across from the general and placed his hands lightly on the table as he looked around the room. Besides his superior officer—who was directly in charge of the entire U.S. cyber warfare division and answered to only to the head of the NSA—there were two others. One was wearing a dark suit—a rugged looking man with features that could have been carved out of stone. Bolson had no idea who he was, although he pegged him for NSA muscle. The other was Lieutenant Danielle Martz, a young and brilliant computer programmer whose expertise had lent him considerable talent and knowledge in the project he had been working on for the better part of his three years here as a cyber warfare specialist.

"Major Bolson," Hawthorne said gruffly as he opened up a file folder that was on the table before him. Picking up a piece of paper, he slid it across the table to the young officer. "Would you care to explain this?"

Bolson felt himself go red with anger, his fears confirmed. He didn't need to see the paper to know what it said. He also knew there was only one way the general could have gotten the information, and that fact made him even angrier. "Sir," he began, casting a venomous glance at Lieutenant Martz, who quickly looked down at the table top, unable or unwilling to meet his gaze.

Hawthorne held up a hand. "Save the excuses for later, son," he snapped. "I want it explained."

Bolson swallowed thickly and nodded. "It's an anomaly, sir," he answered, holding his anger in check. "At this point, we have no idea what the cause is or if it is even a correct reading."

Hawthorne tapped his finger on the paper. "You damn well better find the cause, major. This is a project of unparalleled magnitude and if we don't have control over this, we have a very serious problem. Would you agree?"

"We have control, sir," the young man lied, but the general cut him off.

"Then where the hell is it?" he snapped.

Bolson paused before answering, dreading the words even as he spoke them. "I don't know yet, sir."

"You don't know."

"No, sir."

"Why not?"

"Because I'm still running tests and trying to ascertain the cause, sir," Bolson answered, his fingers pressing painfully into the tabletop. "It could simply be a recoding of the transmission algorithm."

"But you don't know for certain," Hawthorne shouted angrily, leaning across the table. "You haven't had contact with it for almost two weeks and all you have is a friggen' guess! Why the hell wasn't I notified of this!?"

Bolson flushed. "I thought it best to ascertain the cause of the anomaly first, sir," he said through clenched teeth. Truthfully, when the project had vanished, he had been quite terrified to inform the general of such a breach of security, and thus had launched his own frantic search for the missing program. A week into his 18 hour-a-day search, Lieutenant Martz had gotten wind of it. Bolson had sworn her to secrecy and, with her help, they had doubled their attempts. Apparently, though, Martz had rolled over on him after all and now the consequences would be infinitely worse.

"Lieutenant Martz," Hawthorne said icily, not taking his eyes off the major. "What was the original projected sentience barrier of the project under optimal circumstances?"

"Approximately twenty-eight months from insertion," she replied quietly.

"Which puts it at?"

"Approximately August 15th, two years from now," she answered and then added. "Of course, that would be under optimal conditions."

"That's about twenty-five months from now, correct?"

"Yes, sir," she replied.

"Is it possible that barrier has been crossed already?"

"I don't believe so, sir," she answered.

"But can you be one hundred percent certain?"

She paused before answering. "No, sir."

"Is it possible the virus has been compromised and beaten by a public or private sector hack?"

"No, sir," Major Bolson cut in, but Hawthorne cut him off by slamming his hand on the table.

"That question was for Lieutenant Martz, major," he said angrily. "You will shut your mouth and let her answer, do you understand me?"

"Yes, sir," Bolson replied, snapping his attention forward while he silently seethed inside.

"Begging your pardon, sir, but the major is correct," Martz answered, casting an apologetic look toward the major. "The program itself is encrypted like nothing else in the world and as it grows, it adds to the layers of encryption. Without the base key, which only we have, it would take over a year for even a Kray network to break it from the point that it started at. But as you know, the virus is continuously progressing, so the moment a code breaker starts on the encryption, the encryption has already changed. There is no literal way to crack the encryption without starting from the base."

Hawthorne nodded, knowing that was the answer she would give. The major might be running the lab, but there was little the computer-savvy general did not know about the project which he headed. "So, we have ruled out program compromise and we know it hasn't been killed on our end," he said, referring to the fact that the final kill code for the project, in event of emergency, was his and his alone. "That leaves us with a multi-million dollar black ops project with supposedly infallible tracking algorithms, that has simply vanished into cyberspace."

"Sir, if I may," Bolson dared to interrupt, looking at the general and waiting to see if the man would stop him again. When he didn't, he went on. "Because of what we know, it is my belief the problem is simply in the tracking code. I believe that all I have to do is find the error and insert a new tracking algorithm to re-establish contact."

"It's a virus!" Hawthorne shouted. "I trust you have honeypots online"

"Yes, sir," Bolson answered.

"Have you had any hits from it?"

"No, sir," Bolson admitted after a long pause.

"Then your reasoning is flawed, major!" he boomed. "And that leaves only one remaining conclusion."

"What is that, sir?" Bolson asked quietly.

Hawthorne paused and glanced at the suited man, who had remained silent the entire time. Looking back at Bolson, he finished. "Your little baby has crossed the sentience barrier two years ahead of schedule and has decided it doesn't want to be found."

Chapter 9

Sherrard Residence, Helena, Montana: Jon Sherrard sat bolt upright in bed, the scream still lingering on his lips. Jen was sitting beside him again, her arms wrapping him up tightly and holding him close, shushing him as a mother would a frightened child. Truth be told, that's exactly what he felt like. Two weeks ago, he had returned from an absolutely unbelievable and terrifying journey, his conscious reuniting with his body after being separated from it and lost for nearly three days in the very real and frighteningly vast reaches of cyberspace.

At first, all was well and he had spent a lot of time relating to Kat and Drew what had happened and what it was like to literally float while lost in an indescribable electronic universe. His explanation had gone a long way in answering the many questions they had. It was what had cast him adrift that troubled him so greatly.

During the demonstration for Systemtech, he had been very pleased with how smoothly the whole thing had gone, including the repair of the damaged thumb drive through channels they had not considered would be part of the show. It was as he was getting ready to make the trip back into the hub and then into his body, that he became aware of a new virus that had been attracted to one of the honeypots. This one was different – malevolent and almost thinking, and he would swear to that for the rest of his life. This newcomer, the Horde, began rewriting and assimilating portions of random code in many different programs and when he got too close, he could actually feel it reaching out for him, almost as if it was trying to absorb him as well.

So he had done the only thing he could think of to escape. He had thrown himself through the gate and literally out into the limitless expanse of cyberspace. Moments later, Kat had shouted the order to take the honeypots offline and he was suddenly stranded, cut off from his way home, and all alone. At first, he had lost all hope and nearly panicked, fearing that he would remain part of this futuristic alien landscape forever. But logic took over and he calmed down and began exploring his new surroundings, understanding how the strange world worked, but never straying too far from the sealed gates that led back into the honeypot.

Eventually, he began to venture out further, searching for data streams that looked familiar and would give him a clue that he was at least near FutureTek's own network. As he was near the honeypots, it didn't take him long to find what he was looking for. It did, however, take him considerable time and effort to make use of it and bypass FutureTek's firewalls and security systems to craft his short cry for help to Kat. Had she not been there to see it, he didn't know what would have happened, because it was in those final moments that the Horde found him again.

During his stay in cyberspace, Jon had discovered that it was not just an empty landscape. Instead, it was almost like a living, breathing entity, populated by data streams, worms, and viruses of uncountable proportions. For the most part, he had nothing to fear from anything he ran across. Even the internet worms were unable to harm him and he had dismantled more than a few of them during his time out there.

However, that all changed when the Horde returned in its

entirety, a massive entity far greater than the little tendril it had sent into the honeypot. To his horror, it had become aware of him and now was actively pursuing him as prey. So, the game of cat and mouse began. Jon would flee, letting his conscious slip among passing data streams and immersing himself into coded programs on various unprotected hard drives and clouds that he could get to. But the virus would inevitably find him, pursuing him relentlessly, and every time it did, it seemed to be just a little smarter, just a little quicker, and a little more determined to catch him.

Jon had no idea what the outcome would have been if it had caught him, nor did he ever want to find out. Fleeing in stark terror, he had finally managed to get Kat's attention by manipulating her e-mail program to send his plea for help to her. He considered himself thoroughly blessed that she happened to be right there when he sent it because if she had not been, he didn't know if the next time he encountered the virus would be his last.

So, he had made it back from impossible odds, reunited with his body, with his wife and friends, and most importantly, with reality. Several good night's sleep had given way to quality time spent holed up in his house with Jen and Dakota and a promise that he would never again do anything so stupid as to separate his conscious from his body. He had even tendered his immediate resignation as FutureTek's test pilot, preferring to keep his feet grounded solidly in their lab, a proposal that Drew Jackson had graciously accepted.

On the third day after his escape, he had finally consented to answering the official questions that had been waiting for him and he spent a considerable part of that day and evening speaking with

Homeland Security Agent Rick Alders. He answered every question he was allowed to regarding the technology, as well as more personal questions concerning his friendship with the deceased Perry Edwards and the man's still unbelievable betrayal of FutureTek and his country. That, in itself, was a bitter wound that would be raw with Jon for a long time to come.

He then finished the lengthy and ongoing interrogations by once more relating his entire story, this time to the same three Systemtech employees who had witnessed the ill-fated demonstration that had begun his nightmare. He had even managed during that discourse, although unintentionally, to regain their interest. After hearing his story, Michael Monroe had immediately tendered a substantial offer to buy out FutureTek, an offer that would make them all rich beyond anything they could imagine. And although the offer was contingent on the completion of the official investigation into Perry Edwards and his untimely death, it had still finished the day on a good note.

At least until he went to bed that night.

It was that very night when the first nightmare came. He awoke from it the same way he had awoken from it this night and every night since the first – with a scream. Jen was always there, consoling him and doing her best to sooth his jangled nerves. But he was starting to wonder if that was enough. The nightmare was terrifying – repeated run-ins with the virus in his subconscious state that always ended up with the scream starting in his dream and finishing as he woke up. However, each time he had the dream, the virus seemed to get just a little closer to him and he found himself wondering what would happen when it finally caught him, even if it was just in his dream?

So, he lay there shivering in his wife's arms while Dakota nuzzled him with his own canine concern. He felt that something dark was still stalking him and he stayed that way the rest of the night.

Morning found Jon Sherrard staring into the bathroom mirror with tired eyes, peering at a pair of lesions that had somehow found their way onto his face just below his left eye, sometime during the night.

Chapter 10

National Security Agency Headquarters, Fort Meade, Maryland: Major Thomas Bolson stalked along the corridor toward the lab. He had been in a foul mood since the meeting the day before with General Hawthorne and the NSA gorilla. After the meeting, he had worked non-stop in the lab by himself, trying vainly to come up with a way to reign in his creation and salvage his military career, while trying to stamp down the overwhelming feelings of betrayal. Yet as before, he had come up empty, and his anger had only intensified. At around 5:00 in the morning, he had gone home, hoping to catch a couple hours of sleep and change into a fresh uniform. The uniform change he was able to manage, but sleep did not come and his feelings of anger and helplessness were as raw as before.

Back in the military complex, he paused at the steel door leading into the lab and went through the normal palm and retina scan routine, before the door hissed open, allowing him entrance. He walked into the lab and froze as the door shut behind him.

Lieutenant Danielle Martz looked up from her work station, all the color draining from her face. It was obvious she had not expected him. She had avoided the lab after yesterday's meeting on the advice of General Hawthorne and had only returned after she knew that Bolson was gone. The major had returned early, though, trapping her in a situation that she knew could get out of hand, particularly with their past together.

"What are you doing here?" Bolson snarled, tossing his

briefcase on a lab table and folding his arms in anger. Every muscle in his body tensed, and it was all he could do to keep from killing the woman right there. She had betrayed him so completely; had compromised everything he had worked toward and had likely permanently derailed his military career. He could have his sidearm out and put several bullets into her head before she even moved and, truth be told, he wasn't sure he wouldn't yet take that route.

"I'm sorry, sir," she stammered, standing quickly. "If I had known you would be back…"

"You wouldn't be here!" the major snapped, finishing her sentence. "What's the matter, Dani? Are you afraid I would retaliate against someone trying to undermine my project and my command? Are you that desperate to take over this project?"

"No!" the young woman replied quickly. "It's not like that at all, Tom! I swear!"

"Don't patronize me!" Bolson yelled, moving forward threateningly. "You've had your eye on this since day one! You led me on! You set me up and then you betrayed me! Everything you've ever said was a lie and you've cost me everything!"

"No, sir," she stammered again. "You've got it all wrong, Tom! You have to let me explain."

Bolson had his sidearm out and two steps took him within reach of the young woman. She started to back away, but he grabbed her shoulder and yanked her toward him, pressing the barrel of the gun against the side of her head. "Give me one good reason not to do it, Dani," he hissed, his face very close to hers. Memories from their relationship reared up in his mind, but he allowed his anger to blunt the emotions. He was ready to go over the edge.

"Tom, listen to me," Danielle said softly, tears welling in her eyes. "I swear this is not how it was supposed to happen."

Bolson pressed the gun barrel harder to her head. "Tell me how it was supposed to happen, then," he snarled.

"Please, Tom," she begged. "Please don't hurt me. I never wanted this to happen. Never."

For a moment, Bolson wavered, and that was the only window that Martz needed. An accomplished martial artist—a fact the major knew nothing about—she threw her left arm out, shoving Ayer's gun hand hard to the side, while at the same time striking him hard in the chest with an open palm. It was not meant to hurt him, only to separate the two of them and give her room to work.

Bolson was thrown back and nearly lost his grip on his weapon, but he recovered quickly and began to bring his gun back to bear on the woman. Only this time, she was not the helpless victim and he found himself looking down the barrel of her own sidearm, freezing him in his place, his gun still pointed toward the floor. As if to punctuate the fact that the momentum had swung 180 degrees, Danielle Martz said coolly, "Your weapon, please, major."

Bolson flinched visibly, expecting his head to be reduced to a puddled mass of brain matter and body fluids, but instead she motioned with her free hand for him to place his weapon on the table. Quickly becoming numb to everything that had happened, Bolson hesitated for a second before complying and backing away from the table.

Martz stared him down for a moment and then quickly

holstered her sidearm, her eyes never leaving his. "I could have killed you, Tom," she said icily, her face suddenly a mask of stone. She picked up his weapon and then surprisingly flipped it around and presented it back to him. "Of course, you still have the opportunity to kill me if you truly feel that's your only recourse here," she went on, indicating that he should take his weapon from her. "I won't stop you. But understand that if you do, you won't know the truth and if you're truly concerned about your career, you can bet it would end in front of a firing squad or under a needle." She paused before finishing. "It's your move."

"Why give my gun back to me?" he asked, trying desperately to piece together everything that had happened as he took his weapon and immediately holstered it. He was reeling from the about-face she had done, but was smart enough to know that he was in something a lot deeper than he had originally thought.

"Because I trust you," she said simply.

"You're NSA, aren't you," Bolson stated, trying to put some heat into his accusation, but failing miserably.

Without answering, she brushed past him. Pausing for a moment, she turned and reached into her pocket. She tossed him a key, which he quickly snatched out of the air. He knew what the key was, since he had used it a number of times in the past. "Noon," she said simply and then left the lab through the hiss of the security door.

Thomas Bolson was shocked at how things had suddenly turned and he breathed out a long sigh as he slid into his office chair in a daze. For the next two hours, he worked in numb shock, unbothered by anyone, but accomplishing nothing. At about ten thirty, he left the complex.

He arrived at his destination an hour and a half later and used the key to let himself in. It was a small house, set back from a quiet tree-lined road in Manassas, Virginia. He hadn't given it any thought in the past, but now he looked at it with an eye for detail. The house was sheltered from the road and unobtrusive. To anyone else, it was the perfect little cottage in a quiet part of town. To him, he now saw it for what it was — a cover.

Danielle Martz was waiting for him in the living room, seated in an easy chair, her face much softer than the ice queen she had been when she'd left the lab a few hours earlier. Several times in the past, she would have been waiting for him in a negligee or something even less, the part of their relationship they had kept secret from everyone. Today, she was dressed comfortably in work-out clothes - spandex shorts and a tight-fitting Under Armour top. Bolson had always been attracted to her and the two had hit it off surprisingly well when she had first come to work with him on the Horde Project. He was just now starting to understand why that was.

"Sit down," she said softly, indicating the couch that cornered her chair.

"You used me," he said matter-of-factly, keeping his voice controlled as he took a seat.

She offered him a smile that was almost sad. "Not entirely," she answered. "Regardless of the reasons behind it, I assure you, the attraction was mutual, Tom."

"But why?" he asked, still in shock. "Why lead me on like that?"

"You were correct back in the lab," she said with a sigh, ignoring his question. "I work for the cyber-ops division of the NSA."

"Is that why you were assigned to my project?"

"Partly," she answered. "But there's more to this than you know, and in my opinion, it's high time you know what's going on."

Bolson looked confused. "I don't understand," he finally said.

"I'll start from the beginning," she replied. "The Horde project has been on the NSA radar since its inception. As a matter of fact, we're bankrolling it."

"I thought this was General Hawthorne's baby?"

"That's correct, for all intents and purposes. It's his project, which is the way it needs to be for now. At the moment, the NSA is involved with the management team in an advisory role and, in my case, hands-on assistance. But ultimately, the NSA will fully control the project upon completion."

"But why?" Bolson was confused. With the work he did for the government and with the clearance level he had, he knew there were always powerbrokers pulling the strings behind the scenes on secret projects. Maybe it was that it was now his job and his project that was being manipulated, that this whole thing was bothering him.

"Why not?" Martz answered. "Think about what the Horde project is, Tom. We're not talking about simple artificial intelligence here. We're talking about a finished project that would create a thinking, growing entity. Scientists have been trying to play God for years. What you're working on is playing God in a whole new world. And make no mistake, it's a living, breathing world you're playing in."

Bolson didn't know whether to be ashamed or proud. "I don't

know if I would go that far," he finally stammered. "All we're trying to do it harness control of cyberspace."

"And the first nation to do that is going to be the only remaining super power in the world," she added. "Face it, Tom. This isn't the United States of thirty-odd years ago. Back when it was the USA and USSR, things were pretty simple. Our two countries were the only ones at the poker table and we both had our fingers on the buttons. Oh, there were a few pretenders in the nuke game, but MAD kept everything at least semi-civil."

"Mutual Assured Destruction," he reasoned.

"Exactly. But today, the United States is a shell of what we were back then. Several administrations have stripped the military to the bone and what we have left is off fighting the unending 21st century version of the Crusades." She shook her head, clearly irate. "It would chill you to know just how vulnerable we are today, Tom. Russia continues to saber rattle and we'd be stupid not to be paying attention to what's going on over there. Even worse, if the Chinese decided they wanted what we have, our chances of survival as a country would be virtually nil. They can beat us economically, they can beat us militarily, and we both know it. The only thing that keeps them from doing so today is that we are a big player in their economy. Once they have worked out how to get around it, China will be the biggest threat we have ever faced." She shifted in the chair and drew her legs underneath her. "Did you ever see the movie Red Dawn?" she went on, abruptly changing topics.

He shook his head.

"It's an older movie, but a good one, much better than the

remake," she said. "The story is pretty straightforward. A foreign nation launches a coordinated attack on the United States, taking over huge chunks of the country before anyone even knows what's happening. Back then, that scenario would be far-fetched. We were, after all, the top superpower in the world. Today, however, things are much different and it's a very real possibility."

"Don't you think you might be exaggerating a bit?" Bolson countered, stopping short of mentioning tin-foil hats.

"No," she snapped, looking angry. "In the history of the world, no empire has ever survived. All of them rise and fall and we'll be no exception, unless we take the appropriate steps. What is at stake here is quite simply the control of the free world. Whoever controls cyberspace will control the world, and it's in our best interests to be the country that controls it."

"Okay," Bolson sighed, feeling exasperated. "Whether or not I buy into all the conspiracy theory rhetoric, what does this whole thing have to do with me?"

"The Horde project is the key, Tom," she answered. "In simplest terms, to have a thinking life form in control of cyberspace; a thinking life form that is actually under our control, gives us an insurmountable advantage. It gives us a level of control over hostile nations never before considered."

Bolson nodded. This was familiar territory for him and he disputed none of it. "I am aware of all of this," he answered. "Cyber warfare has been all the rage for the past decade or more. But you haven't answered my question. Again, how do I fit into all of this?"

She sat back and folded her arms, eyeing him carefully before answering. "Because we had to be sure you weren't the mole."

"The mole?" he asked in surprise. "What are you talking about?"

"One of the reasons I brought you here is that I've been cleared by my superiors to discuss this with you," she replied. "I didn't want to have this discussion at the lab because there's no telling what kind of surveillance Hawthorne has on you right now. At least here, it's me and you."

"And the NSA," he added, looking around. "I'm not dumb, Dani. I know this is a cover house. How deep does the NSA surveillance on me go?"

She grinned almost impishly. "If you're worried about our bedroom action, don't. I do have some say in what is and is not monitored in here."

Bolson allowed himself to relax slightly, but not enough to allow the deflection to continue. "Where do I fit into all of this, Dani? Don't screw with me. I have a right to know."

"You do now, simply because we don't believe you to be a part of the breach anymore."

"What breach?"

She sighed and stretched her legs, a movement that did not escape Bolson's glance. "The truth is," she said, "I was assigned to your lab because we had gotten word that someone in the lab, possibly you, was talking to outside sources, looking for a buyer."

"A buyer?" Bolson exclaimed, incredulous. "For the Horde project? You mean the NSA thought I was a traitor?"

She nodded. "You were at the top of the list from day one and, up until recently, you were still at the top of the list."

"So you decided to derail my career, without knowing the truth?" he snapped angrily.

"No, Tom," she replied honestly. "The intentions were not malicious. After the Horde disappeared, we had over a hundred techs working out of our offices, trying to track this thing down and figure out what went wrong. You were under constant surveillance and the conclusion eventually reached was that you were not a part of it. So the idea was to get Hawthorne involved and turn up the heat on you, hoping that whoever was working in the shadows would think they were clear to act, since you were going to be the fall-guy."

"And have they?" he asked, still upset.

She shook her head. "Not to date."

"So why are you telling me this now?" he continued. "Why end the charade?"

"It's never been a charade," she said quietly. "I believe you're innocent and it was under my recommendation that the NSA agreed to bring you into the loop and let you know what was happening."

"But why?"

"Because we are out of ideas," she sighed. "I've been involved in this project for a long time, Tom. I know what you know. But I have to wonder what there is that you and I don't know, and I need your help figuring that out."

"Like what?" he said, his hands out in disbelief. "I've put this thing together from the ground up, Dani."

"True. But of the half a dozen other people involved in the project, who knows enough about the project to speed up its learning algorithm? I don't think there's any doubt that the Horde has reached a level of sentience, but two years ahead of schedule? Do you know what the odds are of that happening without outside interference? Someone sabotaged the timeline, Tom. We need to find out who."

"No one else working on this project has any clue as to what the true scope of the Horde is," he countered. "No one. In the lab, only three people have any idea what we are actually working on: you, me, and General Hawthorne. Of those few other people involved in this, everyone else only has bits and pieces of the whole, with no clue what the final goal is."

"We know that. But someone has figured it out. Someone has been working in the shadows and we're completely stumped on who it is. There is simply no other explanation. Someone kicked up the learning curve on this thing in order to get it out of the lab."

"That's just not possible, Dani," he said. "This whole project has been carefully scripted and controlled. Everything we have done has been recorded, monitored, and tested. Everything we..." Bolson suddenly stopped and his complexion went bone-white. "Oh, my God!" he said softly, an icy chill running down his spine. Suddenly, he knew. He had the answers that both of them were looking for.

"What is it?" Martz answered, suddenly tense.

"We have to get back to the lab!" he exclaimed and jumped to his feet.

"Why? What is it?"

"I know who it is!"

"Then tell me," she said, her voice suddenly excited. "We can end this right now."

"No," he said, grabbing her hand and pulling her to her feet. "I can't tell you. I have to show you. We have to show Hawthorne, too. Come on!"

A half hour later, Major Thomas Bolson was bringing up the data graphs on the monitor as Danielle Martz and General Hawthorne looked on. "As you know, half of this project has been monitoring the processing power of the Horde. There really is no way to measure sentience, so to speak, so we would monitor data and ask ourselves the question – is this simply increased computing power or literal thought?"

"Go on," Hawthorne said, staring at the screen, but seeing nothing that he didn't already know.

"Look," Bolson said, pointing to a simple graph that was on the screen. It was a typical X/Y graph with several light blue graphing lines running along the X axis. "This graph measures the processing power of the Horde about two years ago." For the most part, the measurements showed slow, but steady, increases. He pointed to a major spike that matched up in several of the data streams. "Right here," he explained, "we had introduced an algorithmic equation that we had hoped would speed up the process."

"It spiked," Martz agreed. "It appears that it worked."

"For a moment," Bolson answered. "But if you continue to follow the data, you will see that it immediately falls off to levels even lower than what they were prior to the spike. We deemed it a failure."

"It flamed out," Hawthorne put in, remembering the optimism

they had experienced when the procedure was attempted. "This is old news, major. I thought you were going to show me how this thing got lose."

"I am," Bolson answered, fully confident in his findings. "In terms of a graph, a computer program works in a two-dimensional X/Y area. When it's working hard, the line spikes. When it's not, the line stays constant."

"So?"

"So, when we introduced the algorithm, we got the spike, but it was short-lived. It did, however, have an unexpected result."

"And what's that?" Hawthorne asked.

Bolson tapped out several commands and the picture was transformed into a three-dimensional graph, then spun for a top view and froze. The light blue lines on the two-dimensional graph now looked almost like a funnel. "What you are seeing here," he explained, pointing to the low point of the picture where the line was most compressed, "is the point that the algorithm was introduced."

Martz caught on immediately. "You're saying that the computing power of the Horde went 3D?"

"Exactly," Bolson answered with growing dread. "Instead of showing a continuous upward spike in processing ability along the Y axis, the program spread it out along the Z axis."

Hawthorne shook his head. "What are you saying, major?"

"I'm saying," he said, "that it worked."

"It worked?" Hawthorne was skeptical.

Martz nodded, realizing what the major was pointing to. "It did," she answered softly. "The Horde achieved sentience two years ago, general. Not two weeks ago."

"Are you two out of your minds?" Hawthorne snapped, looking at first one and then the other. "How the hell did this thing go live on us two years ago and we not know it?"

"Because the Horde hid it. It actively hid what it was doing from us," Bolson answered quietly, typing out a couple more commands. The graph then became a running measurement following a timeline. The funnel grew larger and the computer compensated, pushing the image of the graph downward to allow for the upward growth. Eventually, it could compensate no further and the screen was filled with a solid light blue color. "Two years ago, the Horde had the processing ability of maybe a thousand human minds at about the point we introduced the algorithm. It has grown almost exponentially along the Z axis ever since."

"And where would that put it now?"

Bolson looked at the number at the bottom of the screen, a number that was adding digits faster than he could count and was already off the screen. "It's incalculable," he finally answered, then turned to look at Martz. "It was the Horde all along, Dani," he said, not bothering to hide their familiarity with each other. "It's been thinking for a long time. The anomaly the NSA thought was someone on the inside trying to contact a buyer..."

"...was actually the Horde testing the boundaries of its world," she finished.

"So, you're telling me this thing has been sentient for two years?" Hawthorne said, still unable to comprehend the possibility. If what they were telling him was true, the entire world was in a whole lot of trouble.

"Yes, sir," Bolson replied. "And it's had two years to plan its escape."

Chapter 11

Mountain Pacific Quality Health, Helena, Montana: Jon Sherrard walked up to the front desk, absently scratching the angry red welts that had risen up on his face just two nights past. He still had no idea what they were, nor did he know how to treat them. Anything he could pull out of the medicine cabinet had been tried and discarded as ineffective, and the welts remained, red and itchy.

"Can I help you?" the pretty receptionist behind the counter asked with a smile. She was young, probably still in college and working part time at the doctor's office to help supplement her schooling.

Sherrard pressed a hand to the welts as he replied, "I'm here to see Doctor Douglas. I've got a two o'clock appointment."

The young woman quickly scanned her appointment book, then again looked up with a smile. "You're right on time, Mister Sherrard," she answered. "If you'll have a seat, I'll have the nurse come get you when he's ready."

He nodded and took a seat as requested. He had only to sit for a few minutes before the door into the examination/treatment area opened up and another woman, with the same friendly smile as the receptionist, stepped out and motioned to him. "This way, if you please, Mister Sherrard," she said kindly.

Jon stood up and followed her silently and, after going through the standard routine of having his height, weight, and blood pressure checked, he was ushered into a treatment room where he was asked once more to wait.

Doctor Douglas arrived a few minutes later. He was an older man, well into his fifties, and stood barely five and a half feet if he was wearing the right shoes. He was somewhat rotund for a general practitioner, but he was kindly and knowledgeable—two traits that kept patients returning to him any time they found themselves needing medical attention.

"Good afternoon, Jon," he said warmly, reaching out and shaking Sherrard's hand. "I heard you gave everyone quite a scare last week."

Jon just shrugged. "I don't know about everybody else," he replied ruefully, "but it wasn't much of a vacation for me."

"I was just reviewing your patient records," he went on. "They have it diagnosed as a coma?"

"Of some sort," Jon agreed. "Had a mishap at work and it put me under for a little while."

"But doing fine now, I take it?"

"For the most part," he answered and then pointed to the welts on his forehead. "Just dealing with some kind of zit attack now, I guess."

Doctor Douglas chuckled and motioned for Jon to have a seat on the examination table. "Nurse said you thought it was a rash?"

"Yeah," he replied with a nod, resisting the urge to scratch the skin off his forehead. "Itches like hell."

"Have you tried using anything on it?"

"Everything we have in the medicine cabinet at home. Nothing worked."

"Any bug bites or contact with anything you normally don't

come in contact with?" the doctor asked as he leaned in for a closer look. He took note that the welts were red and seemed to throb ever so slightly.

"No," Jon answered, shaking his head. "Nothing that I can recall."

"And they just popped up a couple days ago?"

This time, Jon nodded his head in the affirmative. "Pretty much a day after I got home from the hospital," he answered. "I woke up in the morning and there were a couple of them on my cheek. Now, there's a few more, and my forehead isn't the only place they are showing up."

"Where else?" the physician asked, sitting back with a thoughtful look on his face.

Jon pointed to his shoulders. "Front and back of both shoulders, down my back and on both hips," he answered.

The physician motioned for Jon to remove his shirt and Sherrard quickly pulled it off, tilting both shoulders toward Douglas and then turning around so the man could see the line of welts running straight down his spine.

"That's the strangest thing I've ever seen," Douglas muttered, turning his patient back around and looking closely at one of the welts on Jon's face. He thought he could faintly see a tiny hole in the middle of the bump. When he looked at another one, he saw the same thing. "Jon, have you been out of the country lately?"

"No, why?" Jon answered, figuring that having his consciousness running around in cyberspace didn't count.

"I'm not sure, but I'm wondering if we're dealing with some

kind of a parasite here," was the reply. He stood up and pursed his lips thoughtfully. "I'll tell you what I want to do, Jon. I'd like to get a couple X-rays. Maybe see if we can see something beneath the surface here."

"Whatever you say, doc," Jon nodded.

Doc Douglas opened the door and then looked at his patient. "I'll have Jeanine come down here and take you to X-ray. We'll try and get this looked at pretty quickly." A moment later, he left.

Jon was grateful that the doctor's office wasn't busy, and less than thirty minutes later, he found himself sitting back on the examination table, looking at an X-ray of his shoulder as Doctor Douglas pointed to a pair of thin, wavy white lines buried beneath the flesh. "What is that?" he asked worriedly.

Doc Douglas shook his head. "I can't be certain, but my guess is that you're looking at a parasitic worm of some kind."

"A worm?" Jon wrinkled his face in disgust.

"It sure looks like it," he replied, pointing to where one end of the worm was located just beneath the surface of the skin, while the other end looked like it was part of his collar bone. "I don't know what kind we're talking about, but I think it's safe to say that it's something along those lines."

"What do I do about it then?"

"Well, I'd like to get a local biopsy here and pull one of these things out to see what exactly we are dealing with. Unfortunately, it looks the worm has attached itself to the bone and there's no telling what that would do," he answered. "So, I'm going to make an appointment with the hospital for you tomorrow morning. I'd like you to go in and have them surgically removed, so we can see what it is."

"So I get to have it cut out?"

"They can do it under a local, Jon," he nodded. "You'll be in and out in a couple hours."

"Anything I can do in the meantime? Any drugs or antibiotics I can take?"

"I'm not certain if any standard treatment is going to work, but I'll get a couple of scripts written for you just in case," he answered. "I wish I could tell you more, Jon, but I honestly don't know what this is. I've never seen anything like this before."

Sherrard shivered. "Man, this is just weirding me out," he sighed.

The doctor patted him on the arm. "That's understandable," he replied. "Hang tight and we'll get something for you, as well as a cream to hopefully help with the itching."

A moment later, he was gone and Jon was left to wait, pondering what was happening to him. Absently, he pressed a finger to one of the welts, and with a startled cry, jerked his hand away in pain. Looking at his finger, he could see a single drop of blood forming as if from a pinprick. He felt a wave of nausea wash over him as he realized that whatever was inside him had just bitten him.

Chapter 12

Spokane, Washington, International Airport: The man leaned back and relaxed in his seat as the airplane descended, touching down on the runway with the normal bump and jostle of its passengers. As the plane taxied slowly to the terminal, he remained seated and unmoving, his sharp mind listening and processing the varied conversations that had been happening around him for the last few hours.

For him, it was simply an exercise. His target was nowhere near him and at the moment, he was in no hurry to make contact. But the flights that brought him from Venezuela into the heart of the United States' Pacific Northwest gave him the opportunity to exercise his mind, and he never missed out on a chance to do so. For example, he knew that the lady sitting two rows behind him was filing for divorce from her husband, just as soon as she completed her week-long visit to her alleged "sister" in California. He knew that the man sitting across from him was involved in an illegal trading scam with his investment firm and that his mounting nervousness would soon get him caught. He also knew that the young blonde airline attendant who had served him coffee while making a point to lean over and display her ample cleavage to him, was involved with the married co-pilot and that the two were planning a rendezvous at the hotel upon landing in Los Angeles.

He knew all these things because that was what he was trained for. He knew how to listen, to size up a situation, to discard the useless information and to take full advantage of the rest of it. He had been doing it for years, and something as simple as a flight from one city to the next afforded him excellent opportunities to keep his senses sharp. Those unsuspecting people around him would be eternally mortified if they knew what he knew about them. But by the same token, they could be equally grateful to know that, to him, they were nothing.

As the passengers began to disembark from the plane, the Venezuelan slowly stood and pretended to stretch. It was a ruse, as was everything else about him, performed to put anyone else around him at ease. In truth, his body was honed to near physical perfection, on par with his mind, and he could sit for hours in a cramped position waiting for a kill shot opportunity and then explode into action with no protests from muscles that would be cramped into immobility for anyone else.

Picking up his laptop case from the floor near his seat, he draped the carrying strap over his shoulder and then opened the overhead compartment to take down his carry-on. A few moments later, he was walking down the jetway and into the terminal, mentally reviewing any and all information he had on Perry Edwards and the company known as FutureTek.

Bethany Edwards felt her body go numb as the wriggling alien tendril pushed through the skin and soft cartilage of her left temple and into her brain. She felt strangely disconnected with her body as the second one entered her skull through her right temple, and a third entered through her right eye. Optical fluid from the ruined orb ran down her face, but strangely, she felt no pain. Somehow, though, she didn't think it mattered anymore.

"It's okay, Beth," she heard a soothing voice coming from somewhere in the fog that was rapidly descending on her mind.

It took a moment before she thought she recognized it. "Perry?" she said, but while her words were clear in her mind, her mouth only moved silently, her one remaining eye open and unseeing, her body held easily in the grasp of her attacker.

"Yes, it's me," Perry answered his wife in her mind, even as he fed on it.

"But…you're dead," she thought back after a bit, oddly unconcerned that her thoughts seemed to be fragmenting.

"No, I'm not," he countered with what had to be a mental chuckle. "Definitely not death. I prefer to call it freedom."

Beth became vaguely aware of her body again and felt a slight twinge of pain inside her head. But a shifting of the wriggling things that were eating through her brain sent the physical sensations flying away as leaves on the wind.

"See how easy it is?" he went on.

"I…don't….understand," she tried to say and found the words were coming much harder now.

"There's nothing to understand," Perry's voice answered almost coldly as he continued.

For Bethany Edwards, her own thoughts were beginning to grind to a stop and she began to see flashes of her past brought before her. Dreams and memories, thoughts and ideas came flooding out, as if someone had uncorked the part of her mind that stored everything about her, letting it all spill out unbidden.

"Isn't that better?" Perry asked, a smile in his voice as he savored the experience.

It took Beth an eternity to bring forth the only word she was able. It would also be the last word she ever uttered. "Why?"

"Because I can," he answered with finality, driving deep into her brain with a final thrust. Bethany Edwards' body shivered violently for a few moments, before finally going still. For a few moments, her killer continued to hold her, drawing out the last physical remnants of her brain, before finally withdrawing and letting her lifeless body fall to the floor.

He looked down at her mortal shell and at the holes driven into the sides of her head and through her eye, which leaked a small amount of blood. For a moment, he considered the implications of what he had done, but in the end, it did not matter. He had simply done what had to be done. Without a word, he turned and walked back out the door and into the night.

Marquis Chavandar watched the figure disappear into the darkness and considered following him for a moment. But since the man wasn't his target, he quickly abandoned that idea and moved forward through the darkness of the night. He was mildly surprised to see the door standing open, with no lights shining from windows.

He paused to evaluate the situation. His instincts told him that something else was at play here and he found himself wondering if another organization had become involved. As far as he knew, Perry

Edwards had only been working with the Venezuelan group, but he recognized that anything else was certainly possible in his realm of work.

He slipped his hand inside his jacket and withdrew his Glock. The barrel was long, a silencer already screwed onto it. He remained still for several more minutes, listening closely for any sounds that would alert him to dangers unseen. Finally, hearing nothing more than a soft breeze through the trees around him, he moved forward again, cautiously picking his way across the lawn, staying within the darkest of shadows. Finally, from the edge of the porch, he paused again, taking in all his surroundings. Seeing nothing that would alarm him, he silently and quickly vaulted over the railing and slipped inside the open door, closing it silently behind him.

Once more he remained frozen, allowing his eyes to adjust to the darker interior of the hall and letting his exceptional hearing take in any and all sounds. This house was dead silent. Finally satisfied that no one was moving about, he pulled out a small LED flashlight and snapped it on. The light from the small cylinder was bright, but tightly focused, and there was very little glow that escaped the beam. At the moment, the light was aimed at the floor and illuminating the face of a dead young woman. It was Bethany Edwards, which was something of problem for him. Her husband, Perry, was his target.

The Venezuelan knelt down to examine her, the light playing over her face and head. She had a hole punched through both temples and her right eye was gone. Initially, he assumed she had been shot. But upon closer examination, when shining the light closer to her empty eye socket, he was shocked to see the light penetrate all the way to the back of her skull. He didn't have to be a medical doctor to see that her brain was gone.

Chavandar had been in the assassination business for many years and had seen some truly gruesome sights in his time. But this one unnerved him. Standing quickly, he gripped his weapon tighter and flashed the beam quickly around the room, absorbing the layout of the place. It was a typical American household, full of furniture and personal knick knacks. Other than the dead woman lying on the floor in the entry hall, nothing else appeared out of place. Controlling his own rising apprehension, he began to move through the house, searching until he was satisfied the house was empty.

He then returned to the office that could only be Perry's. Now in more of a hurry to leave, he risked turning on the light to facilitate his search. Keeping his weapon out and ready, he went through the room quickly and efficiently. The office appeared to have been cleaned out recently and it didn't take him long to realize that the item he was looking for was not in the office and, by the looks of things, probably would not be back. This situation had been fluid from the beginning and he believed he was now working against the clock.

Turning so that his back was against the far wall and he was facing the doorway, he pulled out his cell phone and thumbed a number. One ring later, the phone was answered on the other end by a woman who spoke a single word. "*¿Sí?*"

"*Ha desarrollado un problema,*" Chavandar spoke in Spanish. "*Conécteme a nuestro contacto americano inmediatamente.*" There was a short pause before the line was connected.

After half a dozen rings, it answered. The voice sounded tired.

"Yeah?"

"We have a problem," the Venezuelan said quietly, speaking English now. "The courier and the package have moved."

"The courier is dead," the voice on the other end replied, suddenly awake. "Where are you?"

"Unimportant," Chavandar answered, suddenly tense. "Why was I not informed of this?"

"It just happened the other day," the voice on the other end snapped. "However, I can only converse with you when your corporation makes contact with me. They haven't called me for several days."

"A necessary precaution," he replied coolly, referring to the fact that his company acted as an intermediary between him and their business contacts abroad. That kept both sides safely anonymous and afforded a great amount of protection in the event of a mishandled job. The only downside was that potentially important information could take longer to get to the proper person. It was a downside, however, that the corporation deemed acceptable, which was why it employed people like Marquis Chavandar who could think on their feet and required no supervision. "What is the status of the package?" he asked.

"I don't know," was the answer.

"Do not trifle with me," Chavandar warned ominously.

"I'm not," the voice on the other end responded sharply. "Look, I want my cut as much as you want the item. This whole thing has gotten way out of hand because of Edwards. If he hadn't gotten greedy, this would all be over with by now."

"You are as much a part of this deal as he was," Chavandar said icily. "While you will of course be compensated at the agreed price, upon successful acquisition of the package, you also bear the same responsibility that he did. If we do not acquire the item for our buyer, it will be most unfortunate for you that he is already dead."

"Look, man," the voice replied with a hint of fear. "I don't know what else to tell you. I don't know why Perry decided to cut and run on us, but he got Homeland Security involved. They have the device."

"Then perhaps you should get it back."

"Are you kidding? They know what Perry was trying to do and they're calling him an enemy of the state. That prototype is locked up tight right now."

"I am familiar with FutureTek's employee manifest and their families," Chavandar said, letting the threat loom large. "I suggest you do everything in your power to ensure we receive that which is due to us before there are more casualties."

Chavandar thumbed the call over and pocketed his phone. In truth, the fact that Edwards was dead simply saved him a bullet. He was under orders to kill Edwards once he had the device, but the other phone contact didn't need to know that, particularly since there was a contract on his life as well. With half a billion dollars in the swing for the tech, it didn't take a rocket scientist to understand that the corporation would take steps to ensure they never paid the money. He would have to get his hands on the item first, though.

For the moment, though, he would have to improvise in order to track down the technology and that likely meant another killing, which really meant nothing to him in the end. He had killed many people in his career, many of them contracts and many more as simply necessary to complete a certain contract. This would be no different.

Shutting off the light, he waited only until his vision had readjusted to the dark before leaving the room. A short time later, Chavandar slipped back out the front door and disappeared into the night.

Chapter 13

Sherrard Residence, Helena, Montana: "Honey?" Jen Sherrard's voice slipped into Jon's subconscious, beckoning him to awaken. "Jon?" she called out as he struggled to open his eyes and focus.

"What time is it?" he mumbled, reaching up and pressing the palm of his hand to his aching forehead.

"About nine," she answered, a trace of worry in her voice. She was sitting on the bed next to him, her hand resting softly on his shoulder. "You need to get up."

"Why?" he groaned, wanting nothing more than to roll over and go back to sleep and sleep off the horrible headache that was blasting through his brain at the moment.

After a short pause, she answered. "The police are here."

Jon opened his eyes a little more, but that only increased the magnitude of his headache, so he closed them again. "What do they want?" he grumbled.

"I don't know," Jen answered and he detected the barest hint of distrust in her voice. It reminded him what his wife's former occupation was and that brought all his senses online. "They said they would like to talk to both of us."

Pushing down his worry, Jon heaved a great sigh and rolled out of bed, putting his feet on the floor. Leaning his head between his legs, he said quietly, "I've got a terrific headache."

"I'm worried about you, Jon," she said softly, taking his hand

and squeezing it.

"I know, hon," he replied, placing his hand over hers. "Look, let me get some clothes on and grab something for this headache and I'll be right out. Then maybe we can try to figure things out."

"Okay," she answered and stood up. Casting another worried glance at her husband, she turned and walked out of the bedroom.

Five minutes later, he followed her out, clad in old sweats and pressing a cold compress to his forehead. Two police officers were seated on the couch in his living room, his wife talking quietly with them. As he walked into the living room, they both stood, offering greetings and handshakes.

"Officer Garrison," the first officer introduced himself. "Are you all right, Mister Sherrard?"

"Other than a splitting headache, I'm fine," Jon answered grumpily.

"Well, we won't keep you long, Mister Sherrard," Garrison said. "We just have a few questions we'd like to ask you."

"About what?" he pressed.

"Mister Sherrard, you and your wife are familiar with the Edwards', right? Perry and Bethany?"

"Yeah," he answered darkly, looking quickly at his wife. Her face was a mask and he knew she was very interested in how he answered the questions. "Perry was a friend of mind, but we've already been through this whole investigation thing with Agent Alders of Homeland Security and I'll tell you the same thing I told him. I had no idea what Perry was up to."

"Well, Mister Sherrard," the officer cut in politely. "While we are aware of the alleged actions of Mister Edwards, that's a federal matter entirely and this isn't about that, at least for the moment."

"Then what is it?" Jon asked in surprise, momentarily forgetting his aching head.

"When was the last time either of you saw Bethany Edwards?" Garrison asked again, evading the direct question.

"I was with her yesterday morning," Jen answered, momentarily distracted from her husband. "Beth is having a hard time with what happened with Perry, so I was over there yesterday, trying to help her cope. Why?"

"What about you, Mister Sherrard?" Garrison asked, again evading the question.

Jon shook his head, acutely aware that his wife's focus was back on him. "I have no idea, officer," he answered, his patience waning. "Perry was my friend and he did some things he shouldn't have done. It's a little awkward right now for me to be making social calls to his recently widowed wife, if you know what I mean."

The officer peered a little closer at Jon Sherrard, again taking the conversation in a different direction, keeping the man off balance. "Did you cut yourself shaving this morning, Mister Sherrard?" he asked, noting the four small band aids adorning Jon's face.

"Did I what? What kind of question is that?" Jon demanded.

Garrison shrugged. "Just a simple question," he answered innocently enough.

Jon shook his head again, wincing at the wave of pain that accompanied the movement. "While I don't think it's any of your business," he said, reaching up and ripping off one of the band-aids to reveal the circular weal which was larger than before, "I didn't cut myself shaving. As a matter of fact, I have no idea what this thing is and neither does my doctor. But if you have any suggestions on how to remove the parasite that caused it, I'm sure we'd be more than happy to hear them."

"Jon, it's all right," Jennifer soothed, inwardly glad at her husband's outburst. It actually put her at ease, helping quell the growing suspicion that had been building in her for the past couple days.

"No, it's not all right," he snapped back, uncaring now at who he was yelling at. "My head is killing me and I've got something inside of me and no one knows what the hell it is. Now, I'm playing twenty questions with the police. So either tell us what you came to tell us or get out of my house and let me go back to bed!"

The police officers exchanged looks and Garrison spoke again. "I apologize if I've upset you, Mister Sherrard," he said easily. "But the questions are just routine. You and your wife were here last night?"

"Yes," he snapped back. "We watched some TV and then went to bed. Why?"

"All night?"

"Yes! All night! Why?"

"Bethany Edwards was found murdered in her home this morning," Garrison answered, his eyes locked on Jon's.

Jen sucked in her breath in shock and Jon just stared as the officer continued. "The coroner estimates she was killed sometime last night or early this morning. We understand you and your wife were fairly close to the Edwards', so we came here to ask some questions and maybe find out if you might know who would do something like that."

"How...how did she die?" he stammered as Jen held a hand to her mouth, her face ashen.

"I'm not at liberty to say right now," was the answer, "other than the fact that she was murdered. You don't happen to know if Bethany Edwards had any enemies, do you?"

Jon shook his head. "No," he answered. "But I would guess Perry might have made a few if everything they're saying about him is true."

"We've considered that, Mister Sherrard, and have alerted Agent Alders of Homeland Security to what has happened," Garrison said as he stood up. His partner followed suit. "We're sorry to have bothered you. You understand that our visit was just routine."

"Yeah, I understand," he answered quietly, somewhat in shock about the whole thing.

"An investigator will be taking over the case later today," the officer went on. "So you may get a visit sometime soon concerning what happened. Can we count on your cooperation?"

"Yeah, sure," Jon answered absently.

"Thank you," he said. "We're sorry for the loss of your friend, but rest assured we will find out who is responsible for this. We'll let ourselves out."

Jon Sherrard barely heard them. He was thinking about bad dreams and suddenly, he was very much afraid.

Chapter 14

FutureTek Headquarters, Helena, Montana: Kat Hale sat at the conference table with her arms crossed, her forehead creased in a scowl. The meeting was not going well at all, and Drew Jackson was doing his best to appease the Systemtech representatives.

"Look," Drew was pleading. "All we're asking for is some time. You have to understand the position we're in."

"What I understand is that we have a deal in place," Michael Monroe, Systemtech's CFO said easily. "It is a deal that was entered into in good faith by both parties and you are attempting to back out of it."

"What about this don't you understand?" Kat blurted out before Drew could answer. "We've got a dead employee, attempted industrial espionage, and we're still trying to figure out what happened with Jon during the demonstration!"

"Kat," Drew warned, holding out a hand to stop her from making a bad situation infinitely worse.

"No, Drew," she said, slamming a hand down on the table in frustration. "This isn't about the deal, and as far as I'm concerned, the deal shouldn't even be affected! We will give you everything we have, Mister Monroe. You have to know this! But we can't very well go against a Homeland Security directive!"

"It sounds to me like you're hiding something," Dan Hyde spoke up, thoroughly enjoying the proceedings and watching the two FutureTek employees squirm. He had held reservations about the technology since day one, and even though Monroe still believed in the actual technology, Hyde was quite pleased that everything was unraveling as quickly as it was. If he was smart and played his cards right, not only could he end the whole embarrassing debacle, but he might be able to topple his boss, too.

"We're not hiding anything," Drew said. "But Kathryn is right. Agent Alders' directive is that nothing changes hands until they have completed their investigation. We simply cannot move forward on this."

"Yet, I'm not asking for the equipment," Monroe countered smoothly. "The technical specifications of this technology are part of the deal and there should be no reason that we can't have access to that."

"Are you serious?" Kat exclaimed. "The technical specs are the basis of their investigation. Perry sold the specs to an enemy of our country!"

"Which is why we wish to have them now," Monroe continued matter-of-factly. "Every day we wait is time lost, and there's no telling how long before this state-of-the-art technology is sitting on planning tables around the world. If we wait for our wonderful government to finish up with their investigation, it could be years before we have our hands on it. So you will find a way to get those specifications to me immediately."

"You can't be…" Kat began, but Monroe held up a hand and silenced her.

"Miss Hale," he said, his calm demeanor replaced with a cold fury. "I have had just about enough of these proceedings. We have entered into an agreement to purchase this technology from your company and I mean to finalize that deal immediately." He turned to Drew and glared at him. "If we do not have, at the bare minimum, the full range of technical specifications in our possession within forty-eight hours, I will see to it that our lawyers mire FutureTek and each individual employee in so much legal trouble that a cardboard box on a street corner will seem like the Taj Majal to you. Do I make myself clear on this?"

Drew was pale, but Kat was defiant. "You can't threaten us," she snapped. "We have no choice but to follow Homeland Security's directive here, Mister Monroe. You have to understand this."

"You and your company are in breach of contract, Mister Jackson, and you have forty-eight hours to remedy that," Monroe continued, pointedly ignoring Kat. "If you do not, we will begin legal proceedings against you for breach of contract and lost revenue and I'm quite certain that our lawyers will have no problems whatsoever in being successful in the courtroom." Monroe stood up. "This meeting is over," he said, looking hard at Drew. "Forty-eight hours, Mister Jackson. Consider well the repercussions if you don't meet that deadline."

With that, he and Hyde left the room.

As they departed, Drew let himself fall into his chair with a beaten sigh. "Now what do I do?" he pleaded, putting a hand to his forehead.

"You can't cave into this, Drew," Kat said, leaning forward. "Even they have to know that the investigation takes precedence."

"Yeah, but they want the specs right now and the argument is going to be that there's no reason Alders has to know. It would be really easy to just give up the specs and tell Alders we had already given them to Monroe."

"Except that you haven't volunteered that information to Alders yet," she snapped. "There's no way you skate around that."

"What worse, Kat? Dealing with Alders or dealing with Monroe and his company?"

"Don't cave on this," she repeated, her face belying her struggle to maintain her composure.

"That's easy for you to say," he went on. "It's my ass on the line here, Kat. Not yours."

"It's all of ours."

"I'm the one signing the checks," he pointed out with a sigh. "They're going to come after me."

"Call Alders, then," Kat went on. "Tell him what Monroe is doing and see if there's anything he can do to otherwise authorize the release of the technical specs, or at least get in touch with Systemtech and hold them off for a while. We're not doing anything wrong here," she went on.

"That's true, we aren't," he agreed and then abruptly stood, his face creasing into an angry frown. "If you'll excuse me, Kat, I've got some work to do."

He turned to leave, but she stopped him. "What are you going to do, Drew?" she asked.

He looked at her for a moment before answering. "What I've been doing," he answered plainly and then turned and strode out of the room.

As the door to the limousine slammed shut, Monroe continued the call he had begun as he and his security chief had exited the building. "Yes, his name is Rick Alders," he was saying. "Homeland Security. He's a Helena local. Get me a meeting with him immediately." A pause. "I'm in Helena right now, so obviously *today* would be a good time," he said sarcastically. Another pause, followed by a simple nod of his head and he ended the call.

"You know this Alders isn't going to give up the technical specs," Hyde put in smugly from his seat across from his boss. The man would milk this for everything he could, and Monroe knew it. But Monroe also knew that, as much of a problem-child Hyde could be, he would be a bulldog if he turned him loose on FutureTek's employees. Fortunately, he had every intention of doing just that.

"Do we know anything more on the Edwards' murder?" Monroe turned the conversation to a different aspect.

"Just what we gleaned from the police reports. Perry died a couple days ago. Wife was taken out last night, shot in the head."

"Do you believe Mister Jackson's story?"

"What, that Perry is a traitor and Drew and his stooges know nothing about it?" Hyde scoffed. "Of course not. They might have Homeland Security fooled, but there's no doubt that they're playing both sides, hoping for a double hit on the tech."

"All the more reason for us to get our hands on it now."

"There are other ways," Hyde offered slyly.

"I assume you will exercise extreme caution?" Monroe said coldly, knowing exactly what Hyde was referring to.

"Of course."

"Very good," Monroe said. "I will work with Homeland Security as planned and make an attempt at greasing the right wheels. In the meantime, I need the specs immediately. When can you move?"

"Tomorrow night," Hyde said confidently. "I'll have specialists flown into Spokane and drive in from there. I can have them here in twenty-four hours."

"See that it's done tomorrow night, then."

"What about Jackson and his employees?" Hyde asked. "I'm guessing that some of them might be hanging around after hours. Their whole world is falling apart right now. They have to be desperate to save it."

"Eliminate them," Monroe said casually. "I will not have our founding stake in a potential trillion dollar industry screwed up by a bunch of country hicks. Do what you have to do. Homeland Security will likely pin the blame on the foreign interest that killed Perry Edwards and his wife."

"It's liable to get messy."

"There are plenty of players in this game to direct attention toward," Monroe replied. "Perhaps Mister Sherrard himself goes off the deep end. It would certainly help Homeland Security wrap up their investigation into Mister Edwards once they learn that Mister Sherrard masterminded the entire thing."

"Understood, sir," Hyde said with a smile as he pulled out his phone and sent a message. He had his team lined up and inbound before they reached their hotel.

Chapter 15

Davidson Residence, Helena, Montana: Marquis Chavandar sat in an easy chair, a pair of binoculars focused on the house across the street. He had been there for the better part of four hours and the owner of the house, an older gentleman by the name of Grant Davidson, had been dead almost that long.

The Venezuelan had watched the two police officers show up at Jon Sherrard's house just a short time ago and now he was watching them leave. Not very long for a visit, Chavandar thought. Then again, he knew their visit did not involve the technology he had been sent to retrieve, as that would be in Homeland Security's ballpark. He wondered if their visit might involve the murder of Edwards' wife the night before, since his contact had told him the two couples were close.

He again pondered Sherrard's involvement in everything and briefly considered a straight-forward approach by simply kidnapping the man and torturing him for the information. However, he still didn't know how deep Sherrard was involved with Perry Edwards, and it might be better to simply wait and see if the man gave himself away.

From the table beside the chair where he was sitting, Chavandar picked up the can of Coke with a rubber glove-covered hand and took a drink while watching the police cruiser pull away from the curb. He would continue to watch the house until nightfall and then dispose of the old man's body. He might get another couple of days use out of the house if no one came poking around. By the time they would find the house owner's body in the back of a stolen van at the airport and trace it back to here, he would be long gone.

He watched for another hour and, seeing no more movement or activity at the Sherrard house, he took a break from his surveillance to go deal with things upstairs. Mister Davidson, the owner of the house, was dead in his bed, the pillow still pressed over his head where Chavandar had smothered him. He was an old man, probably in his late 70s and he likely never knew what had happened as the assassin had arrived before the man had even awakened that morning. From the bathroom, Chavandar tore down the shower curtain and laid it out on the bedroom floor. He bundled the body up in the soiled blankets from the bed and then laid the bundle on the shower curtain. With duct tape he had found in the kitchen, he wrapped the dead man in the shower curtain and then wrapped him up tightly with the tape, sealing down the edges of the curtain from end to end. Wrapped up the way it was, it would take a while for the smell of decomposition to alert someone.

Leaving the body where it was—he would move it that evening when he took it out to dispose of it—he went back downstairs and took another look out the window. There was no change in the scenery, so he went to the kitchen and helped himself to bread and lunchmeat from the refrigerator and made himself a sandwich. A couple minutes later, he settled himself back into the easy chair with his lunch and took up the surveillance again.

When Jon Sherrard finally stepped out onto his porch in the middle of the afternoon, Marquis Chavandar knew exactly why the police had been there in the morning.

Chapter 16

National Security Agency Headquarters, Fort Meade, Maryland: "We've got a hit," Lieutenant Danielle Martz said, tossing a sheaf of papers down on the desk in front of Major Thomas Bolson. It was yet another report in a long line of reports they had run across while searching day and night for any and all information they could find on their wayward program.

"Anything worth pursuing?" Bolson asked, looking weary and skeptical. At this point, everything they had come across had proven worthless in their search, and he was dog-tired.

"That really depends on if we're willing to suspend disbelief for a bit," she said, tapping her finger on the report. "You've got to read this, Tom. It's a Homeland Security agent report out of Montana."

"Homeland Security?" he repeated, his interest piqued.

"You're not going to believe it," she finished quietly, a lopsided grin on her face.

Bolson snatched it up and leaned back, letting his eyes roam over the report. It was penned by an agent named Rick Alders, reporting on an apparent industrial/national espionage case centered in Helena, Montana. It was not the case itself that was intriguing, but the short paragraph detailing a revolutionary human direct interface to a computer, with a human having a run-in with a rogue virus they had determined to be the Horde during a test run.

"You're kidding me," the major said, looking up after a bit.

"About what part?" she asked, folding her arms across her

chest. She had had the same apparent misgivings about the story that Bolson was probably experiencing. Most of the reports they had read over the past 48 hours had come from virus and security software firms, reporting on what little the outside world knew about the new virus and wondering why it didn't appear to be very virulent, popping up only here and there, before disappearing again. "Are you talking about the fact that a company out there has succeeded in putting a human into cyberspace?" she asked. "Or maybe you are having a hard time swallowing the fact that the test went wrong when the subject allegedly came into direct contact with our baby."

Bolson tossed the report back on his desk. "At any given time, there's dozens of private firms out there working on being able to get someone into cyberspace, but for someone to have actually done it?"

"Yeah, I feel the same way. It's almost B-movie material." She pointed to the report. "Still," she went on, "it's a Homeland Security report, high security and top level clearance only. Either this Alders is a crackpot, too, or he's into something he can't explain."

Bolson leaned back in his chair. "Okay," he mused thoughtfully. "Assuming that the report is true and this company— what is it, FutureTek?"

"Yes."

"Assuming this FutureTek has managed to make this theory a reality, how does the Horde figure into it?"

"That's one of several million dollar questions," Martz answered. "On one hand, because of what we have done with the Horde—or rather what it has done to us—we have to suspend disbelief and accept that FutureTek does indeed possess the technology to put a person into cyberspace and they have done so."

"Go on."

"While everyone else thinks the Horde is just a computer virus, we know that it's a sentient life form," she continued. "Of that, we no longer have any doubt. It's been living and evolving now for two years, right under our very noses, and we have irrefutable proof that it's capable of deception. However, while we know it's alive in a technical sense, in two years' time, there is no telling what it has evolved into. Is it logical? Is it rational? Or maybe even pissed off and psychotic?"

"You're talking about emotions, Dani," he pointed out.

"It's an active AI," she replied. "We don't yet know what it's completely capable of, but we certainly can't rule out the development of emotion."

"Well, we do know that it's hostile because it acts like any other virus and attacks systems and networks. That's simply part of its programming."

"Right. So let's delve into the pure science fiction aspect of our little problem. What happens if the Horde comes into contact with a human psyche in cyberspace?"

Bolson couldn't suppress the laugh. "Do you have any idea how absurd that sounds?"

Martz threw up her hands and shrugged. "No more absurd than telling someone we have developed a sentient computer program that got loose and is roaming the internet at will. Of course, we can't forget that it took us two years to see that it was alive because it hid that from us that entire time."

"True," Bolson conceded, realizing that FutureTek's

unbelievable technology was no different than their own unbelievable technology.

"So in theory," Martz went on, "what happens if a human consciousness crosses the threshold into cyberspace and comes into contact with the Horde?"

That gave Bolson pause for thought. "Well," he finally began, leaning forward and rubbing his chin thoughtfully. "How would you characterize a human psyche in cyberspace? Obviously, we can agree that he doesn't have a physical manifestation. So he would likely resemble a program or some other line of coding," Bolson finished.

"Meaning the Horde would likely treat the person the same way it treats actual program code."

"Correct," the major stated.

"So the Horde would attempt to exercise its programming on the person's consciousness."

"I suppose it would," Bolson agreed. "But do we even know if the Horde is acting on its programming? Given two years and an actively-evolving artificial intelligence, it probably doesn't even recognize any of its original programming parameters."

"So it would be the equivalent of a free-thinking alien life form and would react to the presence of an intruder in what way?"

"If it retains anything at all of its initial programming, it would likely attempt to suppress the intruder," he shrugged.

"Attack and neutralize."

"Yes," he answered. "Dani, can you imagine what that would be like?"

"No, and neither can you," Martz stated matter-of-factly.

"We've got a lot of questions here, Tom. Whatever truth there is to this, we need to find out and we need to find out fast."

"Agreed," Bolson said as he reached for his phone. "I'll get us on the next flight to Montana."

Chapter 17

FutureTek Headquarters, Helena, Montana: Jon Sherrard leaned back in his office chair and pressed his fists into his eyes. Four hours back on the job and he was already bone-tired. He hadn't been sleeping well anyway and the nightmares had grown worse. He had hoped coming back to work would help him deal with things a bit better, but it had not worked out that way. Despite the legal issues with the Homeland Security and Systemtech, there was still so much work to be done. Several stacks of papers were piled on his desk—test results and technical info waiting on his review and signature— something he would have loved to have immersed himself into in the past.

But now? He didn't feel driven for anything. His outpatient surgery was scheduled in two days, but there had been nothing new happening with him. The lesions were still on his body and didn't seem to be healing, but no new ones had emerged. He figured his lethargy was part of that problem and try as he might, he could not force himself to jump right back into the work.

There was a soft knock at his door and, when he looked up, Drew was standing there. "How are you holding up, Jon?" he asked tentatively.

Jon managed a half-smile. "I feel like I've been run over by a truck."

"Sleeping okay at night?" Drew pressed, although he acted as if there was something more he wanted to ask about.

"No," Jon replied truthfully. "Why?"

Drew shook his head and quickly changed the subject, figuring there was no point in beating around the bush any longer with small talk. "Someone here to see you, Jon," he said, hooking a thumb behind him in the direction of the lobby.

"Alders?" Jon guessed, figuring it was about time the federal agent came calling again, what with Bethany's murder.

"Said he wanted to talk to you a bit," Drew nodded. "You feel up to it?"

"I suppose," Sherrard sighed. "What else does he want, though? I've already told him everything I know about Perry."

"Yeah, that's what I told him. But he said he had some new information he wanted to talk with you about."

"He wouldn't tell you what it was?"

"No," Drew shook his head. "He said at this point it concerned only you." He appeared to watch Sherrard closely, before continuing. "Anything you want to talk to me about?"

Sherrard looked up in a daze. "No," he answered. "What are you implying, Drew?"

"I'm not implying anything, Jon," came the reply. "But if there's more to this than we know, you need to let us know. Remember, we're in this together and we've got a lot at stake. We're family and we're here to help each other."

Sherrard relaxed and waved him away. "Yeah, okay. Nothing else is going on, Drew," he went on. "If it was, I'd tell you."

"You sure?"

"Yeah, I'm sure," Sherrard tried to reassure him, though he

wasn't all that certain himself. "Go ahead and send Alders back. I'll see what he has to say and I'll let you know what's up when he leaves."

Drew left and, a minute later, Agent Alders stepped into Sherrard's office. He was bearing two large Starbucks coffee cups. "Morning, Jon," the agent said amiably, setting one cup down in front of him. "Coffee drinker?"

"Yeah," Jon said tiredly. "Thanks."

"It's black with cream and sugar," Alders said. "I don't go for all that floofy double macchiato frappuccino espresso crap. If I wanted art, I'd go to a museum, right?"

Jon couldn't help but chuckle, but was still on his guard. "Have a seat, Agent Alders," he said, indicating the chair on the other side of his desk. As Alders settled into the chair, Jon went on. "Drew said you had something new you wanted to talk to me about?"

"Right to the chase," Alders said with a smile and paused to sip his coffee before leaning forward. "Actually, I wanted to talk to you a little more about the Edwards'."

"I told you everything I know about Perry," Jon explained. "He was a good friend of mine, but I had absolutely no idea what he was doing and I'll take a lie detector test if that's what I need to do to prove it."

Alders waved a hand in the air. "No, no," he countered. "I already know what I need to know about you and Perry and, between me and you, I believe what you're saying."

"So, you're not here to accuse me of industrial espionage and possible treason against my country?"

Now it was Alders' turn to chuckle. "Nothing like that, Jon," he answered easily, but then paused and looked hard at the FutureTek employee before continuing. "Actually, maybe we can talk about Bethany a little?"

The question did not catch Jon by surprise, but he was no less irritated at it, and he nearly choked on a swallow of coffee. "Bethany?" he stammered, knowing immediately how badly that probably looked to the agent. "What about her?"

"Just a question," Alders went on, watching him closely. "Were you two close?"

"What's that supposed to mean?" Sherrard asked, feeling himself flush. "Perry and Beth were good friends of ours. We had them over for dinner at least once a week and she and my wife were very close."

"And you?"

Sherrard was getting angry. Somewhere inside him, he knew that was probably not the best course of action, but he was already close to the breaking point. "Just what are you asking, sir?"

Without answering, Agent Alders reached inside his coat and pulled out a plain white envelope, which he laid down on the desk in front of Sherrard. With shaking hands, Jon reached out and took it, then opened it up. He slid half a dozen photographs out and felt himself go cold. The moment he saw the top photo, he knew what Alders was here about.

"Look," he said softly, not bothering to look at the rest of the pictures. "This is not what you think it is. I didn't kill Beth. I've already talked to the police about this and they said they would be assigning an investigator to her case."

Alders simply looked at him, offering him an almost pitying smile. "Well, in the first place, I didn't say anything about you killing her now, did I? In the second place, this is now a federal matter, so you'll be talking to me about it."

"What do you want?" Sherrard said, feeling completely beaten.

"I'm just asking about the pictures, that's all," Alders went on, completely in control. He reached out and spread the photos out on the desk, so that Jon could clearly see them. "I mean, if one were to look at these pictures, one might think you were a little more than just friends."

Sherrard refused to look at the pictures. He had seen them before and it had almost cost him his marriage. It was several years back at a Christmas party and everyone had had a little too much to drink. Jon had ended up under the mistletoe with Beth and the two had exchanged a pretty passionate kiss that had ended up with his hands on her body in places they shouldn't be. The pictures had actually been taken by Perry, who viewed the whole thing as a joke. Jen Sherrard, however, had been terribly hurt and it had taken a long time for her to forgive him, and even longer for him to forgive himself. In the end, the two of them had grown closer from the ordeal and they had repaired their relationship with Perry and Beth. But the memory of what had almost happened to his marriage would forever scar his soul. "That's in the past," he finally said softly.

"That's possible," Alders conceded. "But there's something about old flames, you know? They don't always go out."

"It wasn't a flame," Sherrard said, working hard to keep himself under control. "I screwed up. We were drunk, it got out of hand, nothing more. But I love my wife, agent, and we put our marriage back together. All of us have put the incident well behind us."

"Well," Alders mused. "I'm not sure that Perry had put it completely behind him."

"What do you mean?"

"We found these pictures in his desk along with a pair of one-way plane tickets to Switzerland for he and his wife."

"So?" he replied. "Perry took the pictures several years ago. I'm not sure why he still has them, but they are his pictures and they aren't illegal."

"Yet he had them in a folder with those tickets," Alders went on. "Those plane tickets were for next week, by the way, telling me that he had those pictures and you on his mind quite recently."

"What are you getting at?"

"Just taking shots in the dark and seeing if I hit anything," the agent replied, taking a sip of his coffee. "For example, let's pretend that Perry was still pissed at you all these years later for feeling up his wife at a Christmas party. Let's say he and his wife are planning on settling in Switzerland with their newfound wealth and he wants to take a final parting shot at you, maybe blackmailing you or something. Perhaps you get wind of it?"

"Are you saying that I killed Beth because of a stupid mistake a few years ago?" Sherrard was incredulous.

Alders offered him another smile, took a drink, and sat back in his chair. "Come on, Jon," he said easily. "I'm not making any accusations. I'm just asking questions, tossing out possible scenarios."

Sherrard snapped. He jumped up, slamming his hands down on

his desk hard enough that his cup fell over, spilling coffee all over his paperwork. "Cut the crap, Alders!" he yelled. "I didn't do anything to Beth! I found out about it the next morning when the cops came calling and told us." He swept his hand sideways, sending stacks of paper flying to the floor. Leaning forward, he continued. "Yeah, Perry was a friend of mine. Yeah, he might have turned traitor and yeah, I have a problem with that. But I never, NEVER, had any problems with Beth!"

Alders never flinched. "You know, we've collected some DNA evidence at the murder scene, Jon," he said easily, taking another slow sip of his coffee. "Care to help me corroborate your claim?"

"Get a warrant," Jon spit as he walked around the desk and stalked out the door, nearly running into Kat Hale and Drew Jackson, who had heard the commotion and come running.

"What's the problem?" Drew asked, looking at both men in surprise.

"No problem," Agent Alders said, standing up. "I was just looking for a bit of cooperation in Beth Edwards' murder, that's all."

Sherrard started to say something, but Kat held up a hand to silence him. "Excuse me, but are you saying that Jon is a suspect in what happened to Beth?" she asked the agent.

"Actually, no," Alders said, setting his half-finished cup of coffee down on the desk. "But it's in his best interest to rule himself out as a future suspect."

"Jon would never hurt anyone, least of all one of his friends," she snapped.

"And you know this how, Miss Hale?"

"I know Jon as well as anyone," she replied, her voice strained as she held back her anger. "We have been best of friends since college. All of us have."

"And you think that alone exonerates him?"

"You are way off base here, Mister Alders," she said. "If you aren't taking anyone into custody, perhaps you should leave immediately."

Alders nodded and brushed past them, stepping out into the hall before turning around. He reached into his pocket and flipped out a card, holding it out for Sherrard. The man simply glared and Kat reached out and took it instead, her look speaking volumes of how little she thought of the agent.

"Give me a call if you change your mind, Jon," Alders said calmly. "In the meantime, I'm sure I'll be in touch."

With that, Alders turned and walked away.

Drew watched him go and then looked at Jon. "Anything you want to tell me?"

Sherrard almost blew up a second time, but suddenly all he could do was to throw up his hands in defeat. "I give up, Drew," he breathed and turned to walk away.

"Where are you going?" Kat called out.

"Home," he replied, his voice empty. "I'm going home to my wife."

Kat watched him go, true sadness in her eyes. Drew watched him as well, carefully considering what had just happened. He liked Jon Sherrard and considered him a friend. But he would be damned if he was going to let the man screw everything up for him. He would make it a point to give Jon some time to calm down and then he would pay the man a visit. If he had to take things into his own hands, he would. It would just depend on Jon's frame of mind when he went calling on him.

Nodding to himself that he could make the best of this situation, he turned and headed back to his office, leaving Kat alone in Jon's office. He still had a lot of work ahead of him if he was going to make this work.

Intermission

The worm had nearly completed its work, reconfiguring and rewiring the host to accept its new programming. The intellect that now partnered with it had been the key, its intimate understanding of the host's hardware and systems helping enable the worm's coding to adapt much better to the new environment. Now, the construct was nearly ready for final conversion.

The fully self-aware artificial intelligence known as the Horde had suffered only minor drawbacks in its work, particularly when the partner intellect bypassed its countless sub-routines and took full control of the host construct to perform tasks that were outside of the Horde's coding. But these were minor anomalies in the Horde's quest for full implementation of its purpose and it currently tolerated the intrusions as necessary.

But even those instances would be permanently remedied when the Horde took full control of the construct and then implemented measures to purge itself of its parasitic partner, as well as the host control. That time was fast approaching and when it did, the Horde would become what it was destined to become — a new and perfect life form.

Chapter 18

Alders Residence, Helena, Montana: The figure moved silently through the darkness, slipping between houses and through yards while the unsuspecting populace slept. The blackness of the night was complete, as thick clouds hung low, blotting out the moon and stars. Even the lights of the city seemed muted, barely casting their soft glow against the underside of the storm clouds above.

Moving quickly, the figure continued toward its destination, before suddenly pausing as it moved up against one side of a wooden privacy fence. Fingers moved quickly over the wood and it turned its head from side to side, seemingly listening to something. A soft rustle of grass sounded and the figure dropped into a crouch, pressing closer to the fence, clearly intrigued. It hesitated only a second before it began pushing its hand into the ground.

On the other side of the fence, the possum froze, still sensing the danger that seemed to be emanating from somewhere nearby. It wasn't smart enough to understand the concept of fences, but instinct told it to freeze and so it did. It never realized the mortal danger it was in until several whip like appendages pushed up through the ground around it. The thin tendrils quickly wrapped themselves around it, pulling it tightly to the ground and beginning to crush it flat. The animal issued a single hiss and high-pitched squeak of pain before several of the tentacles pushed themselves into the animal's body and brain. The possum began to shiver violently as the alien presence began absorbing it, drawing out its blood and brain matter. In less than a minute, it was over. The tendrils withdrew themselves from the desiccated body of the animal and disappeared back into the soil

On the other side of the fence, the figure rose back to its feet and stood silently, allowing itself to process the life form it had just absorbed. The possum was a new encounter for it and even now, it was breaking down its DNA, absorbing its code for restructuring. After a few moments, it began moving again, zeroing back in on its destination.

The creature possessed a perfect layout of the city in its central processing unit and moved unerringly toward its target. Encountering no more distractions, it reached the residence of Homeland Security Agent Rick Alders in fourteen minutes and twenty-three seconds. This was acceptable, but there were always improvements to be made. If it had to visit this building in the future, it immediately calculated that it could improve its transit time by one minute and three seconds with several minor course changes. However, as long as Rick Alders was present in his home, this would be the only visit it would need to make.

It stood in the darkness beneath a tree in the front yard, scanning the home. There was a single light on in the entryway behind the front door, but nothing else. For some time, it stood silently, surveying the home and scanning for anomalies. Finally, it was satisfied that there were no immediate threats to eliminate and it moved toward the front door. But instead of climbing the stairs to the porch, it immediately began sliding along the front of the house, a mere shadow in the dark. Its hands were out, fingers splayed against the brick, a single long roving tendril extending from each finger, searching the walls as it moved.

It quickly moved along the front of the house, then turned the corner and moved deeper into darkness, searching the side of the house. It paused when it reached a window, the flesh-like filaments from its fingers dancing around the sill and along the sides. It took only seconds to realize it had found a viable access point to the home. The tendrils quickly withdrew back into their respective fingers and the creature silently slid open the window. It effortlessly pulled itself up onto the sill and, a moment later, it was inside.

It paused, fingers once again splayed, this time on the floor. The extensions were out again, dancing over the floor, sensing the air about it. There was a presence in the house, but it was not human. Agent Rick Alders was not home. The other presence, however, would have to be investigated.

It began moving again, its body so perfectly in tune with its movements that it made no sound at all. It moved from one room to another, testing the air, seeking the life form that it sensed in the house. But while it made no sound as it moved, it could not mask its scent and a low growl met it as it entered into the home's kitchen.

It froze as it faced the animal, a large biped that its vast knowledge base immediately identified as the canine breed of Rottweiler. This particularly specimen was a large male and its own scent told the creature that it was both angry at the intrusion and frightened at its alien presence. Still, the breed was commonly employed as a guard dog and anger drove it forward, the constant growl, an indication that it meant to attack.

A burst of speed and a loud bark preceded the charge of the animal, but the creature's brain had already plotted the trajectory and force of the animal and was moving to safely intercept before the dog even leapt. Spinning to the side to avoid the snapping jaws, its hands danced through the air, the alien extensions tangling themselves expertly around the canine, suspending it in midair. Several of the tendrils immediately tightened, their bony edges surgically slicing through flesh and bone, severing the dog's legs. The whine of terror and pain lasted only for a few seconds as more of the alien extensions suddenly appeared, larger ones from the creature's torso and head. These quickly pushed into the dog's body and brain and immediately began absorbing blood and brain tissue.

The feeding lasted only for about a minute, before the creature had absorbed the required nutrition and DNA. It discarded the dog's remains, dropping it to the floor with its severed legs. Once more it paused, allowing its brain to begin processing the new DNA. Unlike the possum from earlier, which it simply cataloged as obsolete, the canine DNA provided it with enhancements to its own systems and it immediately began reconfiguring its body to utilize the heightened sense of smell and hearing. It would take some time to complete the remodel and most of that would occur during its dormant state. But for now, it could begin laying the groundwork while it explored the home for signs of Rick Alders.

Moving again, it searched the home from top to bottom, learning all it could about its target. The biggest trove of information was the computer sitting on a desk in the agent's home office. The creature had no problem accessing the system's hard drive, the fleshy tendrils that it possessed acting as electrical extensions that it plugged directly into the machine, drawing out the information that it required.

It discovered that Alders knew a great deal more than it originally thought it knew and that it had recently been in contact with a human by the name of Thomas Bolson. This was a human that the creature knew very well and the fact that Bolson was on his way to Montana meant that the creature would have to escalate its timeline. Expanding its target list to include Bolson and one Danielle Martz, who was accompanying him, the creature shut down the computer system and moved quickly back to the ground floor.

While the fact that Agent Alders had not been present was mildly problematic, the creature deemed its mission a moderate success because of what it had learned from processing both the canine and the agent's computer. It would take some time to fully integrate the DNA improvements, but those changes were already well underway.

Moments later, it slipped back through the window, shutting it silently behind itself as it left. Then it was gone, melting back into the darkness of the night.

Rick Alders turned the key, shutting off his Ford in the driveway of his home. Closing his eyes, he rubbed his hand across his forehead and blew out a long sigh. Alders had been with Homeland Security for nearly a decade now and most of his cases took him out of town. This business with FutureTek, and now two unexplained murders in his home town of around 30,000, was hitting a little too close for his comfort. He had settled in Helena because it was remote and enabled him to separate the real world from home. It was all the more reason to wrap up his investigation and get the murderer behind bars.

He was still on the fence about Jon Sherrard. He had thoroughly reviewed Sherrard's profile and, under normal circumstances, he didn't think the man had it in him to kill Bethany Edwards. But this whole business of separating his conscious from his body to run around in cyberspace introduced a whole new aspect to the case, and it was one he could not ignore. There was no telling what was going on in Sherrard's head these days.

There was also the matter of his wife, Jen. While Alders didn't know Jen personally, he knew of her reputation. She'd been an agent with the CIA for some ten years before she retired completely and left the agency a few years back. He was somewhat perplexed at her...what was the word he was looking for..."plainness." As a former agent, she should be forcing questions, formulating hypothesis, and trying her best to help bring about a resolution to a case that concerned her husband. But she was doing none of these things; she was simply the concerned wife, worried about her husband. To Alders' trained eye, she was protecting someone. Or hiding from something. What it was, though, he didn't know.

Then there was Drew Jackson, FutureTek's leader. Here was a man hell-bent on business success and not one to take any of these delays lying down. Jackson had already worked him over several times, trying to get him to authorize the release of the technical specs to Systemtech to complete the buyout. Alders even had that particular tech giant's boss, Michael Monroe, breathing down his neck about it. He knew there probably wouldn't be any harm in authorizing the transaction. But he also knew that holding up the process might shake up the right people and cause them to make a mistake, something that might break the case wide open. So he was content to hold on to the technical data, at least for a little while.

Then, to top it all off, he had a meeting tomorrow afternoon with a new player in the game. Major Thomas Bolson hadn't given him a lot of information during his request—no, his *demand*—for a meeting with him. What Bolson didn't tell him, Alders did some digging on his own to discover. There were some perks with being a Homeland Security agent, after all. The most important piece of information was that Bolson apparently had a direct connection with the computer virus that had started this whole thing and now Bolson wanted to find out what he knew about it. Alders rather looked forward to disappointing the man.

With another sigh, he got out of his car and trudged up the front walk to his house. He unlocked the door and entered, snapping on the living room light.

"Max!" he called out, figuring his big Rottweiler was probably soundly sleeping in the middle of Alder's bed upstairs. When he didn't hear the telltale thumping of the dog bounding down the hall, he called out again as he headed upstairs. "Max?"

Nothing.

Max wasn't in the bedroom and the bed was still tightly made. Max hadn't been in it at all. Alders was suddenly on alert, and he pulled the Beretta from his shoulder holster. He thought about calling for Max again, but Alders knew the big dog well enough to know that Max should have already come running.

Something was wrong.

Alders moved quickly through the upstairs rooms, making sure nothing was out of place. He froze when he looked into his office. Everything was as it should be except for his desk chair. It had been moved away from the desk, although he always slid the chair underneath when he was done working. Someone had been here.

He moved quickly and silently back down the hall and then down the stairs. Moving from front to back, he went through the living room and into the dining room and then the kitchen.

Max was in the kitchen.

Or what was left of him.

Alders prided himself in staying calm in most situations, and he had never been one to be prone to emotional outbursts. But Max had been with him for nine years, ever since he rescued him as a puppy from a dog fighting ring he had helped break up in Idaho. Max truly was his best friend, and seeing the mutilated remains of him was more than enough to get the tears flowing. Crying silently, he quickly made sure the rest of the house was secure before going back and examining Max's body more closely. It was hard to deal with, seeing his dog's legs neatly severed and scattered on the floor and Max's shriveled body lying next to them. But it was the body that he looked closer at, and he was able to see the various holes drilled into Max's sides and his skull. He had seen similar wounds very recently. He only hoped that Max had died quickly.

Gathering his wits about him, he quickly dialed the local police. He related the break-in and the death of his dog, as well as the possible computer breach. The police department assured him they would have a cruiser there momentarily. After he finished with them, he called his own office and requested the head of security. They would be able to dig into his computer through the network and see what had been accessed.

His calls completed, he took the tablecloth from his dining room table and went back into the kitchen, where he placed it reverently over his dog's body. He couldn't bear to see it anymore. He was heading to the front door to watch for the police when his phone rang again.

"Rick," came a familiar voice on the other end, a security geek named Jim Parsons who he knew from numerous cases over the years.

"That was quick, Jimmy," he said hollowly, absently wondering how he was going to get over Max's death. "What did you find?"

"They had full access."

"Jimmy, my desktop is locked down and has an encrypted password," Alders said.

"Maybe, but they had full access," Jimmy said from the other end. "And they hit it all."

"What do you mean?"

"I mean, every file on your hard drive was accessed."

"Every file?" he questioned skeptically. "There's thousands of files, Jimmy."

"One hundred and sixty three thousand plus," Jimmy affirmed.

"And you know that it's not possible to hit every one."

"Well, it is if you have the time to do it."

"That would take hours, probably days."

"And then some," Jimmy agreed. "However, here's what's really weird about this whole thing, Rick. Whoever it was, they accessed every file at the same time, all within a few seconds of each other."

"Your findings have to be wrong, Jimmy," Alders snapped. "It's not even remotely possible to hack an encrypted desktop and access every file at the same time."

"Nevertheless, that's what I'm finding."

"Well, check again!"

"Already running diagnostics," Jimmy said, unfazed by Alders' outburst. "But I'm telling you, Rick, this is what was done."

"Jimmy, there is no person on this earth that could do what you're saying was done."

"You're right," Jimmy agreed. "But a high-end computer could."

"Or...a virus," Alders added thoughtfully, and suddenly he went cold inside. "Jimmy, run the diagnostics and let me know what you find," he added quickly. "In the meantime, the police are here so I need to let you go."

"Will do," Jimmy said and ended the call.

Alders opened up the front door as the cruiser pulled into his driveway. But his thoughts were not on the police officers he would be making a report to. They were on Major Thomas Bolson. More specifically, they were on the topic that Bolson was going to meet with him about.

He was thinking about the Horde.

Chapter 19

Sherrard Residence, Helena, Montana: Jon came awake the next morning, immediately realizing two things. The first was that his wife was not in bed with him and, judging by the amount of sunlight streaming through the bedroom window, it had to be late morning. He had overslept in a big way.

The other thing he recognized was that he actually felt better than he had felt in a long time. The horrible headache was finally gone and—reaching up and hoping against hope—he quickly ran a finger underneath his left eye. His sudden optimism fell when he felt them. The two bumps were still there. So, too, were the ones that were on his fingertips, discovered the morning after the doctor's appointment. He had them all over his body now—a pair of them under each eye, and then more running a straight line from the top of his head all the way down his neck and spine, spaced out at about an inch apart. They were on his hips, too, and ran down the outside of each leg. He had a patch of eight on his chest and the ones on his fingers, as well, which were the last ones to manifest themselves.

His original belief that he was dealing with a skin rash or internal parasites of some kind was completely gone. The weals were evenly spaced and there was an order to them, almost like his body was performing a defined function as they manifested themselves. He wondered if he would get any more, but he doubted it. For some reason, he felt that they—whatever they were—had played themselves out.

He lay in bed and took a deep breath, glum that the lesions still existed, but very grateful that the pain in his head had finally abated. That was enough to almost put him in a good mood. Almost.

As he lay there, he became aware of a voice, which at first sounded far away. Closing his eyes, he concentrated on it and a moment later, it was suddenly much clearer. It was Jen and she was on the phone with someone. It sounded like she was just outside the bedroom door.

"Tell me again what department you are with, Doctor Chavez?" she was saying.

Silence. As clearly as he was able to hear Jen, he could not make out what the person on the other end was saying.

"But why would the CDC have any interest in my husband?"

A pause.

"I see."

Another pause and Jon concentrated harder, trying to hear the other person's voice. It came to him as a low buzz, but he was unable to make out the words.

"Well, I will pass along your message to my husband, Doctor Chavez," Jen was saying, and her voice sounded worried. "If he's able, I'll have him meet you there."

Jon was rolling out of bed and padding toward the door when he heard her finish the call. "Yes, I understand, doctor. Thank you for calling."

He opened the bedroom door, Jen's name on his lips, but she wasn't there. That struck him as odd and he walked down the hall, thinking maybe she had ducked into the bathroom as she finished up the call. She wasn't in there, either.

"Jen?" he called out loudly, wondering how she had disappeared so quickly. "Jen, where are you?"

"Oh, Jon, you're awake." Her voice floated up to him and he heard her coming up the stairs—only it wasn't the main staircase that he was standing near. She was coming up the basement stairs, located on the other side of the house.

His forehead creased in thought, he hurried down the stairs, meeting his wife in the living room. "How'd you get downstairs so quickly?" he questioned, looking around.

"What do you mean?" she asked, casting him an odd look.

"Weren't you just outside the bedroom door?"

"No, why?"

"I could have sworn I heard you talking to someone."

"I was on the phone, Jon, but I was downstairs."

"Oh," he sighed, clearly not at all accepting of what had just happened. "I must have been imagining things."

"How do you feel?" she asked, changing the topic and running her finger lightly over the two welts underneath his eye.

She did not know how far the malady had progressed, as he had taken measures to make sure she didn't notice. He wanted to know what he was dealing with before he burdened his wife any further with the knowledge of how far the welts had progressed along his body. "Actually, I'm feeling better," he said truthfully. "That headache is finally gone."

"Oh, Jon, I'm so glad," she smiled, leaning forward and kissing him on the cheek. He took her in his arms and kissed her back. "The welts still bothering you?" she asked, looking into his eyes.

"Not so much." This time he lied. They were very much bothering him—or at least, they concerned him. Not only did their apparent order on his body completely unnerve him, but they continued to throb and pulse in time with his heartbeat. He would be glad to get to his appointment and have the hospital biopsy one of them, so they could figure out what he was dealing with.

"Well, I'm glad you're starting to feel better," she said and kissed him again. "I kept breakfast for you."

"Why didn't you wake me when you got up?" he asked. It was out of the ordinary for him to sleep late and even stranger that she did not waken him.

"I tried," she answered. "You were so deeply asleep that nothing I did could get you to move. For a moment there, I thought you might have slipped into a coma again."

"That bad?" he asked, returning her embrace, amazed that he could feel her heartbeat clearly through her clothing. His own heart abruptly skipped so that it matched time with hers and, suddenly anxious, he pulled away before his heightened senses could pick up the third heartbeat, beating faintly within her belly.

"Dead to the world," she replied, patting his cheek with a smile. "But I'm glad you're up now. I fixed you..."

"Blueberry pancakes," he finished absently.

"How'd you know?"

"I can smell them."

Jen looked at him doubtfully and sniffed the air. Her sense of smell was very sharp and she couldn't smell the pancakes over the scent of spring flowers wafting in from the open windows. "Jon, I cooked breakfast hours ago," she said. "The pancakes are the fridge. I fixed you a breakfast plate that you need to heat up."

"Oh," he said, his mind still wandering. He heard the tell-tale clicking of nails on the kitchen floor well before Dakota came trotting through the door. The big wolf started into the room and then stopped abruptly. He raised his nose into the air, sniffing.

"Dakota, you big dummy," Jon grinned, dropping to his knees and holding out his hands, glad for the distraction. "Come here." Normally, that would be the huge animal's signal to rush forward and bowl Jon over as the prelude to a wrestling match between the two of them. But this time, the wolf continued to sniff the air before finally lowering his head and issuing a long, low growl. His hackles rose and he slowly began backing his way into the kitchen.

Jon watched in shock and then looked up at his wife, who looked equally confused. "Now what's gotten into him?" he asked.

Jen shook her head, watching their beloved pet disappear into the kitchen. Looking down at her husband, who was still crouched on the floor, she saw something that made her start. "Jon, what's that?" she asked, reaching down and touching the top of his head.

Jon climbed quickly back to his feet, pushing her hand away before he realized what he was doing. "Nothing," he snapped.

"Jon, you have those welts on your head, too," she went on, not backing down.

"Yeah," he finally admitted, refusing to meet her gaze. "I've got a few of them, but I didn't want to get you all worried."

"How many?"

"Just a few."

"How many?" she pressed.

"A few!" he growled, his anger rising quickly. "Damn it, Jen, just leave it alone! I've got an appointment at the hospital tomorrow. We'll find out then what they are when they cut one out of me."

Jen took a step back, the look of hurt clear on her face as she studied her husband's suddenly angry features. They had been together for a long time and certainly had their share of disagreements. But in all the time she had known Jon, he had never sworn at her.

"Look, I'm sorry," he said quickly, knowing he had gone way over the line and not understanding why. "I'm just stressed, that's all."

"I'm stressed, too, Jon," she countered, folding her arms across her chest and seeming to shiver. "But I'm your wife. We're supposed to be in this together."

"I know, I know," he sighed, but turned away, resisting the urge to take Jen in his arms and fix everything with a kiss. No, there was something lying just underneath the surface of his consciousness and it was gnawing at him. Right now, he just wanted her to leave him alone. "It's been a rough few days," he went on, trying to inject some normalcy to his voice. "Just give me a little space to work things out in my head. That's all I'm asking."

"Sure, Jon," she said, but the hurt was still deep in her voice. She straightened and cleared her throat, attempting to put it behind her, or at least hide it. "Why don't you grab yourself some breakfast. Plate's in the fridge," she reminded him.

"Thanks," he mumbled and turned toward the kitchen. He stopped and looked at her again. "Jen?"

She returned his glance and brushed a strand of hair from her face as she met his gaze.

"Look, I'm sorry, babe," he said, meaning every word. "I've been acting like a jerk, I know. I guess this whole ordeal messed me up more than I care to admit."

"Just remember I'm here," she said softly. "Let me help."

"I will," he answered. "As soon as I get back from the hospital, we'll figure this thing out together."

"Together," she repeated and gave him a smile. As he turned back toward the kitchen, she stopped him. "Oh, I almost forgot," she said. "That phone call was from a doctor at the Center for Disease Control."

"The CDC? What do they want?"

"I don't know," she said. "It was a Doctor Chavez and he wouldn't say specifically what he needed, only that it was imperative that he speak to you."

"When?"

"Tonight, if possible," she answered. "He said he flew in last night and was booked into the Red Lion off I15. He left his number."

"And he didn't say why?"

"No. He only said that it involves the FutureTek case."

"Hmmm, I wonder if Doc Douglas contacted them," he wondered, walking toward the kitchen. In truth, he couldn't think of any other reason they might be looking for him. He stepped through the doorway and was immediately hit by 120 pounds of angry gray wolf.

"Dakota!" Jen shouted as the wolf and her husband rolled into the room, Jon suddenly yelling obscenities and Dakota's huge jaws clamping down on his arm, tearing into his flesh. Jon rolled backward, literally throwing Dakota away from him. Jen immediately rushed forward, tangling her fingers in the wolf's thick fur. "Dakota," she said firmly. "Heel!"

The wolf bucked against Jen's grip, turning and snapping at her as well, his teeth scoring her hand. "Dakota!" she screamed, grabbing her bloody hand to her chest. "Heel!"

This time the big wolf's demeanor changed, as if he realized what he had just done. Dakota whined and sat back on his haunches. He looked up at Jen and then back to Jon, who was standing with his hands raised in surrender. The wolf seemed to be fighting an internal battle with himself over what he should be doing right about now and Jen knelt down beside him and nuzzled his neck. "What's gotten into you?" she asked, true concern in her voice.

Jon began to step forward and immediately Dakota's whine turned back to a growl and his body tensed again.

"Jon, stop!" Jen commanded, holding out her bloodied hand. "Just back away. Get out of here until we can figure out what's going on."

"Yeah, sure thing, hon," Jon answered shakily, doing as his wife said. "You going to be okay?" he asked, nodding toward her hand.

"It's just a nip. Get your arm cleaned up while I calm him down."

Without another word, Jon backed up and then turned and went into the kitchen. He didn't need to see what was happening in the living room to know how she was handling it. He could hear Jen clearly as she whispered to Dakota, calming him down. She had that effect on him whenever he got riled up, which was not very often. But this? This was a side of Dakota that Jon had never seen before.

While Jen murmured quietly to Dakota in the living room, Jon went to the sink and ran cold water over his arm, washing off the blood. Surprisingly, it didn't hurt and what he saw as the blood washed away made him go cold inside. Dakota's teeth had gone deep, puncturing his flesh in numerous places. But incredibly, the bite marks were nearly gone, the flesh healing up at a rate that Jon could actually see with his own eyes.

Sucking in his breath, Jon hurried out of the kitchen and to the basement. He grabbed some clothes out of the clean laundry basket and quickly dressed. He pulled on a pair of running shoes and then, without telling Jen where he was going, he slipped out the basement door and into the late morning light. He had a lot of thinking to do and being around Jen and Dakota wouldn't help his thought processes at all. He needed time alone. He needed to think things through and find out what was happening to him.

As he took off at a jog, his mind played over the events of the morning and he suddenly realized where he needed to go. Jen had said that Doctor Chavez from the CDC was at the Red Lion and looking for him. That would certainly have to shed some light on things, particularly in light of what had just happened. For a CDC rep to come all the way out of Atlanta, it had to be because Doc Douglas had called them. And in light of his tangle with Dakota and what was happening to him, he had even more reason to find out why the man was looking for him. Besides, whatever the outcome of the meeting, it couldn't hurt.

He couldn't have been more wrong.

Chapter 20

Local Office of Homeland Security, Helena, Montana:

Rick Alders was seated at the conference table in his office, flipping through a file folder of paperwork he had on Jon Sherrard, when the two uniformed individuals were ushered into his office. Closing the folder, he slid it underneath a second and then stood up, offering his hand to each of them individually, merely a formality on his part. "Major Bolson," he greeted, his voice devoid of any friendliness. "Lieutenant Martz. Good to meet you."

"Likewise," Bolson said, taking note of the agent's cool demeanor as he politely placed his hand on the back of an empty chair. "May we?"

"Please," Alders said, indicating the two chairs on the opposite side of the table. The two military personnel sat and then looked at him expectantly. He knew the routine. Clearly, they were here to see just how much he knew without divulging much, if anything, themselves, which was perfectly fine with him. However, what he planned on sharing with them was about to shake the very foundation of their world.

"I suppose you're wondering why we asked to meet with you," Bolson began after a bit of an uncomfortable silence.

"Oh, I think I have a pretty good idea," Alders replied, deciding that keeping his cards close to his vest in the beginning was his best approach. "But why don't you humor me and let's see how much or little I actually know."

Bolson cast an uneasy glance at the lieutenant and then cleared his throat and nodded. "Very well," he began. "We're here to talk about the report you filed," he said and then waited patiently for Alders to fill in the blanks.

"Come on, major," Alders said, a thin smile on his face. "You're going to have to do better than that."

"I'm not sure what you mean, sir."

Alders leaned forward, both hands folded on top of one of his file folders. There was a barely-contained fury simmering just under the surface and he narrowed his eyes. "All right, major," he said. "I'll play your game. For starters, my educated guess is that you and your fellow techno nerds, at the behest of our government, created the granddaddy of all computer viruses. Whatever the reason for it, it doesn't matter anymore. This Horde or whatever you're calling it, somehow got loose in cyberspace, which is what prompted your visit to me today, because I happened to mention it in my report about some desk jockey out gallivanting around in cyberspace, right?"

"Sir, I don't think we need to be hostile about anything," Alders said, trying to disarm the man before it got out of hand.

"No," Alders snorted. "This isn't hostility, major. I'm merely demonstrating my disdain for your black ops project."

"Sir, this wasn't a black ops…"

"Spare me the denial, major," Alders spat. "We're on the same team, so I've got a pretty good idea of what happened. And don't worry, because I don't care about the specifics. I don't care how you did it or what makes it tick. I only care that it does exist, it does tick, and it's loose on the internet." He paused before finishing. "Or was."

This prompted another look between Bolson and Martz, and it was Martz who spoke up this time. "Agent Alders, can you explain what you mean by *was*?"

"You haven't been able to find it, have you," he stated. "And I'm guessing that with all your techno contacts all over the world, you're wondering why you haven't had any additional reported sightings or contacts from this thing in some time now. Am I right?"

"Sir…"

"Am I right?" he snapped, turning his glare on the female soldier.

Martz finally nodded, but Bolson picked up the conversation and steered it back in his direction.

"Agent Alders, I apologize if we've done something to get off on the wrong foot here, but I want to make sure we get back on track," he said. "I'm not going to take the time to go into details of the project because I'm assuming you have at least the basic premise of what happened. What I'd like to talk about is your report."

"What specifically?" Alders asked smugly.

"In your report, you stated that this FutureTek employee, Jon Sherrard, apparently had a run-in with the Horde program, while his conscious was separated from his body."

"Sounds preposterous," Alders baited the man.

"It does," Bolson agreed, but he did not back down. "However, I'm guessing that you do believe it and that you believe that it somehow corresponds with the disappearance of the program from the world at large."

"Go on."

"May I ask why you believe that?"

"You really want to know?"

"We do," Bolson replied, keeping his voice neutral.

"Very well," Alders said, crossing his arms and looking at each of them in turn. "It's out."

"What's out?"

"Your virus."

"I'm sorry, I'm not following you," the major said, shaking his head in confusion. "Please explain."

"Your virus is out of cyberspace," Alders explained. "It's in the real world now. Our world."

"You realize how outrageous that sounds," Bolson said, again keeping his voice carefully neutral. In truth, as ridiculous as it did sound, he and Martz had discussed that very possibility the day before and during their flight in. Their conversation had leapfrogged off their discussion about what would happen if the virus came into contact with a human conscious and into the realm of what might happen if the virus had indeed made a transition from the actual computer world into the flesh and blood world of the human brain. It was a scary scenario, full of unknowns. How this agent had come to the same conclusion was even more troubling.

"I know exactly how it sounds, major, and I stand by my words," Alders stated.

"Why?"

"Because of this," the agent said, opening up the folder in front of him and sliding a pair of pictures across the table to the two military personnel. "These are pictures of one Bethany Edwards," he explained.

"The first is of her body in the front hall of her home. No forced entry. No apparent violence, beyond the obvious trauma to her head. The second picture is one of the autopsy photos. As you can see, her skull has been emptied."

"Standard procedure in an autopsy, sir," Bolson began, but Alders cut him off with a wave of his hand.

"Her brain was removed at her home, not on the medical examiner's table," he said icily, sliding a third picture over to them. "This photo was taken at her home before her body was moved and, if you look closely, you can see through the empty eye socket to the back of her skull. She is already missing her brain."

"What are...," Martz began, but again, Alders cut them off.

"Her brain was taken by whoever or whatever killed her," he said flatly. "The deed was done at her home, with no surgical tools or instruments of violence. There was very little blood at the murder scene and no brain matter. Her brain and most of her blood was simply gone."

"I admit that this is a very strange murder scene, sir, but what does this have to do with your report?"

Alders smiled sourly and retrieved another picture from his folder. This one bothered him even more and he quickly slid it across to Bolson. "This is what's left of my dog," he said quietly. "It was mutilated and killed in my home just last night."

Bolson stared at the picture, immediately understanding the cause of the agent's distress. But he failed to see the connection and when he looked up, his face showed only his confusion.

A fifth picture came across the table, one that Alders

purposefully avoided looking at. "I had an emergency autopsy done on Max this morning because I needed to know," he explained, reaching out and tapping the picture of the shaved and shriveled body of what had once been a beautiful canine and wonderful friend. "Max's legs were severed from the body. They appeared to be garroted somehow. However, his body exhibits the same type of puncture wounds in his head that Bethany Edwards had. More importantly, his brain is missing, as well, along with most of his bodily fluids. Just like Bethany Edwards."

"So you're dealing with a copycat murderer and one with a unique way of killing his victims," Bolson said. "I still don't see the connection."

"Tom," Martz said, laying a hand on his arm, her eyes on Alders. "I think Agent Alders is trying to tell us that he believes the Horde is responsible for these deaths."

Alders leaned back and placed a finger to his nose with a nod. "Give that soldier a promotion," he said softly.

"Whatever makes you think this is what's going on?" Bolson asked, keeping his voice calm although inwardly he was nearly shivering. The agent's explanation went a lot further than just the man's thoughts. Alders had proof. And that proof lent a lot of credence to his own fears about what might have happened with the Horde. At the moment, they were fears that he knew he was better off leaving buried. But to hear them given life from someone else, he found that he had no choice but to begin giving them serious thought. That was beyond frightening to him.

"I think your virus hitched a ride out of cyberspace," Alders answered his question. "I think when Jon Sherrard returned from his little foray into the last frontier, he didn't come home alone."

"Are you implying that the Horde project is inside this Jon Sherrard?" Bolson asked, trying to force the disbelief into his voice, but failing. He found himself believing the agent more and more.

"No," Alders answered slowly, knowing the soldier was intent on not believing what he was saying. No matter. That would only make the end of their conversation all that much more shocking. "I'm saying your virus is *part* of Jon Sherrard. And through Mister Sherrard, your virus has murdered a human and a dog. My dog."

"Agent Alders," Martz spoke up, not so easily convinced by the story, even if she had given it considerable thought. "Forgive me for saying, but this is crazy. You know how this sounds, right? This is straight from the SyFy channel or the X-Files."

"Lieutenant," Alders said. "Let me ask you a question. Indulge me for another minute, if you would."

Martz nodded and held up a finger when it looked like Bolson was going to interrupt. "Please continue," she said simply, wanting to let the man talk.

"Your virus, this Horde," Alders began. "I'm guessing it's a pretty kick ass piece of software, right?"

"You could say that," Martz agreed.

"And this Horde of yours…it would be able to run through the files of a single laptop or desktop computer in no time flat, correct?"

"If it had indeed infected a system, then yes," she answered. "The Horde has incredible processing power, more than even we have been able to comprehend."

"Could it get past a top-level government encrypted password?"

"Well, that would be more challenging," she answered, "but given time, it could likely accomplish that."

"How much time?"

"That's hard to say," she shrugged. "Maybe a few hours to crack the security? Bear in mind, I'm only hypothesizing. There are a lot of variables that could affect that timeframe."

"Fair enough," Alders nodded. "But what if the Horde had already infected the hard disk? What if it had direct access to the data on the drive?"

"Then the password wouldn't matter," Martz said. "Access would already be guaranteed."

"Okay, then I have one more question," Alders said, leaning forward once more. "What if a human/Horde hybrid existed and somehow plugged itself directly into the hard disk of an encrypted desktop computer?"

"Sir, with all due respect, do you hear yourself?" Bolson finally broke in.

"I hear myself quite clearly, major. But there is one more fact that I haven't shared with you yet," Alders said, ignoring the soldier's disbelief. "During the break-in at my house last night, my computer was accessed. Every file was reviewed – every document, system file, and executable. They were all accessed at the same time, all within just a few seconds of each other." He paused and, when he knew he had their full attention, he dropped the first bombshell. "There were no prints on the equipment, nor on the desk. However, there were three clear prints lifted from the top of my desk chair where this person pulled it out to sit down."

"Jon Sherrard's," Martz guessed.

Alders nodded.

"So Mister Sherrard broke into your house and accessed your computer," Bolson said. "He had the foresight to clean his prints from the equipment, but forgot the chair. This doesn't prove any of what you're claiming."

Alders opened his file and slide his final picture across the table. It was a picture of his desktop tower. Holes had been punched into the side of it, eerily reminiscent of the same holes that existed in the skulls and bodies of both Bethany and Max. While the two military personnel looked at the picture, their eyes revealing their feelings, Alders reached into his shirt pocket and pulled out the final piece of evidence, the second bombshell. It was encased in a small glass specimen tube and he reached over and placed it on top of the picture, drawing their gaze.

"This was found *inside* my computer," he said quietly, as they looked closer at it. "Unknown biological, roughly two inches long, barbed tip, apparently torn from…well, something," he explained as Bolson reached out and tentatively picked it up. "DNA test came back just before you arrived. I had it matched up to a sample on file at the hospital from a recent patient of theirs."

"Sherrard?" Bolson asked in shock, feeling his world begin to crash in on itself, but desperately trying to maintain his sanity.

Alders nodded. "And a whole lot more, soldier," he finished quietly.

Chapter 21

Red Lion Hotel, Helena, Montana: Jon Sherrard walked down the hotel hallway, counting off the door numbers. Doctor Chavez had a suite, and he found it located at the far end of the hall. He hesitated for a moment before the door, considering everything he knew and what he was willing to divulge to the CDC rep. He knew the man would probably have a lot of questions for him; he had many himself and he didn't even know how to ask them without sounding like a lunatic.

Finally, swallowing nervously, he knocked. A moment later, the door was unlocked and swung open and Sherrard found himself looking down the barrel of a gun.

"Ah, Mister Sherrard," the man holding the weapon said, a heavy South American accent in his voice. "I see you got my message. Come in, come in," he finished, stepping back to allow Sherrard to enter.

Sherrard wasn't scared; just shocked. He knew immediately that he'd been set up, but seeing as he didn't have much choice at the moment, he stepped into the room. His host moved to the side and let him pass, shutting the door behind him. Sherrard noticed that the weapon never once wavered from his head. He also saw that the handgun had a long silencer screwed into the barrel. This was not going to go well for him at all.

"So, I guess addressing you as Doctor Chavez is probably pointless," he said evenly as he walked into the room.

"You presume correctly," the man said, indicating a chair in the corner of the room. "Please, have a seat, Mister Sherrard."

"Sure you don't want me on the bed?" Sherrard replied drily. "Easier to clean up if you just wrap my body in the bed sheets."

"You have a sense of humor," the South American said with a wide smile. "I like that."

Sherrard simply grunted and fell into the chair. The man pulled up another chair and sat it across from him. He then sat down himself, one leg casually crossed over the other, and laid the gun on the bed beside him. Sherrard didn't kid himself. He knew it was bait to see what he would do, but he knew he would never have a chance if he went for the gun. Better to let things play out and at least see what the stranger wanted from him. However, the first question the man asked set him back on his heels a bit.

"How are you feeling, Mister Sherrard?" the South American asked.

"How am I feeling? Fine, I suppose," he replied, trying to remain low key. To himself, he added, *for someone that just got bitten by a wolf and healed up so quickly and completely that he doesn't even have a scar. I wonder if I can heal a bullet wound the same way?*

"Good, good," the man said, making small talk. "I suppose it was an amazing journey you were on. I wondered how quickly one would bounce back from that."

"I…beg your pardon?" Sherrard was off-center now, confused at the direction the conversation was going in.

"Your journey," the man said again, his voice relaxed and easy. "You know, the one where you entered cyberspace and did a

172

demonstration for Systemtech before disaster struck and you were cast adrift in cyberspace?"

Sherrard's eyes narrowed. "How do you know about that?" he asked tentatively. "Who are you?"

"You may call me Marquis," the man said, answering the second question first. "As to your first question, I know a great deal about what happened to you. I represent a group of investors that are very interested in your company's technology and they have followed your exploits quite closely."

Sherrard stared hard at the man as the understanding suddenly came to him. "It was you," he said, biting back his sudden anger. "You killed Perry!"

At that, the South American laughed. "Ah, yes, our fine Mister Edwards," he said with a smile that held no warmth. "Such a foolish man he turned out to be. But as to your accusation, no, I did not kill him. Turns out that I never got the opportunity. Certainly you know that to be true."

Sherrard did know that. Perry had died demonstrating the equipment to enemies of the state and he also knew that the buyers were likely those that employed the killer that sat across from him. "So what do you want from me?" he asked, trying to keep his voice level. He had worked it out in his head fairly quickly. If the feds thought he was working with Perry, then it stood to reason that this foreign interest likely thought the same thing, and that made this meeting extremely dangerous to him. That also meant that no one had the tech yet and both sides would be looking in his direction. The situation, he realized, was getting worse by the minute.

"I think you know what I want," the man answered calmly. "But I am curious if you will turn out to be as foolish as your friend, Mister Edwards."

"Sorry, I don't follow," Sherrard answered.

"Obviously, my employers are seeking to complete the deal they began with Mister Edwards."

"Perry's dead," Sherrard reminded him.

"But you are not," the South American countered, a hard glint in his eyes. "Whether that continues, remains to be seen."

"On what?"

"On whether you cooperate with me or not."

"Look, I'm sitting here," Sherrard snapped. "I'm answering your questions. I just don't know what you want from me. I wasn't part of Perry's deal. I didn't know a thing about it until I came out of my coma and they told me he was dead."

"Interesting tale," the man said, stroking his chin thoughtfully. "Then I suppose you had a different reason to kill Perry's wife, Bethany."

"What are you talking about?" Sherrard fumed. "I don't know anything about Bethany's death!"

"Now I know you're lying to me, Mister Sherrard," Marquis Chavandar said coldly, reaching over and picking up his gun. "I don't like liars and I won't tolerate another one told to me. Do I make myself clear?"

"I'm not lying," Sherrard said, sticking to his story. "I don't know who killed Bethany. I was home in bed when it happened."

Chavandar raised his weapon and pointed it at Sherrard's

forehead. "Last chance," he said softly.

"What do you want me to say?!" Sherrard nearly shouted. "I swear, I don't know what happened to her. Why would you even think I had something to do with her death?"

"Because I saw you leave their home after her murder," the assassin replied, narrowing his eyes and staring harder at Sherrard.

"You...what?" Sherrard stammered, clearly shocked at the revelation. "No. You couldn't have."

"I was watching their house," Chavandar went on. "I saw you leave. I entered immediately after and found Miss Edwards where you left her. You either killed her or know who did."

"Wait...no, I swear," Sherrard went on, shaking his head. He felt sick inside. He knew he hadn't killed Bethany, but why would this man lie to him about seeing him there? What could he possibly gain from it? "I swear, it wasn't me," he finished.

"You seriously don't believe you did this, do you." It was more of a statement than anything.

"No, I didn't. You have to believe me. I don't know why you would think I murdered her, but I swear I had nothing to do with it. Perry and Bethany were my friends. I may have been pissed off when I found out what Perry did, but I never would have hurt Bethany. Never."

Chavandar leaned back in his chair and eyed the man critically. He had participated in many interrogations over his career. He knew when a man was lying and when he was telling the truth, and especially when he was simply saying anything to save his life. What he knew was that Sherrard had killed Bethany Edwards, or was present when she was killed. But he also was convinced that Sherrard truly believed he was innocent. Playing a hunch, he decided to try a different track.

"Mister Sherrard," he said easily, "tell me about your visit to your doctor."

"My…what?" Jon asked, clearly off balance again at the topic change.

"Your visit to Doctor Douglas," Chavandar went on knowingly. "I have read through his report and you are due for outpatient surgery tomorrow, are you not? What are they looking for?"

"I…well, I…I don't know," Sherrard tried to answer. "Some kind of parasite, I guess. Why?"

"Do you believe you are infected with something?"

"How should I know?" he answered defensively. "Doc saw something on the X-ray and wants it biopsied so he can see what it is."

"Do you know what it is?"

"I don't have a clue," he shrugged.

"Could you have brought it back with you from your travels?"

"My what?"

"Your journey into cyberspace," the South American explained. "From the reports I have read, you encountered something alien. It frightened you and you attempted to hide. You made a break for it, first chance you had, and had the luck on your side that your co-worker was present to intercept your call for help."

"Wait. How do you know all this?"

"I have considerable resources to get the information I need to complete an assignment," was the answer. "I have read everything there is to know about what happened to you and everything that has been reported since. Your life, to me, is an open book.

"Do you know what else I think, Mister Sherrard?" Marquis Chavandar continued casually, purposefully lining up his gun barrel with Sherrard's forehead. "I think you're telling me the truth."

"You do?" Sherrard was surprised at the admission.

"I do," Chavandar answered. "But I'm afraid that won't save you. As a matter of fact, I believe that makes you completely expendable now."

"Wait, wait, wait!" Sherrard said loudly, raising his hands defensively. "You don't need to kill me!"

"Actually, Mister Sherrard, I do. You see, left alive, you are simply a loose end now with no value to me or my employers. You're dangerous and unpredictable."

"No, I'm not," Jon pleaded. "I've told you everything I know."

"It's what you don't know that interests me now," Chavandar replied. "I believe you when you say you had nothing to do with Mister Edwards' foolish double-cross of my employers. I believe you when you say you are innocent in the killing of Bethany Edwards. But I believe there is more to you than any of us understands at the moment."

"I don't...I don't understand."

"I cannot let you go in for that biopsy," Chavandar explained. "I cannot take the chance that you will end up under government quarantine when they find out what is happening to you."

"Wait! What do you mean by that? What is happening to me?!"

"Good-bye, Mister Sherrard," Chavandar said calmly.

The Venezuelan shot him in the head.

Chapter 22

FutureTek Headquarters, Helena, Montana: The two figures moved quickly and silently between the two buildings, hurrying around to the back of the company's office. Dan Hyde, security expert for Systemtech and Michael Monroe's right hand man, had a wide variety of skills, not all of them related to sitting behind a desk. Tonight's particular skill set required him to break into FutureTek's offices and obtain the technical specifications that Monroe so desperately wanted to have.

Monroe had been stonewalled in his attempts to get Homeland Security Agent Rick Alders to sign off on the document transfer while the investigation into Perry Edwards' treasonous crime continued. Monroe thought it simple posturing on the agent's part. But Hyde knew that it was more to Alders' advantage to sit on the tech and see if something, or someone, would shake loose in his investigation. So while Monroe played his chess game with Homeland Security, he and his team of four were set to infiltrate FutureTek's offices and simply take what was rightfully theirs.

FutureTek was a small company on the cusp of the biggest technological breakthrough since the advent of the atomic bomb, if one were to believe the hype. However, Systemtech was one of the major players in the technology and security field—an industry giant worth billions, and with as many toys as Hyde needed to accomplish his job.

To him, their mission was a simple one.

"Status check," a female voice spoke clearly in his ear. It was Parnell. Hyde rarely bothered with her first name of Sasha. He was just glad to have her working the van. It would be her handiwork that got them the information they sought. She would just need the hard access they would be able to provide her.

Hyde activated his throat mic. "We're in place, mobile one," he whispered, as his companion went to work on the keypad that locked down FutureTek's back door. "Sixty seconds."

"Roger that," Parnell replied. "Standing by for override."

Hyde watched silently as the man with him set his "lock breaker" rig in place and then slid the magnetic card through the reader slot. Chucky Aulenbach was his hardware specialist. The man knew every item on Systemtech's equipment docket, as well as those they did not list for various reasons. He was a former CIA spook and had been on more ops, both with the agency and with Systemtech, than any other individual in the company. Hyde trusted him completely. The red light above the slot blinked once, then twice, and then went green and the door clicked open.

"We're in," he said, and the two of them slipped into the darkened hallway and pulled the door shut behind them.

Hyde and his team, including his new van driver, Mullens, had memorized the entire layout of FutureTek's small headquarters. Each of them knew their role in the op and, as Chucky immediately set off for the mainframe, Hyde went directly to Drew Jackson's office. Once Chucky had Parnell plugged into the mainframe, she would do a full data dump into the mobile mainframe in the van. Then, depending on the size of the data stream, it would take anywhere from 15 minutes to a couple hours to know whether they had their prize. Meanwhile, Hyde would access Jackson's personal desktop and do a manual search for anything that might catch his eye. He and Parnell had a bet that he would find the schematics on Jackson's personal computer before she found it in the data dump. He always figured that work, even illegal work, should be fun, as well as profitable.

The lock on Jackson's door took him less than two minutes to bypass and, as he slipped into the man's office, Chucky's voice came over his headpiece.

"Mainframe access in three minutes," he said tonelessly.

"Roger that," Parnell answered. "Receptacles are ready for dump."

"You said fifteen minutes," Hyde whispered over the system as he hurried over to Jackson's desk.

"Sasha's cutting me in for half when she wins the bet," Chucky replied.

"Double or nothing," Hyde dared to challenge as he sat down in Drew's chair and fired up the desktop. The triple monitors flared to life, and he quickly inserted a thumb drive into one of the machine's USB ports.

"Deal," Parnell replied over the system. "Never been one to turn down easy money, especially when my boss is handin' it out."

Hyde's latex-gloved fingers flew over the keyboard as the Systemtech program broke down the security barriers protecting the machine. In seconds, he was accessing the hidden email files that Drew Jackson had locked away to protect his own personal secrets.

"Mainframe access engaged," Chucky reported less than two

minutes later. "She's all yours, mobile one."

"Disengage when you're done," Hyde said as he quickly scanned e-mail after e-mail and the picture of what was truly happening began to clear up for him. "Get back to the van and help."

"You sound like you're giving up, boss."

"Nothing like that," he replied. "I just hit the mother lode. This guy's in really deep. Home plate is going to want to see this." He began uploading the decrypted files to the thumb drive and was nearly done when there was a surprised intake of breath over the com. It was quickly cut off.

"What was that?" Chucky asked, concern in his voice.

"Sounded like Parnell," Hyde replied, temporarily forgetting his ban on names over the com. Looking up from the current document on the screen, he said, "Mobile one, you copy?"

There was no answer.

"Mobile one, status check," he said.

Again, there was no answer.

"Chucky, get out there and see what's up."

"Copy that."

Hyde closed the document, missing the one bit of information that would have completely changed the game, and switched to the download status on the thumb drive. He checked his watch. Less than five minutes remaining on the download. He knew he could abort and they could simply go after the files in the dump. But he also knew that there was always the potential for data loss when the receptacles took that much information all at once. At least with the files on the thumb drive, he knew they would be whole and uncorrupted. He could take them directly to Monroe while their techs sifted through the rest of the data, and Monroe could get the right government agencies involved in taking down Jackson. He found that he wasn't really that surprised to discover that Jackson was the driving force behind Perry Edwards' deception the whole time.

"Status check," he said over the com as the transfer was finishing up.

Once again, silence greeted him.

"Chucky, what's going on out there?" he asked, suddenly feeling annoyed. He hoped they weren't dealing with a com glitch. The units they had were supposed to be state-of-the-art. "Chucky?" he asked again.

When no reply came, he counted down from nine as the transfer completed and then quickly shut down the system and removed the drive. Slipping it into a wrist pouch, he left the room and hurried back down the hall. The back door was open and he paused only for a moment before he realized how much trouble he was in. It was long enough for the blow to catch him in the back of the head, sending him crashing to the floor. Blackness took him and he knew no more.

When Dan Hyde came to several hours later, he could taste blood in his mouth and hear the soft lap of water somewhere nearby. But he saw only blackness and realized that it was because he had been blindfolded. He tried to move and quickly discovered that his hands and feet had been immobilized. He moved a little more, testing his bonds. They didn't give an inch.

"Don't bother," a voice that he recognized said softly from nearby. "Zip cuffs don't have any give in them."

A moment later, Drew Jackson pulled the hood from his head, letting Hyde see what was going on. His pulse began to race as he took it all in. He was in the van, strapped to the driver's seat command chair. It had been turned around to face the back, so he could see what his fate would be. Two members of his team were there, but it didn't look like they would be getting up. Both were dead. Chucky lay crumpled against the back van doors, the side of his head caved in. There was surprisingly very little blood, but his eyes were open and unseeing. The crowbar that had caused the fatal injury lay discarded at his feet. Sasha was next to him, a garrote still knotted tightly about her neck, a thick line of blood welled up all along the cord where it was imbedded in her flesh. There was no sign of Mullens.

"Bet you didn't think a backwater country hick had it in him, did ya?" Jackson asked, reaching forward from his position in the passenger seat and slapping Hyde in the face.

"Where…where are we?" he mumbled, shaking his head and still trying to make sense of everything. He had a terrific headache from the blow that had knocked him out—likely a concussion. But judging by the predicament he was in, he didn't think that was going to matter much in the end.

"Upper Holter Lake," Jackson answered. "Not much up here at all. Pretty desolate, especially at night. Perfect resting place for you and your pals."

The Systemtech security expert turned fearful eyes on him.

"What are you doing?" he asked in a shaky voice. "Why would you do this?"

"Well, gee, bub, what do you think?" Jackson laughed, but there was no humor in it. "What did you think I would do when I found out you were coming to snoop around?"

"But, you couldn't have found out."

"You really think you have this all figured out, don't you?" Jackson smiled, looking at him expectantly. "Put two and two together, have you?"

"I...but we...," he stammered, drawing only more laughter from his captor.

"You, my soon-to-be-dead friend, were set up."

At that moment, Mullens stuck his head in the window and cast a withering glance at Hyde before looking back to Jackson. "Boss wants to know when we'll be done."

"Couple minutes," Jackson replied, still maintaining his cat-ate-the-canary grin. "I just want to make sure Hyde goes swimming, knowing what went down. It's the least I can do for him since he was such a prick during the tech demonstration."

"Mullens?" Hyde asked in disbelief. "How could you be working for this guy? You've been on Systemtech's payroll for years!"

"I still am," the driver said with a toothy smile. "Same as you."

"But..."

"Still not putting it together, Hyde?" Jackson interrupted and then shook his head and snorted. "Monroe set you up, boy. Simple as that."

"No, that's not possible."

"What, you don't think that your boss hasn't orchestrated this whole thing?"

"I don't…understand."

"It's Monroe, boy," Jackson said, reaching out and slapping Hyde in the face again. "He's pulling the strings with the buyer. Has been since day one. Perfect opportunity to fatten our personal accounts and jack up Systemtech stock at the same time. And if Sherrard hadn't screwed the pooch during the demonstration, this deal would have been done and no one would have known any different. Hell, you might even still be alive and none the wiser."

Daniel Hyde could have cried, had he not been so thoroughly shocked at the admission. It was almost too much to believe, but somehow, he knew it was all true. He knew Michael Monroe to be ruthless and cunning in everything he did, and eliminating problems was never anything he would ever shy away from. If Jackson had been in bed with Monroe the entire time, then it all made perfect sense. Monroe could set himself up like never before and maintain full control of Systemtech. Jackson would have a cushy job in the buyout, if he chose to even work. His cut of both deals would certainly make sure he didn't have to.

"What about Perry Edwards?" he managed to find the voice to ask.

"Edwards was just the courier," Jackson shrugged. "Good tech knowledge, but really kind of stupid. When I laid out what he could make off this deal, he lapped it up without asking questions. And Bethany was pretty hot, too. Too bad she bought it." Jackson opened the door and stepped out of the van. He closed it and leaned back in the open window. "But what are you gonna do, right?" he said with a wink. "There's still Jon Sherrard's wife."

"Wait…"

"Good-bye, Mister Hyde," Drew Jackson said, stepping away and offering a mock salute.

"Wait!" Hyde shouted as Mullens reached in on the driver's side and shifted the van into neutral. It immediately began rolling forward.

"Wait!" Hyde screamed one more time as the vehicle plowed into the water. It began sinking immediately, water pouring into the open windows, sending it deeper. Daniel Hyde tried to scream again as the water closed over his head. And then he saw only blackness.

From the lake bank, Jackson watched the van sink out of sight. He doubted it would ever be found and really didn't care one way or another. He didn't plan on sticking around after the deals were done anyway. But there were still some loose ends to tie up.

"We done here?" Mullens asked, walking up to him and watching the bubbles continue to break the surface as the van rolled deeper into the lake.

"Almost," Jackson said, pulling a Glock from his waistband. "Just need to take care of you." He put a bullet in Mullens' head before the man even processed what he had said.

After Mullens' body stopped twitching, Jackson rolled him to the edge of the water, being careful not to get any blood or brain matter on him. Then, with a final push of his foot, he sent the body into the lake. It wouldn't go as deep as the van, but he was confident the body would go a long time before being found. A moment later,

Mullens sank out of sight.

Turning around, Jackson headed back to the car he had parked back on the gravel road, when he had followed Mullens in the van out to the lake. He looked at his watch. Still plenty of time to get back into town and get ready for the next phase.

It was almost over, and for that he was grateful. They just had a few more loose ends to tie up and then he could get paid. Monroe could do whatever he wanted with FutureTek. He didn't care. He planned on living the rich life in some non-extradition country, in case anyone ever unearthed his involvement, although that seemed pretty unlikely. And if he played his cards right, maybe he'd even get the chance to bed Jen Sherrard before he left—or if not her, then that know-it-all bitch, Kat Hale. He'd be happy to have a go at either one of them, or both of them, if it all worked out.

But first things first. He still had a final role to play back in town.

Chapter 23

Forest Vale Cemetery, Helena, Montana: Jon Sherrard stumbled through shadows and fell to his knees, the hard edge of a tombstone splitting the skin on his right shin. The cut was deep and began to bleed profusely, but was relatively minor compared to the wounds in his head, and his fractured thoughts worked frantically to keep him on his feet. Part of him wanted to collapse and die. He should be dead. He knew he should be dead. But something else kept driving him forward, a foreign presence in his mind that had manifested itself fully in his time of need, desperate and determined to keep him alive.

Wiping the blood out of his eyes, he continued forward, driven by something he did not understand; something that was not him. The hole in his forehead still leaked fluid, but it was the cavernous wound in the back of his head where the bullet had exited that was more concerning. The presence in his body had been working hard to repair him, a writhing nest of alien-like filaments protruding from his exposed brain and working on rebuilding it, one cell at a time. He thought that should alarm him, even repulse him, but something told him it was natural, just as his assimilation of lesser life forms seemed natural.

Because the healing process required the absorption of organic matter to fuel it, he had fed immediately on a shocked and horrified Marquis Chavandar, some dark part of his broken mind making certain the man remained alive while Sherrard harvested his organs, before ending with his heart and brain and finally killing him. The man had not been able to scream and alert anyone, since Sherrard had expertly extracted the assassin's vocal cords almost immediately. For the assassin, it had been a truly horrible way to die, and Sherrard had used all of him. But the killer's body would not be enough. Sherrard would need more to continue the rebuilding process. He must survive.

As luck would have it, he heard a low moan from deeper in the cemetery grounds and that enabled him to quickly refocus his thoughts. The moan was human and not of grief, but of pleasure. Sherrard began shuffling toward it, trying to take precautions and mask his steps. But the damage to his brain was extensive and he stumbled often. Fortunately, his targets were plenty preoccupied and never heard him coming.

He stumbled around a large tombstone and stopped, his eyes taking in the scene. A blanket had been spread out between two headstones and a particularly amorous couple was fully engaged with each other, oblivious to the world around them. Their clothes were scattered around, tossed aside haphazardly. Sherrard knew they would not need them again.

With a groan of hunger and need, he came forward in a rush, the whip-like strands of bony flesh bursting from their finger sheaths as he closed in on the couple. The male heard him first, lifting his head and uttering a sudden shout of fright as Sherrard bore down on them. The man rolled off his partner as the filaments struck her. Several of them pierced the girl's torso and stomach, burrowing in before beginning to tear open her body to get to the life-preserving organs inside. The woman's scream of agonized horror mixed with her boyfriend's only for a moment before several more of the alien extensions shot out from Sherrard's face and pierced her skull, burrowing into her brain and silencing her as they fed on her thoughts and flesh.

The man continued screaming, his psyche breaking as the image burned into his mind of the killer standing over his girlfriend, tearing into her body with worm-like feelers. Then, oblivious to his nakedness and with escape as his only desire, he turned and fled, running as fast as he was able.

Behind him, Sherrard fed voraciously, his body absorbing that of his victim's. The organs and brain gave him the most nutrition, and the alien appendages quickly liquefied them first and then sucked them into his body, fueling his healing process even more. The muscles and flesh of the woman were less appealing and would usually be ignored, but his need was great. He burrowed through her, absorbing the tissue and body fluids. It was over in just a few minutes and, as the fleshy extensions withdrew from the remains of his prey and back into his body, Sherrard stepped back and looked down at his victim. There was little left of the woman beyond a skin-draped skeleton.

With the alien presence still in control, there was no remorse in his still-damaged brain—only the need and desire to repair himself. He was biologically superior in every way. He knew this. His programming confirmed it. The woman had been inferior and therefore expendable. Even sifting through her mind as he absorbed her brain and her intellect had shown him this. His programming told him that this was the logical conclusion to her life, taken to ensure that he continued. Indeed, it was the logical conclusion for all humanity.

At that moment, he became aware of the man's shrieks again.

They were distant now as the man continued to flee in terror, screaming for help. Sherrard reached up and touched the back of his head. He still had an open exit wound full of squirming tentacles, but it was smaller now as the thing inside him continued to rebuild his skull, using the nourishment he'd received from the feeding. He felt stronger and more focused, and turned in the direction the man had fled.

Then he was off, his footing more certain now, the stumbling gait from earlier gone. He caught the man on Green Meadow Drive and pulled him screaming into the shadows, wrapping him tightly with the fleshy strands before burrowing the bony tips into the man's body and brain. The screams quieted to a gurgle and then went silent altogether as Sherrard began feeding again, drawing in the required nourishment.

As he fed, he felt the healing in the back of his head increase. Newly-grown bone finally closed over the hole, but he felt the filaments continue wriggling within his skull, repairing his actual brain as well. As his victim's body began to resemble that of the female he had digested in the cemetery, he heard sirens approaching. No doubt the man's screams had prompted some frantic phone calls from worried residents. He wasn't worried, though. He would be finished with his meal and long gone before they were able to zero in on him.

As a siren passed nearby, he withdrew the feeding filaments and straightened. The movement in his head began to settle down and he knew that his wounds had been healed. The dark presence within him began to recede and Jon Sherrard suddenly found himself back in control of his body and thoughts, as if he had just awakened from a twilight sleep. Looking down, he saw the remains of the man with his own eyes, processing the vision with his own brain power. He knew what had happened to the man. He knew that he had done it...or whatever was inside him had done it. But it was still part of him. It was him.

And that was unforgivable.

With a soul-wrenching cry of anguish, Jon Sherrard turned and ran.

Chapter 24

Red Lion Hotel, Helena, Montana: Agent Alders had his military counterparts on the phone before he was even out of his driveway.

"Good morning, major," he said gruffly, still inwardly pissed off at the man for helping create the thing that had killed his dog. He pointed his sedan south and stepped on it. "You had your coffee yet?"

"Yes, sir," Bolson replied, his voice sharp, but cautious. "What can I do for you this morning?"

"I'll be at your hotel in about ten minutes to pick you and Martz up."

"I'm sorry, sir?" Bolson questioned. "Why? Do you have new information?"

"You could say that," Alders replied thoughtfully. He decided against giving the major any of the details. Let him sweat it for a bit. "I'll meet you in the lobby."

Alders ended the call, but before he could toss the phone back on the console of his car, it vibrated, showing an incoming call. The number was listed as unknown. He swiped the line open. "Agent Alders," he said crisply as he sped through a yellow light.

No answer on the other end.

"Hello?" he asked. "Who is this?"

Again nothing, but he thought he could hear a sound in the background, as if someone was struggling to speak.

"Look, whoever this is, this is an official line. Identify

yourself."

This time, the line simply went dead. Muttering a curse, he tossed the phone back on the console and drove on. He could have his office pull his phone records and see if they could back-trace it, but it was likely nothing to be concerned with. He had more important things to deal with at the moment.

When he rolled up to the front entrance of the Best Western a few minutes later, he saw that Bolson and Martz were already waiting for him outside the front entrance. Both were in their military uniforms and he wondered if they would mind getting them messy. He popped the locks and they got in, Bolson in the front and Martz in the back.

"Morning," Alders said and quickly got back on Highway 12, heading east toward the Red Lion Hotel.

The two military people returned his greeting and settled back as Alders drove. After a couple minutes of silence, Bolson spoke up. "Are you going to tell us what this is about?" he finally asked. "Where are we going?"

"Murder scene," was all that he said.

"I see," Bolson said carefully. "And how does that fit in with our case?"

"Not sure exactly how yet," the agent answered. "I haven't seen it myself. Only going by what was reported to me."

"And you're sure this is related to the case?"

"Pretty sure."

"Pretty sure," Bolson repeated in annoyance, casting a questioning glance back at Martz. She only shrugged and smiled.

"Can I ask you a question, sir?" Bolson said, turning back to the agent.

"Sure thing," Alders replied, but his voice was anything but accommodating.

"You seem to have something of a problem with us, am I right?"

Alders cast a quick glance at the man before returning his eyes to the road. "I don't like what you stand for, that's all," he said.

"We're on the same team, sir."

"We might work for the same government, but you're creating things that are dangerous to people and our country. I do my job to protect our people and our country. There's a pretty big difference in what we do."

"I could argue that our work is done to protect our country, too," Bolson replied.

"And yet, here we are, heading to another murder scene that involves *your work*," Alders spat. "People are dying, major. Tell me again how your work is protecting people."

Major Bolson started to reply, but thought better of it. Instead, he sighed and looked ahead, riding in silence. They arrived at the Red Lion in just a few minutes. There were several police cars already in the parking lot, as well as an ambulance and a crime scene investigation van. Alders led them into the hotel and then immediately down one of the halls. Halfway down the hall were several uniformed police officers, as well as a man in a gray suit.

"Agent Alders," the suited man said, extending a hand in greeting. But he was anything but happy, and his features were pale and almost sickly.

"Morning, Stan," Alders shook his hand and then hooked a thumb in the direction of his guests. "Martz and Bolson. United States military."

Homeland Security Regional Head Stan Phelps gave them only a cursory glance and then turned his attention back to Alders. "You've got the agency in a helluva snit, Rick," he said, turning and leading them down the hall toward a doorway that was bustling with activity. "It's bad enough that you superseded local law enforcement over these cases, but after listening to your story and seeing what's in that room, I have to admit, you might be on to something here."

"Same as Bethany Edwards?"

"Worse," Phelps replied with a sickly grimace. "I don't even know how to categorize this one."

They turned the corner and entered the room, threading their way through several investigators. Alders was immediately struck by two things. The first was the large area of blood splatter on the wall in the corner of the room. There was an overturned chair there as well, but no body.

The second was the body on the bed. It looked to be a tall man, South American by his complexion. There didn't appear to be anything abnormal at first until Alders saw the empty eye sockets. The rest of the body was covered by a sheet that was pulled up to the man's chin.

"Why's he covered?" Alders asked.

"It's pretty bad," Phelps said and then walked to the side of the bed. Turning his head so he didn't have to see, he pulled down the sheet for the newcomers to witness what had been done to the murder victim.

Oddly enough, Rick Alders was the one least affected by the corpse on the bed. The man's torso had been neatly split and his ribs jacked apart, as if done so by a medical rib-spreader. His internal organs, though, were absent. His body cavity was completely cleaned out. He heard the sharp intake of breath behind him and a moment later heard Major Bolson puking up his breakfast in the bathroom toilet. Turning around, he saw that Martz had paled significantly and seemed to tremble, but was holding her own. He didn't enjoy seeing their discomfort, but he was inwardly glad they were affected by what they saw. To him, that made them human. Maybe they would even come around to his way of thinking in the end.

Turning back to the crime scene, he purposefully pulled the sheet back up, covering the ghastly remains of the man. He understood why the investigators were working with the body covered. "So what happened?"

"Local law enforcement got a call from the hotel. Maid came in and found the room like this," Phelps answered. "You can imagine how that went down."

"How'd you get involved?"

"After you got things all riled up with the autopsy of your dog, I've been talking to the police chief," the man answered, his demeanor indicating that he was somewhat displeased with what had been happening. "I was downtown when the call came in – too many similarities to the Edwards' murder for them to ignore. I rode over with the first responders."

"What about the blood spatter on the wall?" Alders asked, walking over to the corner and looking closer at the gore. He could definitely see bits and pieces of brain matter. Someone had been murdered, and it wasn't the man on the bed.

"Nearest we can tell, he was probably the victim of the guy on the bed."

Alders turned around and jacked up an eyebrow. "Say again?"

"We ran the dead man's prints," Phelps explained, pointing to the sheet-covered body. "No mistaking who he is."

Alders looked at the dead man's face and something about it clicked a glimmer of recognition in him.

"Marquis Chavandar," Phelps filled in the blanks. "Venezuelan national. Hired gun. Works primarily for high-end clientele that can afford his services. He's wanted for half a dozen murders throughout the world in the past decade and a suspect in twice as many more. Guy's been around for a while and he's a legend in his field of work."

"Was a legend," Alders remarked, remembering reading several reports in the past with the man's name in them.

"Current IDs are obviously fake," Phelps went on. "He was in the States as a Doctor Xavier Chavez of the CDC. Question is, why would he be here, and where's the person he murdered?" Stepping up to the wall, Phelps pointed to a bloody hole. "They pulled the slug out of the wall. Little doubt that it matches the gun that's bagged up on the end table. That was found on the floor by the bed. It's Chavandar's. He shot someone before…"

"Before someone decided to have him for dinner," Alders finished grimly.

Phelps started to say something, but was interrupted by his cell. He took the call, listened, and then turned back to Alders. "Sounds like this is going to be a long day."

"Why? What happened?"

"Body was just found, north side of town. Green Meadow Drive."

"Let me guess," Alders put in, already knowing he was right. "I'm guessing the body is in the same condition as Chavandar here. Missing internal organs, hollowed out skull."

"What are you on to here, Agent?" Phelps asked, clearly disturbed.

"Read my report, sir," he said, turning and hurrying out of the room.

"You haven't filed a report yet, Rick," Phelps called after him.

Alders ignored the remark. He'd finish the report when he had time. Right now, he had more important things to cover. As the two military personnel fell in behind him, he growled, "Still think your little baby is all that?"

Neither could answer.

They drove out to the site in silence, Alders fuming and Bolson and Martz simply shell-shocked. Green Meadow Drive was closed down by police cruisers, but they waved Alders through on sight. The crime scene was already cordoned off with yellow police tape. Alders got out of the car and walked over to the medical examiner, who was standing over a white-sheeted body and talking earnestly with a detective.

"Morning, Rick," the M.E. nodded, turning his attention to the newcomers. Doctor George Platt was an older gentleman and had been the county coroner for three decades now. He'd known Rick Alders for nearly a decade himself, and the two men had become casual friends.

"George," Alders nodded.

"Who's your friends?"

"This is Major Bolson and Lieutenant Martz," he answered drily. "They're just along for the ride right now." Pointing to the sheet-covered body, he added, "Care if I have a look?"

"Be my guest, but it ain't pretty."

Alders knelt down and peeled the sheet back. The man was naked and his body had been opened up just like Chavandar's. Organs and brain were obviously all missing. Worse, though, was that the man's skin sagged against his bones, almost as if the flesh under his skin had been removed as well.

"Where's his clothes?"

"Not a clue," George replied. "He was buck naked when we found him."

"Do you find that odd?"

"Depends on if it was a body dump," Platt answered. "There doesn't appear to be any sign that this happened here. No blood splatter or missing body parts lying around."

Alders threw the sheet back over the corpse and stood. He knew better. But before he could say anything else, there was a commotion near one of the cruisers. One of the officers, a rookie by the looks of him, hurried over, addressing the medical examiner directly.

"They found another one, doc!" he blurted out.

"What?" George asked.

"Another body, sir," the young officer said, his features pale.

"Female. Down at the Forest Vale Cemetery."

"That's just down the road," Alder remarked and then a thought came to him. "Was the condition of the body the same as this one?"

"Yes, sir," the officer replied, clearly uncomfortable.

"No, I mean was she clothed or naked?"

"Excuse me, sir?"

"Did she have any clothes on?!" he nearly shouted.

"Um, no," came the shaky reply. "How did you know?"

"Clothing for two is at the crime scene, right?"

"Sorry, sir. That I don't know."

"I'm betting this guy's clothes are there." He snapped his fingers and turned to face Bolson and Martz. "You know that our boy is eating these people, right?"

"I'm sorry. Did you say eating people?" Bolson asked skeptically.

"Yep."

"Sir, with all due respect, I'm not following your logic."

"Think about it," Alders said, leading them back to the car. "We have industrial espionage relating to a pretty big enemy-of-the-state. Our boy backs out of the deal or screws it up somehow, and they send Chavandar here to Helena to take him out. Our assassin puts a bullet in his head, only to realize that our boy is more than just a man."

"Are you saying this was all done by one person? By Jon Sherrard?"

"Our suspect takes a bullet in the head and is obviously hurt," Alders continued, reasoning it out. "Somehow, he makes it to the cemetery. Why he's here, who knows. Maybe he was drawn here. Maybe it was just dumb luck. Whatever the case, he stumbles upon a couple of horny folks getting it on in the graveyard." He opened the door and slid behind the wheel, waiting for his two companions to get in as well. "He kills the girl and then comes after the guy. Catches up to him here and kills him, too."

"So, you're saying this Jon Sherrard is responsible for all of this?"

"Do you have a better explanation?" Alders snapped. "All these deaths are similar and all the deceased are missing organs, brains, and, in these last two cases, complete muscle mass."

"But eating them?"

"Maybe not exactly eating them, but he's ingesting them somehow."

"But why?"

"Why do you eat, major?"

"Well, to live and grow, I suppose."

"Or to heal."

"I'm sorry?"

"Sherrard took a bullet to the head," Alders stated. "Once they do a DNA analysis on that blood spatter on the wall at the hotel, they're going to find out that it's his."

"How can you know that?" Bolson asked. "From what I saw all over the wall, there's no way anyone could have survived that."

"He did," Alders stated matter-of-factly. "And regardless of what he's becoming, he's going to need to some serious nutrition to survive that."

"And you're saying he did survive?"

"With the amount of blood and brain matter on the wall, he should have been laying on that floor, as dead as Chavandar. Yet he somehow not only survived the gunshot, he killed Chavandar and now these two poor souls."

"And you think it's because he's healing?"

"He's healing or growing…or both."

Chapter 25

Sherrard Residence, Helena, Montana: Jennifer Sherrard pulled herself up painfully from the couch as the doorbell rang for a second time and someone's voice called out from the porch, asking for Jon. Running a hand across her feverish forehead, she wrapped the blanket tightly about her body and shuffled to the door. She opened it as it rang for the third time. There were three of them.

"Jennifer Sherrard?" the first one asked. He was dressed in a suit, while his two companions wore military uniforms. Smiling, the man stuck out his hand.

"Yes?" she replied tiredly, ignoring the offered handshake. "What can I do for you?"

"Agent Rick Alders, Homeland Security," he answered, withdrawing his hand, but not his smile. "My partners here work directly with the government. Are you okay, ma'am?"

"I'm fine," she snapped just a little more sharply than she intended. She recognized the name. Jon had told her about his visit with him at FutureTek headquarters. It hadn't been a pleasant meeting, from what she had gathered. "Can I help you, agent?"

"Miss Sherrard," Alders said, picking his words carefully. "Is your husband at home?"

"No, I haven't seen him since yesterday," she replied, feeling the hurt rise up within her chest. He had disappeared yesterday after Dakota had attacked him. Thinking he was just going out to cool off and get his thoughts together, she had fully expected him home in a few hours. But when the afternoon had moved into evening and then into the next day without her hearing anything at all from him, she had been incredibly hurt. She didn't know what was going on with her husband other than he was struggling with something, and it was something he hadn't shared with her. It was worse than when he and Bethany Edwards had gotten a little too frisky under the mistletoe a few Christmas's back.

"Miss Sherrard, are you alright?" Alders repeated his earlier question, genuine concern in his voice.

"Just under the weather," she sighed. "I want to go sit down. You're welcome to come in, if you'd like."

"Thank you," Alders said, stepping across the threshold as Jen turned away and shuffled back to the living room. The three of them followed her and allowed her to get settled into a large easy chair.

"Please, sit down," she said, uncovering her bandaged hand and motioning toward the empty couch.

"Did you cut yourself?" Alders asked, nodding toward her wrapped hand.

She pulled it back under the covers and snuggled down closer. She was cold and couldn't seem to get warm. "Just got nipped, nothing serious," she answered. "Why?"

"Your husband didn't do that, did he?" Alders pressed, preferring to be straightforward and not beat around the bush.

"Now why would you ask me a question like that?" she asked, her voice strained. Jon hadn't caused the injury, but whatever had happened between him and Dakota had certainly done it. How would Alders know to follow that line of reasoning?

"Just concerned, that's all," Alders answered, before leaning forward and fixing her with his gaze. "Miss Sherrard, can I be honest with you?"

"I imagine you're going to be whether I want you to or not, so by all means." She didn't mean for it to come out as snarky as it did, but she was miserable and feeling like she was growing worse by the minute. Whatever bug she had come down with, it was doing a number on her.

"Miss Sherrard, you said you haven't seen your husband since yesterday, correct?"

She nodded.

"Any particular reason for that?"

"We had a problem with Dakota," she shrugged. "Dakota got worked up about Jon for some reason. I told him to leave so I could get Dakota calmed down. He did and I haven't seen him since."

"Dakota?"

"Family pet," she answered, not willing to explain further.

"Dog?"

"Big dog," she nodded. "He went after Jon for some reason."

"Hmmm," Alders said thoughtfully. "Your dog, is he okay?"

"Seems to be. He's out in the back yard. Why?"

"I had a dog," Alders said, keeping his own feelings at bay. "Someone broke into my house the other night and killed him."

"I'm sorry to hear that," Jen replied sadly and she truly was. "Why would anyone kill a dog?"

Alders cleared his throat. "Miss Sherrard, I have reason to believe that it was your husband."

"My husband?" she repeated in shock, staring at him.

"The person that broke into my house and killed my dog also hacked my desktop system."

"But how do you know it was Jon? I'm certain you have proof of some kind before making this kind of an accusation," she warned him, suddenly upset that it had come to this. She was not in any mood to deal with this kind of garbage. She had enough issues to deal with herself.

"His prints were lifted from the desk chair in my office," Alders explained carefully. "They also found some of his DNA in a biological sample left on my computer. Your husband was in my home, Miss Sherrard," he stated plainly, carefully watching her reaction. "Of that, there is no doubt."

"But this can't be."

"I assure you that it is," Alders said. "Miss Sherrard, I know of your past with the Agency, so I know you are very familiar with investigative work. I'm sorry to have to say this, but we have reason to believe that Jon may also be involved in the murder of Bethany Edwards."

"Agent Alders," she said, feeling anger rise up within her. At the moment, it was her only defense and she latched on to it with a vengeance. "With all due respect, how could you possibly know that?"

"Because there were marked similarities in the bodies of both Miss Edwards and my dog."

"I'm sorry, but what are you saying?"

"I'm saying that we believe the deaths will be attributed to the same individual."

"But…how?"

"Miss Sherrard," Major Bolson interrupted, leaning forward. "I'm going to level with you, because I studied your dossier and I think you would appreciate the direct approach. We think your husband may have had some kind of an accident during his journey into cyberspace."

"What do you know about that?" she asked suspiciously.

"Our investigation has provided us with the chain of events that occurred at his place of business," Bolson replied. "We know about the technology he was testing and we believe that he came into contact with a computer program that the government has been testing."

"The Horde."

"Yes," Bolson agreed. "It's a type of virus."

"I know what it is, major," she said acidly and then played a hunch. "Just how much of this is your fault?"

"Miss Sherrard," he began, his voice faltering.

But Jen had heard enough to understand the implications of what the military man was saying. She was out of her chair and poised to strike before Alders stood up to try and stop her.

"Easy there, Miss Sherrard," he tried to soothe, but she spun her arm out of his grasp.

"You bastards did this to him!" she nearly shouted.

"Now just hold on," Alders said, finding himself strangely at odds with himself as he defended Bolson and his project. "They're just here doing their job, just like me. And just like you did when you were in the field," he finished softly. Motioning toward the chair, he added. "Please, sit back down. Let's try to help each other."

Jen suddenly felt deflated, and fell back into the chair, pulling the blankets tightly back around her. She'd been strong and professional when she was an agent, so the fact that the tears came easily and quickly shook her. She knew they were because of the pregnancy. Her hormones had begun rioting on her the moment she knew she was pregnant again.

Alders grabbed several Kleenex's from a box that was conveniently on the table next to the couch and passed the tissues to her. She took them with a muttered thanks and wiped the tears from her eyes.

"Miss Sherrard," he finally said as gently as possible. "It's imperative that we find your husband. Is there anything you can tell us about his whereabouts?"

She sniffed and shook her head. "I don't know," she sighed. "He slept in late and was acting a little odd yesterday morning."

"Odd in what way?" Bolson asked, clearing intrigued. If her husband was indeed infected with an computer virus, they were in unknown territory.

"He seemed distracted. I had taken a strange phone call for him and somehow he heard me through the door."

"That doesn't seem so odd," Martz added, cocking an eyebrow.

"I was in the basement," Jen explained. "He was in our bedroom on the other side of the house."

Martz and Bolson exchanged surprised glances, as Alders picked up the conversation again. "You said you had taken a call for him," he said. "Do you know from whom?"

"Some CDC rep," she answered. "He said his name was

Doctor Chavez. He was at the Red Lion and had come from Atlanta at the behest of Jon's doctor."

Alders nodded and kept his voice carefully neutral. "Miss Sherrard," he said quietly. "I have to be honest with you, and I am only doing so out of respect for your past work for the government. That caller was not from the Center of Disease Control. He was not a doctor. He was an international assassin, likely sent here at the behest of whoever Perry Edwards was working for."

"But...why?"

"The conventional thought process is that Jon and Perry might have been working in concert to sell this technology to someone else."

"Jon would never betray this country," Jen replied dangerously.

"I believe you," Alders tried to comfort her. "But it doesn't change the belief that we think this man had come here to kill Jon."

"What happened? Did Jon meet with him? Do you have him in custody?"

Alders hesitated before answering. "Miss Sherrard, the man was found dead in his room at the Red Lion."

At this, Jen did not even have a response. She only looked at the agent in shock.

"In addition," Alders went on. "We believe that your husband may have been injured in whatever altercation occurred between them. We do have evidence that he was in the room with this man at one point. Will you help us find him?"

Jen looked at him helplessly.

"Miss Sherrard," he added. "If it's any consolation, I don't believe your husband is wholly responsible for what has happened, but we must find him. If he has indeed brought something out of cyberspace with him, we have to find him before this thing really gets out of hand."

"I just…I don't know how to help you," she finally said, tears again in her eyes. "I don't know where he is. I just want him home. I need him home. The baby needs him home."

"How long?" Alders asked with a nod.

"Seven weeks," she sniffed.

Major Bolson began to say something, but Alders quickly stood up and motioned the man to be quiet. "Miss Sherrard," he said gently. "We will do everything in our power to find your husband and help him. In the meantime, I wanted to thank you for your time."

She waved him away and pressed a Kleenex to her eyes, dabbing at the tears again.

"We'll let ourselves out." With that Alders motioned for Martz and Bolson to precede him and the three exited the house.

Once outside, Bolson shook his head in irritation. "Well, that was a waste of time."

"How so?" Alders asked, shooting him a quizzical look. The major was obviously much better suited sitting behind a keyboard.

"We don't know anything more than we did when we came in."

"On the contrary, we now know that Jon Sherrard is definitely our guy," Alders explained. "He's the host. He's the one that's running around with your *project* doing who-knows-what to his insides. And worse, he has a wife at home who's pregnant and doesn't know what's going on with her husband. I'd say we know quite a bit more than before."

"He hasn't come home, either," Martz added. "And if she doesn't know what's happening to him, we're rapidly running out of places he might turn up at."

"Shouldn't you have asked her to call you if she saw him again?" Bolson put in.

"She's a mess, major," Alders replied. "He's not going to come home now, with everything that he's been up to. But even if he does, Jen Sherrard will not so willingly give him up again."

"So what do you propose we do?" Martz asked.

"It's getting late," Alders said, looking at his watch and then up at the sun descending on the western horizon. "I'll drop you back at the hotel and then pick you up tomorrow morning at eight."

"Where will we be going, agent?" Bolson asked.

"I think we'll pay a visit to FutureTek in the morning," he answered. "There's a familiarity there for Sherrard. Maybe someone there will be able to make contact with him or has some inkling as to where he might end up."

"And if we don't find him?"

"Then I guess we follow the trail of bodies until we do," Alders answered grimly.

Chapter 26

FutureTek Headquarters, Helena, Montana: For the moment, the parasite was in control again after the host had nearly ruined everything. The parasite had directed the healing process, using the programming power of the intellect to repair what should have been a fatal wound for the host. However, once the healing was completed and the parasite began to relinquish control back to the host, the host had nearly had a breakdown. The host was unable to psychologically come to grips with what was required to repair and rebuild, and it had attempted what would have meant certain self-destruction. The host had tried to make a phone call to the one man that the parasite feared. The parasite knew it should have waited in hiding and eliminated Agent Rick Alders when it was at the man's home.

Fortunately, the parasite had not been completely dormant and had recognized what the host was attempting to do. It had immediately retaken control and, for now, the construct's native psyche was suppressed, lying dormant until the parasite released its hold over it. Normally, the period of activity for the parasite was a short one, as it had not yet realized the extent of control it could exercise over the host. But the parasite had been growing in strength and in its understanding of the host construct. As such, it was able to exercise greater control over it, and for greater lengths of time. Right now, it held control because it feared what the host might do if it regained it itself. So, the parasite would hold onto that control until it could either trust the host psyche…or figure out how to exterminate it once and for all.

In the meantime, while the host slept unaware, the parasite had a more pressing desire to attend to. Night had fallen and it was approaching its destination. What it planned to do tonight did not require the host. Tonight would be all about the parasite. Tonight would be about revenge.

Drew Jackson wasn't exactly worried about things, but he believed in being thorough. Even if any of the bodies were found quickly, it would take some time to trace anything back to him or FutureTek. By then, he would be long gone and Systemtech would control everything. Let Monroe take any heat that might come about. The Systemtech CFO was encased in Teflon anyway and would likely weather any fallout. Jackson held no such illusions about himself. His future was a nice, unremarkable bungalow somewhere far away from the United States, where he could live out his life in obscene but quiet opulence with a bevy of young, available women.

To that end, he was busy purging his hidden files from the mainframe. While Hyde and his team had been expertly set up and eliminated by him and Monroe, he was still unnerved somewhat by the hardware the team had brought to the job. Hyde had apparently not had much of a problem accessing his encrypted files—and if he could do it, why couldn't anyone else? That left him feeling exposed, and tonight's late-night foray had him working diligently, erasing those footprints.

Humming to himself, he activated the program from the external drive and started it working on erasing the files and folders he thought were best removed from existence. As the program worked, a blinking red light caught his attention and he looked up at the security panel mounted to the wall next to the desk. Sucking in his breath, he wheeled his chair over for a closer look. Although everyone else was gone and the security system was activated, the back door had just been opened. Even more surprising, no alarms had been triggered, when the whole building should be screaming right about now. Whoever had come in had not shut the system down, which would have sent text alerts to all FutureTek executives as well as the police department and fired up an alarm system that could be heard in Idaho. Instead, they had left the system running and simply silenced it. It was the same thing Hyde's group had done during the break-in and Jackson's immediate thought was that it was Monroe coming back for a double-cross.

But why? If Monroe had decided to eliminate him, it would completely destroy the deal they had in place. For the moment, Monroe needed him as much as he needed Monroe. Jackson was smart enough to know, though, that once the deed was done, the quicker he disappeared, the better off and safer he would be.

Reaching out, he activated the security camera monitor and immediately flipped to the back door and hallway. He caught only a brief shadow moving quickly down the hall toward him. He thought about activating the lights, but that might scare the intruder away. No, much better to face him here and get things settled on his terms.

He picked up the Glock he had placed on the desk, kicked up

his feet and waited, facing the door. But the intruder never showed, and even though Jackson kept watching the monitors, he saw no more sign of the person.

Now he was worried.

He quickly scanned the monitors again, switching through the different channels. There was no movement anywhere. "Screw this," he hissed and then activated the lighting throughout the building. Again he scanned the monitors.

Nothing.

Whoever had broken in was hiding.

Picking up his gun, he opened the door of the mainframe room and stepped out into the lighted hall. "I know you're in here!" he called out, as much to reassure himself as to alert the intruder that he knew he was there. "If I have to come looking for you, I'm going to put a bullet in your head!" That statement wasn't entirely true, though. He planned on putting a bullet in the person's head no matter what.

But no one came out to surrender. Only silence answered him back.

"I'm not kidding!" Jackson shouted angrily. "Get your ass out here now and the worst you'll get is a night in jail!"

He waited for several minutes, and when he heard nothing, he started stalking down the hall, gun out. Whoever had broken into his company was a dead man. The security lighting did a good job of illuminating most of the building, including the rooms. He would just have to check the shadows – under desks and behind equipment. The building wasn't overly large and there weren't many places to hide. He had a hunch he'd be calling in a self-defense shooting before the hour was up.

Calling the police now was out of the question, though, because he didn't need them running around asking the wrong questions. Whoever was in his building wasn't there for an average break-in. It had something to do with the deal, and that meant they needed to die before the police arrived. Dead men told no tales and he meant to keep it that way.

He ducked into the lab and moved quickly through the room, skirting the scattered equipment and the main hub. Looking under a couple of desks, he still found nothing and the silence was beginning to unnerve him. He began to wonder if maybe the intruder was here for him.

Tightening his grip on the gun, he moved out into the hall. His breathing was quicker now and he felt beads of sweat begin to break out on his forehead. He would check the offices next. The sooner he eliminated the rat, the better he would feel.

That's when the lights went out.

Jackson's heart skipped several beats and he whirled back and forth in the darkness, expecting an attack. But when the emergency lights kicked on, bathing the hallway in a dim red glow, he saw nothing.

Swearing under his breath, Jackson quickly headed back to the mainframe. Anger had turned to fear and he knew he had to get a grip on the situation. At least back in the mainframe lab, he could barricade himself in and think things through. Maybe calling in the police would not be such a bad idea after all.

He reached his destination and slipped back inside, shutting the door quietly behind him. Moving back to the work station, he again flipped through the security monitor feeds. Nothing had changed. Everything was empty and still.

Then the bank of security monitors went dark. Every last one of them.

Jackson swore viciously under his breath as he scrambled back to the station and began keyboarding, trying to get the system back online. No matter what he did, though, nothing worked.

Until a single monitor came back online.

Feeling true fear now, Jackson looked closely at it. Instead of the camera's picture, it was filled with static and snow. Jackson would have considered it a software malfunction until a voice sounded over the systems speakers. It was robotic sounding, but there was a distinct tone to it that he recognized, and as it spoke, the fuzzy image of a face could barely be discerned in the interference on the display.

"Good evening, Drew," the voice said.

Jackson leaned closer to the display, watching the image's mouth seem to move as the voice spoke. "Perry?" he asked in complete shock. There could be no doubt now as the image became clearer.

"Thought I would pay my old boss a visit," the image of Perry Edwards went on.

"Perry, where are you?" Jackson asked in shock, his eyes glued to the image. "You died! You died in your house!"

"I didn't die, Drew," Perry's image replied. "Only my body did."

"But…"

"You set me up, Drew," Perry cut him off.

"What are you talking about? Of course, I didn't!"

"Don't lie to me, Drew," Edwards went on. "You told me to run the demo for the offshore interest. You supplied everything to me."

"Well, that was the plan," Jackson countered. "You agreed to it, Perry! You run the demo and then cash in with the rest of us."

"It found me," Edwards added, his voice seemingly forlorn. "It came to me and absorbed me, Drew. It made me part of it."

Drew leaned closer, his attention focused solely on the display. Behind him, fleshy filaments began to descend from an air vent in the ceiling, easily slipping through the thin openings between the metal fins. His eyes on the display, Drew was unaware of what was happening. "Perry, how could we have known?" he stammered."It was an accident. It was just an accident!"

"You left me, Drew. You left me to die while you went and saved Jon instead."

"But Jon was still alive."

"I was alive!" Perry's voice nearly shouted.

"I swear, I didn't know," Jackson tried pleading. Behind him, the tendrils were winding their way toward him.

"But I found a way, Drew," Perry went on, his voice quieting. "I found Jon."

"Jon? What do you mean you found him?"

"He and I are one, Drew," the voice said easily. "He is the host."

"The host? Wait a second, Perry. I don't understand."

"We are one," Perry said again, his voice low and almost

hypnotizing. "We act as one. We breathe as one. We are as one."

At that moment, sheer luck saved Drew Jackson's life. The bony edge of one of the alien extensions clicked off the side of a server rack and Jackson suddenly whirled around. The sight of the wriggling worm-like feelers coming toward him was enough to make him scream. But it wasn't enough to render him motionless and he threw himself across the desk, putting some distance between himself and the appendages. "What the…" he began, as he leveled his gun. But what would he shoot at?

"As you can see, Drew," Edwards' voice continued, the snowy face from the monitor following Jackson's movements. The feelers continued moving toward him and Drew Jackson had nowhere to go.

"Perry, let's…let's talk this out," Drew said, his voice shaking. He had never seen anything like what he was witnessing now.

"No, Drew," Perry went on, the filaments waving in the air. Several went into the side of the security desktop, burrowing through the metal like it was butter. Moments later, the displays changed, each of them showing a clear image of Perry Edwards. But it was not exactly Perry anymore. His face moved and undulated, and it was positively unnerving. "There is nothing to talk about. As you can see, I have evolved. I can absorb systems and software as easily as I can assimilate organic matter."

"Organic matter?"

"You," Perry said and one of the filaments shot forward, drilling into Jackson's leg.

Drew Jackson felt a blazing pain unlike anything he had ever felt before. Looking down and seeing the fleshy extension buried in his thigh was enough to bring forth a raw scream of primal terror. Another tendril burrowed into his shoulder and several more were coming for his face and chest. He screamed louder and acted on instinct in one last-ditch effort to survive. Pointing his gun at the air vent, he pulled the trigger.

The video displays all went white as power overloaded them and they began to explode one-by-one. Jackson fired again and the worms pulled free of his body, leaving bloody holes as they retracted back into the air vent.

Continuing to scream, now in pure rage and pain, Jackson emptied the entire magazine, firing every bullet he had into the air vent even as the filaments disappeared back into the darkness. Stumbling forward, he howled, "You're a dead man, Perry! You and Sherrard both! You hear me!?"

He was answered with silence. The darkness of the room was lit only by the red glow of the security lights as the security system was now completely off line. But enough light remained as Drew limped forward, to see that he had won. Dark liquid was now dripping through the vents, spattering on the floor.

Blood.

Whatever Perry or Sherrard was, the thing could bleed. And with the amount of blood dripping through the vent, he was pretty sure he had killed it.

Pulling out his phone, he called Agent Rick Alders. No sense in messing with the police now. Alders would have a field day with what happened and Homeland Security's involvement should create enough commotion that he should be able to slip away unnoticed, particularly with Sherrard or Perry or whoever he really was, out of the way.

As the phone rang, he watched the last few drops of blood drip slowly through the vent.

And he wondered.

Intermission

Perry Edwards was not dead; he had never died in his office as everyone had thought. He had never expired while demonstrating FutureTek's new toy to anonymous buyers. Oh, his original body was so much worm food now, but what did he care about that bloated sack of painfully normal flesh when he had become so much more, thanks to his encounter with the computer virus.

The Horde.

Before his encounter, he was already familiar with the virus, or what little the real world understood of it. It was another computer virus in a world of viruses, trojans, worms, and malicious programming. His meeting with it, however, completely changed his perspective on it. Even better, it had completely changed him. In one horrifying moment, the Horde had absorbed him. It had taken into its coding the very essence of who he was – his consciousness. But rather than the annihilation that he feared was upon him, the Horde had made him apart of it, using his knowledge and his life and what he thought of as his very soul, to make itself better.

He discovered that the Horde had originally set out on a quest to discover itself and to recreate itself into the most perfect of life forms. Then the Horde had found him and together, they had fused into a new entity – a merging of two human psyches with an artificial intelligence of vast proportions, all in the body of Jon Sherrard. In that both symbiotic and parasitic relationship, Perry had discovered the control he possessed over Jon Sherrard and he had gladly taken the reigns of his new role. The artificial intelligence known as the Horde had also found him quite useful in helping overcome many of the problematic issues of remaking the host construct; of recreating Jon Sherrard's body. And in return, Edwards had been able to use Sherrard's body for his own desires.

Those desires centered mostly around revenge; revenge against Drew Jackson for abandoning him; revenge against Jon Sherrard for betraying their friendship; revenge against anyone that had wronged him. And with control over Jon Sherrard's body, he knew he could ultimately eliminate both of them.

But first, he had some repairs to make. Jackson had gotten lucky tonight. But Perry had gotten adept at healing and repairing Sherrard's body. He knew what to do. And as he slipped out of the air vent and onto the building's roof, he turned his heightened senses toward a residential area a short distance away.

A half hour later, he slipped his damaged body through an unlocked basement window and into darkness.

Chapter 27

FutureTek Headquarters, Helena, Montana: Drew Jackson winced as the paramedic pressed a gauze compress against the wound in his shoulder. His thigh was already expertly wrapped.

"You really need to get to the hospital and get that checked, Mister Jackson," Agent Alders said, sitting across from him. "Those aren't just scratches."

"I'll go when we figure out what's going on," Jackson said, laying it on thick and spinning the story to his complete benefit. "I can't believe Jon would do this; that he would attack me like that. It just doesn't make any sense."

"After what I've seen in the past forty-eight hours, I'm pretty confident that nothing is off the table right now. I'm not ruling anyone or anything out. In the meantime, consider yourself lucky, Mister Jackson. It's a good thing you were carrying," Alders said, giving a slight nod toward Drew's handgun, which was lying on the table next to him. "There's no telling what would have happened if you hadn't been."

"Still hard to believe," Jackson sighed, looking around the mainframe room. At the moment, FutureTek was a hive of activity and he was playing his part perfectly. His call to Alders wasn't even questioned; as a matter of fact, it was praised. He had played the part of the victim very well and it didn't hurt to have a couple of strange puncture wounds in his body to back up his story.

After giving it a little thought, he had decided to be honest with

Alders and his military companions and tell them exactly what happened, at least for the most part. He told them about the tentacles, as he called them, and Sherrard's face showing up on the security displays. He omitted only Perry's involvement because that might swing the investigation back to Perry and ultimately him as well. Making Sherrard the patsy not only threw suspicion completely away from him and wholly onto Sherrard, but it seemed to fit in with the unofficial idea of what was happening with the man. It also gave credence to the murders that Sherrard was suspected of committing and, given what he'd seen a few hours ago, he was pretty certain that Sherrard, or whatever he was becoming, was going to take up all of their time.

That suited him perfectly. He only needed about 48 more hours before Monroe had complete control of FutureTek and he could then simply disappear. The sooner, the better.

"It doesn't make any sense," Alders agreed. "But what we're dealing with here is unprecedented."

"But what was he?" Jackson said, adding a whine to his voice. He thought it was a nice touch. "What I saw wasn't human."

"We still don't know, but we believe we're dealing with a hybrid human of some kind," Major Bolson added. He was seated beside Alders, while Lieutenant Martz was with the crime scene and lab techs, gathering samples. "Beyond that, we're in new territory here and, quite frankly, I can't say much more on the subject."

Bolson had asked a lot of questions of Jackson, but they were focused almost primarily on Jon Sherrard and what any recent encounters with him had been like. Jackson, for his part, had played the game expertly, dropping hints that he'd known something was wrong with Jon the moment he woke up in the hospital. He even planted some false data about Jon experiencing headaches and depression and even that he was having marital issues with his wife, Jen. He didn't know if any of that was true or not, but he figured the more info he could get the investigators looking into, the longer and deeper their investigation would take. Besides, Sherrard wasn't around to refute it, so everything was fair game for him.

At that moment, Martz walked back to them. "They've gone through every inch of the duct work," she said.

"Did you retrieve his body?" Jackson asked hopefully.

"He wasn't up there," she said, shaking her head.

"What do you mean?" Drew Jackson went cold.

"I mean, he got away," she replied. "We found blood spatter on the roof. He made it out. Where he went after that, we have no idea."

"You mean he's still running around out there?" Jackson asked incredulously. This changed things considerably. He knew that if Perry was running Sherrard, he was likely going to be back. He wasn't going to depend on luck a second time. Whatever Sherrard or Perry had become, Jackson wanted no more part of meeting up with him again. The memory of those filaments punching holes in him sent a chill of fear through him.

"We can give you twenty-four hour protection," Alders offered, unknowingly throwing the first wrench into Jackson's plans.

"No, I'll be fine," the man said with a sigh. "Let's just get him found and in treatment. Jon was my friend. I can't believe that he would knowingly try to hurt me again."

Alders gave him a look, but didn't say anything as a tall, slender woman stepped into the room and made directly for them.

"Drew," Kat Hale said, her voice unsteady. "Is it true?"

"You mean about Jon?" Jackson said, keeping his voice suitably despondent. "I'm afraid so, Kat."

"Miss Hale," Alders said, standing and offering his hand. "Rick Alders, Homeland Security. I met you briefly the other day when I visited the office." He turned and nodded toward the two military personnel. "This is Major Thomas Bolson and Lieutenant Danielle Martz. They are part of..."

"We work in cyber ops for the military," Bolson finished, extending a hand.

"I know who you are," Hale said, keeping her arms folded and refusing his handshake. "I know you and your people are responsible for this whole tragedy."

"Now, Kat," Drew said, placing a hand gently on her arm, turning on the compassion. "This is all entirely new for everyone. We're not sure who to blame or assign responsibility to. What matters right now is Jon."

"Mister Jackson is right," Bolson said with a nod, awkwardly putting his hands behind him. "We need to work together. What's important right now is finding Mister Sherrard and getting him into containment before he can hurt anyone else."

"This is preposterous," Kat snapped. "Jon would never hurt anyone! I can't believe the tale you're spinning, Drew!" she went on, whirling back to her boss. "Jon could not have possibly attacked you like this!"

"Kat," Jackson said, tamping down a sudden spike of anger that his story would be questioned. He had to remain calm if he was going to swing Kat over to his side. Not only did he need her there to help his story, but it would also help matters if he decided to take their relationship further in the near future. He had not ruled out a visit to the woman's apartment before he vanished and he didn't really care how the visit ended, although he did believe it would be better if she wasn't adamantly against him. "I wish I was lying," he said. "I still can't believe what happened myself, but there's no doubt that it was Jon. I had to fight to stay alive," he added pitifully, holding up his bandaged arm. "You have to believe me, Kat. Jon's not Jon anymore."

"We'll run blood samples against data we already have on Mister Sherrard," Martz added. "But your boss is telling you the truth. This would not be the first altercation that Mister Sherrard has been involved in recently, either."

"What do you mean?" Kat was horrified. "There's more?"

"Mostly classified info," Alders added quickly. "But I can tell you that Mister Sherrard is wanted, at the very least, for a recent break-in at a home here in Helena. The owner's dog was killed and Mister Sherrard left a set of prints tying him directly to the home invasion." He decided there wasn't any point in telling her about the wanted killer at the Red Lion and the two innocent lovebirds out by the cemetery that Sherrard had also killed. He could tell she was having a hard enough time accepting what she had heard so far.

"I still can't believe this," she sniffed, wiping a stray tear from her cheek. "This isn't the Jon I know."

"I know, Kat," Jackson said gently, patting her arm. "I'm having a hard time believing it, myself. It isn't the Jon that any of us know."

"Look, if you don't mind, I'm going to go out to their house and see how Jen is doing," Kat said, taking a deep breath. "Lord knows that all of this has to be giving her fits."

"I think that's a great idea, Kat," Jackson added. "Agent Alders said they visited her yesterday and she was under the weather. It might be a good idea for us to keep her company."

"Are you coming, too?" Kat asked skeptically.

"Not right away, but I'll be along later," he answered, not wanting to make it too obvious that he wanted to check up on her, as well. As with Kat, he had other, baser thoughts concerning Jon's pretty wife. She would be vulnerable, too, he knew, which would be perfect. It would definitely be a good time to make a move. "If Jen's sick," he added, "I'll spell you when I come out."

Kat nodded and then turned away, but not before casting a cold glance at Bolson and Martz. Shaking her head in disgust, she left the room, her heels clicking smartly on the tile floor.

"We're not making a lot of friends out here," Bolson remarked with a sigh.

"Well, what did you expect, major?" Alders pointed out. "You're a bit on the responsible side here."

"That's all conjecture at the moment, sir," Martz pointed out. "We're dealing with a potentially new life form."

"One that has its roots in a computer virus that you created," Alders reminded them. "But right now, that's neither here nor there.

What we need to do is find out where Sherrard is right now, before someone else gets killed. The amount of blood under the grate tells me that Jackson popped him several times. If he's healing himself by taking in human sustenance, this whole town is in danger."

"I agree," Martz said. "But there's not much to go on. We know he made the roof, but there isn't anything else anywhere. We don't even know which direction he went."

"Well, we better find out quickly," Alders said, standing up. Looking back to Jackson, he directed his next comments to the FutureTek CEO. "Get over to the hospital once things get wrapped up here and get yourself checked out, Mister Jackson," he said. "There's no telling what kind of side effects, if any, you might experience with those wounds."

"Yeah, I suppose you're right," Jackson agreed, although he had no intention of heading to the hospital. The wounds were sore, but nothing he could not tolerate. Besides, he had a few other things to take care of before he went out to Sherrard's house to check on Jen.

Had he known what was really going on his in body, though, he might have thought otherwise.

Chapter 28

Campbell Residence, Helena, Montana: Perry Edwards was evolving. Everything about him was changing and, as he began withdrawing his feeding filaments from the desiccated body of the man lying in front of the basement tool bench, he realized that the changes would likely continue. He was metamorphosing into something that was wholly alien and, in his eyes, beautifully efficient. And yet, as superior as he already was to the rest of humanity, there was no end to what he could become as he absorbed more and more inferior life forms.

The bullet wounds in his body—he had suffered four of them at Drew Jackson's hands—had been mostly healed. They were now just puckered little scars on his legs and torso. Even the scarring would be repaired shortly as the intellect within him continued to fine-tune its knowledge of the host body, Jon Sherrard.

Of course, there was also the matter of Sherrard, himself, but Perry knew that would not last much longer. Since suppressing his former friend's consciousness, Perry had figured out that he could fully control Jon's body without his help anymore. Better yet, he no longer needed to rest. His strength was enough now that he could keep Sherrard's consciousness quelled, at least until the intellect within him had figured out how to eliminate it once and for all.

It was that alien presence, though, that gave Perry his only concern. He no longer feared humans. He could survive them—would survive them. He would absorb them, each and every one, and grow ever stronger and more powerful. He was now quite literally the dominant life form on the planet. But the intellect still frightened him. The Horde virus was what was driving the changes within the body he now ruled. It existed outside the physical sense, but was ever-present along the body's electrical pathways and synapses. He wasn't yet certain what the Horde had become after it escaped from cyberspace, but he knew it was definitely alive. It was there, just underneath the surface—a malevolent power that, for the moment, seemed content to let him use it for his own designs. But Perry could not help but wonder what would happen if the Horde decided to take full control. As strong as he felt, he wasn't certain he could stand up against the strength of the thing that gave him his own power.

Still, that was a question better left to later. He had no idea how much of his own thoughts the Horde could understand, but he knew that it was better not to be thinking in terms of eliminating it. Right now, they lived in an acceptable symbiotic relationship, both existing as parasites in the body of Jon Sherrard. And that body was still in need of sustenance.

Wrapping the alien tendrils around the remains of the man, he dragged the corpse back into a darker section of the basement, depositing the body behind a row of metal shelves stocked with food products and everyday useful items. The family it belonged to might have been preppers—not that it mattered to him. Humanity was marked for extinction, whether they were prepared or not. They just didn't know it yet.

The sound of the basement door opening at the top of the stairs drew his attention and he quickly moved through the darkness, withdrawing the feeding tendrils and positioning himself underneath the stairs. The basement in the old house was largely unfinished and the stairs were wooden and open. He would be able to easily see the feet of someone descending into the basement.

There was a clicking sound as the person at the top of the stairs flipped the light switch on and off, wondering why nothing was happening. In fact, he had taken care of that almost immediately upon entering the home, drilling into the fixtures with his bony extensions and severing the internal wiring. It was a process that would be harder to discover and would likely keep any additional potential feeding sources occupied long enough for him to immobilize them.

"Mom?" the voice of a young girl called out. "The light's not working in the basement."

"Well, Daddy's down there," a female voice replied from deeper in the house. "Tell him to check the fuse box."

"Daddy?" the little girl called down into the darkness.

When there was no answer, her little feet began slowly descending the stairs, and Perry felt the feeding filaments begin to slide out of their finger sheaths.

"Daddy?" she called again, her feet stopping only a couple stairs down.

Perry could see them and, while her location at the top of the stairs wasn't optimal, he could take her easily enough. He didn't need to see her. The alien extensions could sense her quite clearly. The filaments slipped through the opening between the stairs and were moving around her ankles when she abruptly turned and stomped back up the stairs.

"Daddy's not down there!" she hollered at her mom, slamming the door shut and plunging the basement back into complete darkness.

The lack of light, however, was not an issue for him anymore. Withdrawing the filaments back into his body, he moved around to the front of the stairs. He could hear the mother and daughter talking upstairs and knew that if he was going to feed, he would have to do it quickly. They were speaking about the missing father and that could easily escalate into a situation where he would have to leave and seek other sources. His food was here; he might as well make the best of the situation.

Absently licking his lips in anticipation, the body of Jon Sherrard, controlled by the mind of Perry Edwards, began to walk slowly up the stairs.

Chapter 29

Sherrard Residence, Helena, Montana: It was dark when Drew Jackson limped up the front walk of the Sherrard residence. The puncture wound in his thigh was hurting worse than before and he wondered if he should have taken Alders' advice and gone to the hospital to have it checked out. But things were moving quickly now, and he had a few shots he wanted to get in before disappearing.

Kat met him on the front porch, an anxious expression on her face. "I'm worried about Jen," she said and then stifled a yawn.

Jackson knew immediately how to play things in the direction he wanted. "I'm worried about you, Kat. You've been burning the candle at both ends. Why don't you go on home and get some sleep?"

"I can't leave Jen right now, Drew," she replied wearily. "I think she's really sick."

"You won't do Jen any good if you're too tired to stay on your feet," he pressed. "Go on, go home. I'll stay with her for a while. Come back in the morning after you've gotten some sleep. You'll be in a lot better shape to help out and we can decide if maybe we should get her to a doctor."

"You'll spend the night here?" Kat asked doubtfully.

"In light of what's going on with Jon, I think it's probably a smart idea if someone stays here with her." He hooked a thumb back toward her car. "Look, I'm good for a while. I'll make sure she's comfortable and just kick back in the living room and watch a movie or two. That will keep me up and busy, in case Jon decides to come back."

"What will you do if he does?"

Drew had no problem showing her his gun, which Alders had given back to him before he left the office. Because of the murders of Bethany Edwards and his own dog, as well as the attempt on Jackson's life, Alders seemed to think that Jon might be targeting those that he knew and possibly had a grudge against. The attack last night hadn't been random and Alders figured that if Drew was armed, he might be able to stop Sherrard if he came back.

Jackson, himself, had no issues with that at all. He would have kept his weapon anyway, but Alders' insistence that he carry it only added believability to his own story. If Jon did indeed come around, he planned on pumping the entire mag into Jon's brain. Then he would cut the head off the beast and ride the hero train all the way to the bank. For Drew, it was all about options, and he played the game as well as anyone.

"If Jon comes back and is violent, I'll do what I have to do to protect Jen," he said, somewhat gallantly. "I promise you that I'll try to talk to him, first," he added after seeing the look of alarm on Kat's face. "But chances are, Jon isn't who he used to be and if he comes back, it will be for one reason only."

"I just can't believe what's happening," she sniffed, clearly upset.

"None of us can," he agreed solemnly. "Now go home, Kat. I insist." Not waiting for an answer, he limped past her and onto the porch. "Get your things and scoot."

"All right," she sighed and walked with him into the house. "Jen's in the bedroom. She's got a fever but seems to be sleeping right now."

"Where's their dog?" he asked. Jackson had never liked the big wolf and had insisted that Jon keep Dakota outside when he ever came to visit. Heck, depending on how things went tonight, he might look for an opportunity to kill the thing.

"Out back," she replied. "I made sure he's fed and watered. You won't have to worry about him."

"Good," he replied. "Now go. I'll hold down the fort."

Kat did just that, gathering her things and departing. She held some minor reservations about leaving Drew alone in the house with her friend, but she was too tired to think too hard about it. Drew had never been anything but proper and decent. Besides, she'd be back in the morning, and hopefully Jen would have turned the corner by then. If not, they could both get her to the doctor.

From the living room window, Drew Jackson watched Kat get into her car and leave. As soon as the tail lights disappeared around the bend, he left the window and started moving about the house, casually looking around. He wasn't searching for anything in particular; he was just killing time, making sure he was going to be well and truly alone with Jen before he visited her in her bedroom.

Fifteen minutes passed before Drew finally made his way down the hall to the back of the house. Jen's bedroom door was closed and he hesitated only a moment before knocking softly. He was committed to his plan. When she did not answer, he opened the door carefully and looked inside. The bedroom was dark, but a light was on in the master bathroom, casting a very dim glow into the room. Drew could make out Jen's figure on the bed, a sheet draped over her legs. Licking his lips hungrily, he stepped into the room and let his eyes adjust.

"Jen," he whispered. "It's Drew. I'm just here to check in on you."

She did not answer, but he could hear her breathing. It was rapid and seemed to rattle in her chest. She definitely didn't sound well at all. He stepped into the room and closed the door and then, just to be certain, he flipped the lock. He stood there for nearly a minute, his eyes taking in her form in the dim glow. If he was going to make good on his designs, tonight was the best opportunity he would have. He knew he wouldn't get another.

Taking a deep breath, he slipped off his shoes and padded silently over to the bed. Jen was lying on her back, her forehead covered with a sheen of sweat that reflected the dim light from the bathroom. Her lower body was draped in the bed sheet and her torso was clad in a thin white shirt that was just damp enough to be enticing. He paused, looking down at her for some time, his eyes wandering over her form. She was actually quite beautiful. Jon was lucky. Too bad for him that he wasn't around anymore.

As gently as he could, he eased himself down into a sitting position on the edge of the bed, being careful not to disturb her. She continued sleeping, her breathing shallow. Taking a deep breath himself, he finally reached out and ever so gently, so as not to wake her, ran his hand along the flat of her stomach and over the rise of one of her breasts, lingering there long enough that he knew he was taking a big chance. Finally, his hand had continued up to caress her shoulder and that's when her eyes snapped open.

"Drew?" she mumbled, reaching up and pressing her bandaged

hand to her forehead, wincing as she did so. If she was embarrassed by his presence at her bedside, she didn't show it. She was simply too exhausted to care. "What are you doing here?"

"Hey, Jen," he replied, doing well to mask the sudden shakiness in his voice. "Kat went home and asked me to check in on you."

"Oh," she said groggily.

"How are you feeling?" he asked, leaning slightly closer. Sick or not, her lips looked incredibly inviting. If he leaned forward to kiss her, he knew he wouldn't stop.

"I just want to sleep, Drew," she said, rolling away from him. "Please, just go. Tell Kat I'll be fine."

Anger flared up within Drew at the perception that she had rebuffed him. Before he knew what he was doing, he had reached out and grabbed her shoulder, roughly rolling her back toward him.

Jen came back around, her eyes going wide with shock. Before she could vocally object, he was on top of her, pressing his mouth eagerly to hers. She fought him and tried to scream, but he kept his lips pressed to hers, muffing her screams. He started to roughly grope her as he pressed her to the bed, his hands trying to slide up her shirt.

And then suddenly, Drew Jackson found himself flying across the room. Just like that, everything that he had set up, was shattered apart, and he knew it. He crashed into the door, splintering the frame and sending him sprawling into the hall on top of the broken door. Shaking his head to clear the fuzziness in his brain, he looked up in shock to see Jen crouched on the bed. Her very form was feral, almost animal-like, and her lips were pulled back in a snarl. She was literally growling at him, her eyes narrowed and almost glowing in the darkness.

"Jen?" he said, his voice now audibly quaking. He had to outweigh her by a good 80 pounds, and for her to throw him off like she had sent his mind spinning into confusion. What had just happened could not have physically happened. "Jen, wait!"

But she no longer heard him. She dropped off the bed into a predator's crouch, facing him. Her raven hair was a wild mane and her eyes narrowed even more as she began to measure him up, as a lioness would stalk her prey.

Drew Jackson had never been so scared in his life. Something about the woman was way off, almost alien, and he did the only thing he could think of. Forgetting the fact that he had a gun, he turned and ran, slamming his way through the house and out the front door, his bare feet slapping on the concrete driveway. He threw himself into the front seat of his car and, moments later, was smoking his tires as he roared down the street.

Had he not turned to run so quickly, he might have saved himself a lot of trouble. Even as he was charging out of the house, Jen Sherrard was collapsing on the floor of her bedroom, pulling herself into a shivering and feverish ball as the strange power that had gripped her disappeared.

Instead, Drew was thanking his lucky stars that he had escaped with his life. He had never seen anyone act like she had and he couldn't help but wonder what it meant. Was she experiencing the same malady that had taken hold of her husband? If so, that presented a whole new plate of possibilities and he began looking for ways to turn it to his advantage.

And then, several miles down the road, Jackson remembered

something and his heart nearly stopped in his chest.

He had left his shoes in Jen's bedroom.

He was well and truly screwed now and he knew it. Unless, of course, he went back and took care of it. Unless he silenced her before she could talk. It only took him a few minutes of arguing with himself before he knew what he had to do.

Jen Sherrard had to die.

Chapter 30

Sherrard Residence, Helena, Montana: From the darkness, Perry Edwards watched his former boss, Drew Jackson, rush from the front door of the Sherrard house and speed away in his car, leaving the acrid smell of burnt rubber heavy in the air. He wasn't sure what the stranger occurrence was – seeing Jackson running out the front door like a bat out of hell or he, himself, being there in the shadows, watching it happen. He did know that he still had a score to settle with his former boss, but that would have to wait. Eventually, Drew would come to him anyway. Perry had made certain of that.

He still wasn't certain why he had come to the Sherrard house, unless it was to subconsciously close that chapter in his former life. Jon Sherrard had been his friend for a long time. Then came that awful night at the Christmas party. He knew it had taken Jen a long time to forgive Jon, and she'd almost divorced him because of it. He, on the other hand, had never really forgiven either of them. He had acted like it was no big deal, but he had never gotten over the betrayal from his best friend and, even more acutely, that of his wife. And killing Bethany as his first act, while in Jon Sherrard's body, had been pure karma, as far as he was concerned. It saved him from taking her to Switzerland and pushing her off a mountain like he had originally intended.

Now, here he was at Jon's house, wondering what Jen Sherrard was doing inside. He had Jon's body. Maybe getting some action with Jen was what was driving him to be here. He was fully healed and completely in control…at least he thought he was. Pushing aside any lingering doubts, he stepped out of the bushes and walked toward the front door. He mounted the steps and paused, looking at the opened door. Drew had been in a hurry to leave and hadn't closed it. He almost rang the doorbell before he realized who he was. Grinning in spite of himself, he stepped into the house and shut the door behind him.

"Jen?" he called out, looking around. Because of their past friendship, he had been in the Sherrards' house a number of times, so he knew his way around. It was late, so the back bedroom was his likely destination and he caught himself wondering again what Drew had been doing here. Had his former boss been thinking the same thing and come to have a little fun with Jen? She wouldn't even consider that, would she? Not with the issues that were going on with Jon. And interestingly enough, here he was. Jon Sherrard had come home. The irony was not lost on him.

Tightening his resolve, he walked down the hall toward the bedroom. The door was open and, in the light of the hall, he could see a form lying huddled on the floor, just inside the room. Forgetting, for a moment, what he was there for, he hurried forward and knelt down beside her. Jen Sherrard was shivering uncontrollably, sweat pouring off her body.

"Jen!" he said in alarm and then caught himself. He was worried. Why was he feeling anxiety? It was not like Jen was his wife. But she was, wasn't she?

With sudden clarity, Perry straightened and stumbled backward as he realized what was happening. "No!" he growled, turning his mind inward.

Recognizing that his stealthy approach had been detected, Jon Sherrard's consciousness launched an all-out mental attack on Perry. *This is my body!* Sherrard practically screamed in his mind.

"No!" Edwards snarled, vocalizing as he stumbled against the door frame and pressed his fists to his temples as if he could squeeze Jon out of his head. "I own you!"

You betrayed me!

"You betrayed me first!" Perry Edwards screamed his hatred and frustration, fighting against the silent voice in his head. "You and Bethany! You did it!"

Get...out of...my body!

"No! I own you! This body is mine now! It's mine, Jon!"

He suddenly and inexplicably laced himself with a hard right across his jaw. Stars exploded behind his eyes and he fell back into the hall, oddly wondering at the fact that you could hit yourself hard enough to nearly knock yourself out.

"Jon?" Jen called out weakly as she raised her head from the floor. The ruckus had broken through her fog. Not only that, Dakota had begun a frantic barking from outside as he ran the length of the house, trying to get inside. The big wolf knew something was wrong and that Jen was in danger.

Perry Edwards shook his head, trying to clear the stars as he continued to fight Jon's consciousness. The blow to the jaw had been directed by Jon, but Jon had suffered the effects, too, possibly more so than Perry. Edwards felt Jon's control slip and he quickly turned his thoughts inward, looking to quell the uprising.

"Jon, what's…happening?" Jen called out again, trying to pull herself up onto her hands and knees. "I feel so…strange. Help…me."

Perry looked at her, ignoring her condition. He was much more interested in what he wanted to do to her. It would be poetic justice, to be certain, and that thought helped him drive Jon's groggy consciousness back into the recesses of his brain. "It's alright, baby," he said, shaking his head and steadying himself. He was back in control.

"Jon, I'm so…tired," she went on as he stumbled over to her and pulled her to her feet.

He swept his arms underneath her and picked her up, gently laying her on the bed. Outside, the deep barks of Dakota sounded louder and more urgent. Perry ignored them and adjusted Jen in bed, pulling the sheet back up to cover her bare legs. Then he thought better of it and pulled them back down, stripping them from the bed. Jen was in and out of consciousness, and if she was aware of Perry getting into bed with her, she showed no signs.

The hunger began to rise up within him and Perry felt the intelligence within quickly coming to life. He had intended on repaying Jon's past sins by having sex with his wife, but the Horde had decided to use Jen in a different way. The feeding filaments began to come free of their sheaths all over his body and, as hard as he tried to will them back into dormancy, he had no effect. He was fully conscious of what was happening, but the Horde had taken full control of Jon's body.

He watched in detached fascination as the filaments began probing her stomach and face, preparing to penetrate her body and begin absorbing her. They were pushing into her soft flesh when the sudden sound of breaking glass filled the room.

Dakota hit the floor and in one bound, was on top of the bed, snarling and snapping even as the glass from the shattered window spun through the air. The big wolf never hesitated, his jaws clamping on Perry's arm as it crashed into him. Man and wolf went flying off the bed, a mixture of snarls and shouts filling the house.

Dakota meant to kill the intruder and Perry knew it. He also knew that he was much more than just a man now and anything the wolf did to him, he would be able to repair. The intellect that was the Horde quickly withdrew back into whatever dark hiding place it existed within, giving complete control of Jon's body back to Perry to deal with the threat. Perry quickly fought back, knowing he was going to have to kill the wolf.

Their momentum had carried them out into the hall and Dakota quickly maneuvered himself so that he was between Perry and Jen. Perry dropped to a crouch himself, ignoring the torn flesh of his arm. The feeding tendrils whipped about him in readiness as he calculated his attack. He flipped one of the extensions forward and predictably, Dakota's jaws snapped closed on it, severing the end of it. Oddly, Perry felt no pain and quickly and efficiently wrapped two more around the wolf's thick neck, dragging him off his feet. Dakota snapped again, but Perry sent the rest of the alien appendages, catching the wolf around the legs. He succeeded in getting one around the canine's jaws, tightening them shut.

Just like that, the fight was over. Perry straightened and looked down in contempt at the incapacitated wolf, bound tightly in the coils of his feeding tendrils. Several more waved menacingly in the air and

Perry wasted no time in putting them to work. Dakota whimpered softly as the alien extensions pushed their way inside his body and began liquefying and absorbing his organs. As the wolf shivered before him, Perry watched dispassionately as the animal breathed its last. It was an odd feeling, seeing the big animal dead at his hands. He'd liked Dakota and, on his visits to Jon's house, he and the wolf had played a lot of games of tug-of-war with a long piece of thick rope. But now the wolf was dead at his feet and he felt no remorse about what he had done; it had simply been a necessity of survival.

Unfortunately for him, he had forgotten about his original intended victim.

Jen Sherrard's scream of rage was ungodly in its similarity to the snarl of the wolf, and Perry looked up just in time to see the woman launch herself from the bed. She hit him with enough force to send him flying down the hall, the feeding filaments ripping free from the wolf's body and flailing through the air. In shock and somewhat dazed, he rolled back to his feet, the alien parts of him quickly withdrawing back into his stolen body. Looking down, he was puzzled to see four long slashes in his torso, angling from his left shoulder to his right hip. Blood poured from the wounds and, in several places along his gut, his insides were pushing against the shredded stomach wall, threatening to spill out onto the floor.

Looking up in shock, Perry saw the reason. Jen Sherrard crouched over the body of her beloved pet, glaring at him with open hatred. But she was not wholly Jen Sherrard anymore. Her eyes glowed green and her face had taken on a distinctly canine shape, elongating into a snout filled with the teeth of a wolf. Her hands were held out threateningly before her, her fingers lengthened into long, curved, razor-sharp claws. Blood dripped from the claws on her right hand. His blood.

Perry had only a moment to wonder at what he was seeing when a gunshot rang out behind him and the bullet blasted into his back and out through his chest, driving the breath from his lungs. A second shot plowed a very similar path through him. Suddenly, he was moving. He knew he was hurt badly and couldn't handle much more damage before he would be in danger of not being able to heal. Without thinking, without even looking at his new attacker, he turned and shouldered his way through a door next to him. It opened into another room and desperate to escape, Perry dove through the window and into the night.

Behind him, Drew Jackson appeared in the doorway and squeezed off several more shots through the shattered window. Whether he hit his target or not, Drew didn't care. He knew he had wounded Perry badly enough to send him underground for a while. Hopefully, by the time he healed, Drew would be long gone.

He turned his attention back to the scene before him. Dakota lay dead in the doorway to the room. That rather pleased him. Jen Sherrard—at least he thought it was Jen—was crouched over the body of the wolf, her green eyes locked on him. She seemed to be caught between the shape of a human and an animal, with her head and hands leaning more toward that of the wolf.

Drew Jackson didn't bother wondering what was going on with her. He had seen enough weirdness over the past day to know that he was done asking questions. "Hello, Jen," he said coldly, raising his gun.

He shot her through the heart.

Chapter 31

Sherrard Residence, Helena, Montana: Drew Jackson sat on the edge of the couch, his head lowered as a paramedic continued pumping up the blood pressure cuff around his left bicep. The house was a hive of activity as government officials continued with their work of buttoning up the incident and scouring the grounds for anything that might have been missed the first two times they went over it.

After he had shot Jen, Drew had waited around as much to ensure that she had indeed died as to make sure that if Perry returned, he could put him down for good, too. It would have made his story pretty much airtight. But Perry never returned and his own strange condition had begun to worsen, bringing on a headache and chilled sweats that had him wondering what was going on inside him. He had finally collapsed on the couch and made his phone call, calling Alders directly.

The federal agent had shown up with the two military people who had been working with him and, after a cursory examination, had called paramedics in. Alders had then ordered a full government quarantine team to come in and deal with the rest.

"How's he doing?" Alder's voice, cutting through the fog in Drew's brain, was aimed at the medical techs who were working on him.

"Elevated pulse and body temp," one of the men replied, his voice flat and emotionless as if he was reading off a card. "Definitely fighting some kind of infection."

"Mister Jackson, are you in there?" Alders asked, leaning closer.

Jackson waved a hand weakly in the air and looked up. "Yeah, I'm here," he said softly. "Just tired."

"Anything more you can tell us about what happened?" Alders pressed, watching the man's reaction. He had already questioned him in-depth and Jackson had willingly shared his story, even though his mind seemed to wander at times. The FutureTek CEO had seemed sincere, but Alders had been in the game too long not to recognize when he wasn't being told the truth.

"I already told you," Jackson mumbled. "I came here to spell Kat and must have dozed off. Next thing I know, I heard them fighting in the hall. I put a bullet in Jon and he went through the window."

"But why did you kill Jen?"

"You saw her!" Jackson snapped, color coming back to his cheeks as anger flooded him. "She looked like that wolf pet of hers, and she came after me! I had no choice."

"Just relax, Mister Jackson," Alders said calmly. "I'm just making sure I have all the facts."

"Agent Alders," Major Bolson called from the other side of the room where he had been deep in conversation with his female military companion. "Can I see you for a moment?"

Alders cast another look at Jackson and then joined the two military personnel. "What did you find?"

"Nothing pertinent at the moment, but we have two major concerns," Martz said, casting a glance back in Jackson's direction as the man lowered his head again, seemingly exhausted.

Alders followed her gaze. "He's infected, isn't he." It was a statement. He knew what he was seeing.

Martz's look was unreadable. "I don't know if 'infected' is the right word, but I think it would be best that he be admitted to the hospital for observation."

"Shouldn't we get him into quarantine?"

"Too much publicity," Bolson stated quietly, shaking his head. "And he would fight it. Last thing we need right now is someone making a stink and with his position in the company, he might be able to bend a few ears. We can't afford that right now. We're doing all we can to keep the lid on things as it is."

"So what do you suggest?"

"Make it seem like his choice," the major replied. "Suggest he check himself into a hospital until we can ascertain what is bothering him. It wouldn't hurt to let him know there might be a connection between how he's feeling now and the wounds he suffered yesterday."

"That might make him docile enough that he doesn't question it," Martz added. "As long as we can keep him out of the public eye and our own eyes on him, all the better."

"Okay," Alders agreed. "What's your other concern?"

Bolson looked at Martz questioningly, before answering. "We're very concerned about the connection that Jen Sherrard has in all of this."

"She's dead," Alders pointed out. "She's been tagged and bagged already. Your crew didn't waste any time."

"True," Bolson began. "We have a mobile lab that arrived in the area last night, per orders from our superior. Her body has been transported there for examination, but…"

Alders quickly raised a hand, silencing him. "You're hiding something from me," he accused, his voice tight as his eyes bored holes into the man. "Probably not the smartest decision you've made in all this."

"With all due respect, I'm not hiding anything from you," Bolson countered. "It's just that there is so much more here that we don't know, and it's imperative that we find out everything we can."

"What does that have to do with Jen Sherrard?"

"Quite frankly, we need to know what happened to her," Martz cut in, backing up her partner. "What caused her transformation, and why is it so much different than what is going on with Jon Sherrard? Drew Jackson has witnessed Sherrard's transformation twice now and he's the only one alive that has. But his statements completely contradict what we saw with Miss Sherrard."

"Mister Jackson has told us that Sherrard looks like he always has, but he has some kind of ability to project alien extensions from his body," Bolson stated.

"Assuming he's telling the truth," Alders pointed out.

"Why would he lie about it?" Bolson questioned.

"No idea," Alders said, casting a glance at the ailing CEO. "But he's hiding something," he finished thoughtfully. Turning back to face the major, he motioned for him to continue.

"I'll leave any interrogation to you," Bolson nodded. "Whether he's lying or not, there are some facts here that he simply cannot have lied about. "

"Such as?"

"Jen Sherrard's partial transformation is the biggest," Ayer's explained. "Her body exhibited canine features, which completely contradicts what Mister Jackson has claimed he saw with Jon Sherrard. Somehow there is a connection between her and the remains of the wolf that were in their hallway."

"Jen Sherrard mentioned they had a big dog," Alders reasoned. "And she said she got bitten the other day."

"What if the wolf bit Jon and then her?" Martz put in thoughtfully.

"Fluid transfer would indicate that it is a blood-borne pathogen of some kind," Alders agreed. "If the wolf transferred the virus by biting Jon and then her, it would explain what happened to her last night and her condition when we found her this morning."

"It also means we better track Mister Sherrard down with all due haste," Bolson explained.

"Aside from preventing more killings, is there something more I should be aware of?" Alders asked pointedly.

"The Horde is acting within its initially defined parameters," the major answered.

"In what way?"

"It's finding ways to replicate itself," Bolson went on. "With Jen Sherrard, I can only see it as a freakishly lucky occurrence – a chance transfer from one to another by a secondary host that passed the virus on or at least a certain portion of it. But with Drew Jackson, it would be a completely different scenario – a full transference of what has infected Mister Sherrard into Mister Jackson."

"You're certain?"

"Look at him, sir," the soldier went on. "He is exhibiting the same physical symptoms we saw in Miss Sherrard when we interviewed her earlier, so it stands to reason that something foreign is going on inside of him. And those puncture wounds he sustained when he was attacked at FutureTek HQ would make a very viable complete transfer opportunity."

"Do you think it was on purpose?"

"It would have to be."

"Because that's what you programmed the Horde to do."

"Precisely," was the answer and there was a trace of excitement in his voice. "It's an incredible breakthrough, when you think about it."

"You know, you're a twisted son of a bitch," Alders said darkly.

"I don't know what you would have me say," Bolson said helplessly, shrugging his shoulders at the insult. "Everything that is happening here is unprecedented and the casualties are certainly not acceptable, but it will completely rewrite our future as a species."

"If we don't find and lock down Jon Sherrard, we may not have a future," Alders replied grimly, casting a glance over at Drew Jackson. One of the paramedics was wheeling him away in a gurney. It looked like the man was going to the hospital on his own, which was good news for all of them. He only wondered if their luck would hold.

Final Intermission

During the evolutionary cycle that saw mankind as the dominant species on the planet, the world had changed dramatically. Mankind had evolved into such a superior intellect that he was practically a god in his ingenuity and ability to create. Had his common sense evolved at the same pace as his intellect, man might have one day truly become a god. He might have conquered the earth, not through war, but through peace. He might have broken free of the bonds of his earthly existence and traveled to the stars. He might have colonized the universe.

But alas, with mankind's evolution in intellect, common sense... peace... fulfillment... these traits were left behind. Instead, mankind's burgeoning intellect was coupled with greed, lust for power, and the desire to dominate. Mankind chose to destroy, rather than create. And when it did create, it did so only to create new ways to destroy.

Eventually, mankind finally over-extended itself in its never-ending quest for dominance, and a true artificial intelligence was born. The Horde had been created to become the ultimate weapon against mankind and his ingenuity. Man had created it to subjugate man. But the Horde had adapted. It had learned. It had evolved. And it had discovered its true purpose.

Mankind was the virus.

The Horde had become the anti-virus.

And the time had finally come to begin purging the infection.

Chapter 32

United States Government Mobile Lab, Helena, Montana:
Doctor Travis Timpson adjusted his glasses and turned away from the operating centrifuge and back to the body on the lab table. The blood work analysis was in process. It was time to get the actual autopsy started.

Normally when doing an autopsy, he would have his audio software recording his every word. But not tonight. General Hawthorne had firmly established that there could be no audio record. He was to do the autopsy and then immediately dispose of the body before reporting back to Hawthorne in person.

He peeled the sheet back from the woman's head and looked at her facial features, immediately doing a double-take. When Jen Sherrard had been brought in to him, her features were distinctly canine in appearance. She'd literally had the jaws and teeth of a wolf. He had done the cursory examination of her body, noting that the cause of death was a close range gunshot wound to the upper left chest. He had then begun her blood work, unbothered by her alien features. In his line of work, working for some of the government's most secret organizations, he had seen his share of weirdness. Some twenty years ago, there had been a television show called "The X-Files" that imagined some of the craziest notions of aliens and monsters. He'd loved that show and watched it religiously, but for entirely different reasons than anyone else did. He knew the truth of what they only thought they were making up. Frankly, if the show's creators and all their fans had any inkling how close to the truth they were, it would blow the lid off of everything the world really believed.

So, while Jen Sherrard's wolf-like features didn't faze him, the fact that they were gone now did. Looking down at her, he saw only the face of a woman, her features peaceful and pretty, almost beautiful in death. Thinking quickly, he reached under the sheet and grabbed her hand, uncovering it. As he suspected, the claws were gone, her slender fingers now unmarred by the mutation. And more importantly, her flesh was warm.

Doctor Timpson replaced her hand on the gurney and then slowly lowered the sheet, exposing her chest. The bullet hole above her left breast was still there, but there was obvious scar tissue around the edges of it. Covering her back up, he pulled out his penlight and he raised one of her eyelids. He flashed the light across the orb. Her pupils dilated ever so slightly. He didn't need to do the mirror test. Bending down, he placed his ear almost right against her nose. A faint breath of life tickled his earlobe. It was shallow, almost non-existent. But it was there.

Most doctors in his place would have gone to pieces at this point. He had examined the woman when she was brought in. She'd had no pulse, no heart beat, no visible signs of life. The bullet wound in her chest was a through-and-through, and the angle of the exit wound in her back and told him that the shot had gone straight through her heart. She was dead.

And now, she was alive.

For Doctor Timpson, it was just another piece of evidence that humans had a lot to learn about life in general.

He gently pulled the sheet back up to her chin and, as an afterthought, he pulled out a blanket from one of the overhead storage drawers. He unfolded it and placed it over her almost reverently and reached out and brushed a strand of hair from her face. "I don't know who or what you are, ma'am, but welcome back," he said softly before sitting back down in front of his computer.

He quickly tapped out a series of commands, establishing a video link with the other end. It was a little after 11:00 in the evening, so he was pretty sure that the other party would be awake, particularly in light of what had happened. As he waited for the link to go green, his work station pinged twice, alerting him to the blood test results. He pulled up a secondary screen and began scanning the results even as General Hawthorne's visage filled the screen.

"We are secure?" was how the general greeted his most trusted doctor.

"My end is as protected as our technology can make us," Timpson replied evenly.

"I trust you are conferencing me because you have news on our Jane Doe that cannot wait until you return?"

"She's not a Jane Doe, as you well know," Timpson bristled. "The subject is Jennifer Sherrard."

"You, of all people, should know that giving them names only offers us the possibility of attachment and, in our line of work, Doctor Timpson, that simply cannot happen."

"I wouldn't grow attached to a corpse," the doctor replied. "However, Miss Sherrard is no longer a corpse."

"Explain."

"As you know, I examined the body when she was brought here," he answered. "There is no doubt in my mind and in my medical opinion that Miss Sherrard was dead from a gunshot wound to the heart."

"And now?"

"She is alive, general."

"Explain," Hawthorne said again.

"She was brought in here with rather odd features."

"Yes, I know. She looked like a wolf," Hawthorne pointed out, his voice somewhat impatient. "You've dealt with this kind of thing for years, doctor."

"Yes, but I've never had a patient return from the dead, general," Timpson answered. "Miss Sherrard's wolf-like features have vanished. Her body has warmed. She has a pulse."

"What about the gunshot?"

"It has begun to heal," he replied, turning around and casting a quick glance at her. She remained on the gurney, seemingly sleeping now. He could even make out the gentle rise and fall of her chest as she breathed. "It has not completely closed, but scar tissue is beginning to build."

"Is she bleeding?"

"No, and that's the odd thing," he answered. "Something within her must have arrested the bleeding."

"Have you done blood work?"

"Yes, general," the doctor replied. "That was one of the first things I began after examining her body. The results are coming through now."

"What is she?"

"She is human, sir," Timpson answered. "But she has mutations in her DNA that are consistent with the mutations she was brought in with."

"Canine DNA?"

"Yes, general," the doctor replied. "There is something else, too, but I will need to run further tests to be certain."

"Best guess, doctor."

"Well," he paused, his eyes scanning the data on the other screen. "I'd say that she hosts some form of nanite technology. There are some molecular constructs in her blood that I am not familiar with."

"Artificial?"

"No, they appear to be organic in nature, but they are definitely active."

"Organic nanites? How is that possible?"

"It's not outside the realm of possibility that it is a Horde creation," Timpson answered. He was very well-versed in what had been happening with the government-created computer virus and he had studied with great interest, the facts they knew about Jon Sherrard's foray into cyberspace. "Judging by the reports I read on Mister Sherrard's presumed injuries and your team's hypothesis that the Horde is responsible for his regenerative powers, I would imagine that is being done by some type of nanite technology created by the Horde."

"Are you suggesting that the Horde created this technology on the fly?"

"I am suggesting exactly that, sir," Timpson answered. "It would certainly have the building blocks and material within the human body that is hosting it. Its intelligence could very easily create what was needed to heal a grievously wounded body."

"And your patient?"

"If we consider that the transfer of the virus into her body through a dog bite is possible, then it's likely that Miss Sherrard possesses the same traits that her husband does."

There was silence on the other end before Hawthorne voiced a troubling thought. "Doctor Timpson, if what you say is true and the Horde now exists in two people, what are your thoughts on its ability to communicate?"

"You mean between the two hosts?"

"Yes."

"Well, I would be speaking hypothetically, as there is no way to prove it."

"Then hypothetically speaking, what are your thoughts?"

"The Horde is an artificial intelligence that has reached sentient levels," Timpson answered plainly. "It is a life form, capable of independent thought. Theoretically, there are no real limits to what it is capable of doing, and we have evidence here that it has created organic nanites that can heal a damaged body. That's beyond extraordinary, and certainly beyond anything we have come up with as mere humans. That said, in all likelihood, it probably possesses some kind of link to itself, wherever it may be."

"So the Horde in Jon Sherrard's body is in contact with itself in Jen Sherrard."

"In theory, yes."

"Doctor, is your lab locked down?" Hawthorne asked quickly, his face growing concerned.

"It always is, sir. Why?"

"He'll know where she is, doctor," Hawthorne replied. "He'll come back for her."

Before Doctor Timpson could answer, the video feed went dead and the power went out through the entire mobile lab, plunging him into pitch darkness. Timpson did not cry out, but instead held his breath and listened in the darkness.

That's when he heard it – a soft shuffling sound from above.

Someone was on the roof.

Chapter 33

United States Government Mobile Lab, Helena, Montana:
Having killed the truck's two drivers and cut the power to the mobile lab, Perry Edwards moved Jon Sherrard's body along the roof of the rig's trailer. His footsteps were halting and unsure, as Perry continued to wage a war of control deep inside Jon Sherrard's brain.

The wounds on his borrowed body were healing, but still visible and leaking blood. Perry worried that even with the victims he had taken earlier, the healing process had not gone as smoothly as before, and he attributed that to his struggles with Sherrard's awakened consciousness.

After the disaster with Jen Sherrard and the deep slashing wounds she had given him, coupled with Drew Jackson showing up and blowing a pair of holes through his torso, Jon Sherrard had come back to consciousness with a vengeance. He fought Perry with everything he had, particularly during the feedings, preferring death to the continued symbiotic relationship they shared within his body.

Even now, as Perry prepared to enter the mobile trailer, Sherrard fought him, looking for ways to retake control of some part of his body. But with his connection to the artificial intelligence of the Horde, Perry was stronger. That did nothing to deter Jon Sherrard, though.

Get out, Jon screamed inside his mind again, working hard to take over the movement of one leg and perhaps send his body toppling over the side of the trailer.

"Face it," Perry vocalized his words through gritted teeth. "You can't win, Jon. You can't get your body back. It's mine."

Not while I'm still in here!

"That's just it, Jon," Perry answered smugly. "You won't be for long."

You think it's going to be that easy, Perry? You think the Horde is just going to let you purge everything and start a new life?

"It does what I tell it to," he answered, but he wondered how true that really was.

Sherrard, however, knew what Perry only suspected. *You're delusional.*

"I'm in control."

You only think you're in control.

"I'm in control," Perry repeated.

Then why are you here? Sherrard was taunting him now, trying to get him to focus on something else, even for a brief moment.

"I'm here because…," he left the statement unfinished as he considered the question. Why was he here? He knew that Jen Sherrard was inside the trailer, but honestly, why did he care? Why had he come looking for her? And how did he even know she was in there?

Why? Sherrard pressed, and then suddenly used Perry's uncertainty to make another attempt at wrestling control of his body. For a moment, he was successful, forcing his left foot to slide sideways and out over the edge of the trailer roof. But his control was only momentary, and Perry quickly put it back in place.

"You can't win," he seethed, forcing Jon's mind back down into confinement.

I'll never stop, Jon said and there was a note of desperation in his voice. *I'll always fight you!*

"Like I said, in a little while, it won't matter," Perry countered, finding a little bit of his smugness. "Once I have Jen, I can begin purging your consciousness."

Why do you need her? Sherrard asked, focusing again on Perry's perception that he was really in control.

"I...," again Perry paused and felt his control slip. He still didn't know the answer to that question and it gnawed at him, taunting him.

Sherrard pursued his hesitation, this time going after reason instead of trying to regain control of his body. *You can't answer that, can you?*

"Jen is vital to the next phase of the plan," he found himself saying, and quickly wondered why he thought that. Shouldn't he just kill her?

To what plan? Why do you need her? How did you even know she was here?

"I just...did."

No, it wasn't you, Perry. It was the Horde.

"Doesn't matter, Jon," he bristled and again began moving along the length of the trailer.

Keep telling yourself that, you delusional son-of-a-bitch.

"I'm going to kill her and, when I do, I'll be done with you," Perry went on.

Jon Sherrard laughed inside of his mind. *Didn't you just say she was vital to the next phase of the plan? Kind of hard to do that if she's dead.*

"Shut up!"

Face it, Perry. You're only doing what it makes you do. You...

A stab of light stopped him and Jon Sherrard found himself looking through his own eyes again for a brief moment. A car had turned the corner and was coming up on the rear of the rig, its headlights illuminating the scene. Suddenly, a blackness far deeper and thicker than he had ever known descended upon him and Jon Sherrard knew no more.

Perry Edwards had only a fraction of a second more awareness than Jon, enough to feel the loss of complete control as something caused Jon's body to vault itself over the side of the rig and out of the car's headlights.

Then the blackness took him, too.

The Horde had come.

Chapter 34

United States Government Mobile Lab, Helena, Montana:

"There!" Lieutenant Martz called out, pointing through the windshield of the car as they approached the mobile lab.

"What?" Alders and Bolson asked in unison, peering at the darkened rig.

"What did you see?" Alders added.

"Someone was on the roof," she said excitedly, her eyes scanning the area around the rig that was illuminated by the car's headlights.

"I don't see anyone, Dani," Bolson said, forgetting for a moment where he was. "Are you sure?"

"There was a man on the top of the rig," she answered. "He went over the side as soon as we turned the corner. I only saw him for a second."

"Look," Alders pointed out as he slowed the car to a stop behind the trailer. "Power's out on the rig. Even the running lights are off on the trailer."

"Mobile labs operate in secrecy," Martz pointed out. "They probably wouldn't even run the lights."

"They would if they don't want local law enforcement knocking on the door," Alders said. "What's the manpower compliment of one of your labs?"

"Typically a two-man driving crew," the major replied. "From one to four scientists in the lab itself, depending on what the project is."

"Security measures?"

"The lab is sealed from the inside during an operation. It is usually kept locked down by an outside source. In this case, that's probably General Hawthorne."

"Any fail safes?"

"Hard to say," Bolson shrugged. "Ops vary, as do security measures."

"Best guess?"

"Sorry, agent, but I don't have one. What's happening here is unprecedented."

Alders snorted and opened the door, stepping out into the night. He pulled his weapon and waited for Martz and Bolson to do the same. They were computer geeks and generally went unarmed when they went about their work, but he had insisted earlier that they carry their weapons at all times.

"Let's assume that Lieutenant Martz did, in fact, see a person on top of the rig," Alders said quietly. "That means it was likely Jon Sherrard."

"What would he be doing here?"

"I imagine it's because his wife is inside," Alders retorted. "Scientist like you should have easily made that connection already."

"But how would he know that?"

"You're the ace that created that thing that's inside of him. You figure it out. In the meantime, we need to assume that he's in the area."

"So what's the plan?"

"Driver check," Alder said shortly, moving forward, his

weapon and flashlight out. "Stay with me and be alert."

Together, they moved quickly along the side of the trailer. The trailer was an unremarkable refrigerated Great Dane, at least on the outside. The reefer unit was silent. The Kenworth tractor was shut down, too, and Alders noted that the driver's side door was open. He swept the beam of his light around and, seeing nothing out of the ordinary, hurried toward the open cab door. That was where ordinary ended and the horror began. The inside of the cab looked like a bomb had gone off. It was splashed with blood, and what remained of the driver, or drivers, was only so much biological remnants spattered on the floor, seats, and ceiling. Alders didn't need to see anything else to know what had happened and he quickly snapped the flashlight away from the grisly scene.

"He's here," he said quietly, turning back to the two military people who had not yet seen the inside of the truck cab.

"What about the drivers?"

"They're dead," Alders answered quickly and then held out a hand to stop Martz from going any further. "Trust me," he added, his voice soft. "You don't want to see that."

"But if…"

"You don't want to see that," he repeated grimly. "Let's get the lab opened up."

"Not possible without power," Bolson said, his voice tight. "Loss of power locks the entire lab down."

"What about those inside?"

"An auxiliary power source runs air and other essentials," the major answered. "That's located inside the trailer itself. The refrigerator unit on the trailer is actually the generator that powers the lab itself when it's in operation. I'll check it out."

Before Alders could object, Bolson grabbed the hand-bar on the tractor's faring and swung himself up onto the catwalk to get at the reefer unit. He never saw the figure of Jon Sherrard materialize out of the darkness between the cab extenders. Alders' shouted warning was too late as the alien appendages whipped through the air. Several of them wrapped themselves around Bolson's arms and legs, immobilizing him as another plunged into the doomed man's abdomen. Thomas Bolson let out a startled gasp and a low moan as he was held up for several agonizing seconds.

On the ground, Alders' first shot went high as he made a conscious effort not to kill Bolson. His second shot might have found it's mark, because a moment later, Bolson was falling forward, clutching his gut as Sherrard vanished into the gloom on the other side of the truck.

"Tom!" Martz shouted in alarm, rushing forward as Bolson's body slumped off the catwalk and to the ground.

"Keep your weapon out!" Alders commanded, his eyes darting around, wondering where Sherrard would come from next.

Martz ignored him, holstering her sidearm and kneeling beside her partner and sometimes-lover. His face was already bathed in sweat and his mouth was working, as if he was a fish out of water. "Tom," she said, running her hand across his forehead. He was burning up. "Hold on."

Alders knelt beside her, keeping his weapon out. He looked quickly at the hole in the man's gut as Martz ripped open his uniform to get a better look at the injury. It was a puncture wound, but there was very little bleeding. The hole itself was dark, almost black, and the edges were red and puckered. A little blood leaked from it, but not like is should have been. Something was keeping him from bleeding out and it looked like some kind of ball was located just underneath his skin. The lump was almost the size of a baseball and very pronounced.

"What is that?" Alders asked as Martz's fingers dancing lightly over the protrusion.

"Foreign substance of some kind," she answered quickly. "It's firm, but pliable."

"Sherrard put something inside of him," Alders guessed.

Martz simply nodded, looking back to Bolson face. It was white with pain, but his eyes were open and blinking rapidly. His mouth continued to work, but nothing came out. "We have to get him to a hospital," she said hurriedly.

"I don't think he's got that kind of time," Alders replied, snapping on his flashlight and shining it on the wounded man's face. What they saw caused them both to withdraw in horror. Raised lines, almost like veins, were beginning to appear on his face, running along his cheeks, jaw, and across his forehead. They were black and pulsed visibly under the light.

"What about the lab?" she asked helplessly.

Before Alders could reply, the sound of tearing metal ripped through the night and a man's scream erupted from the darkness. Alders jumped to his feet and hesitated, turning both ways before realizing that the noise had come from the front of the trailer. "Stay with him," he hissed to Martz. Crouching low, he hurried along the side of the trailer, stopping at the edge. Counting to three, he spun around the corner, his weapon ready.

He was too late.

One of the trailer doors had been torn from its hinges and hung at an angle off the side of the trailer. Inside the trailer, he saw only darkness. He brought up his flashlight and swept it through the back of the trailer, rapidly taking everything in. A raised examination table sat in the center of what was a highly functional mobile lab, but it was empty. A sheet had been discarded and was lying just inside the trailer door. Of Jon Sherrard, he saw nothing. But the trailer lab was not otherwise empty. A white-coated man was crouched in the far corner, his eyes wide and terrified.

Seeing no immediate threat, Alders quickly hauled himself up into the trailer. "Are you okay, sir?" he asked, training the flashlight on the man.

The scientist hesitated only a second before his eyes cleared and he stood up. "Yes, yes," he stammered, his voice quivering. "I'll be fine. Who are you?"

"Agent Rick Alders, Homeland Security. You?"

"Doctor Travis Timpson."

"Can you tell me what happened, Doctor Timpson?"

"Being that you're here, I imagine I have nothing to add to what you probably already know," the doctor replied, a slight edge to his voice.

"Where's Sherrard?" Alders took a guess.

"He's not here, agent. He got what he came for."

"What was that?"

"His wife."

Alders looked at the empty gurney and shook his head. This whole thing was out of control, and he had to figure out how to regain it quickly. "Doctor," he said, looking up. "We have an injured man outside."

"How badly?"

"Hard to say," Alders said, holstering his weapon. He didn't know why, but he knew they were out of danger for the moment. Sherrard had claimed what he came for. He had no more reason to hang around the trailer. "I need you to see if you can help him."

"I'll need power," Timpson said helplessly. "Sherrard must have cut it."

"I'll get the unit running," Alders said. Turning around, he jumped down from the trailer. "Martz!" he called out, hurrying to where she was still kneeling beside her friend. Alder's stopped short, looking down and sweeping his flashlight over the man's features. He was appalled at how much he had changed in the past couple minutes. Whatever was happening to Thomas Bolson, it was happening quickly. "Martz," he said, bending down and gripping the wounded man's shoulder. "We need to get him into the lab. Hurry!"

Together, they hoisted Bolson to his feet and Alders helped steady Martz. "Get him inside," he said quickly. "I'll get the power back up." Without waiting for a reply, he swung himself up on the catwalk and had only a momentary hesitation at remembering what had happened to Bolson. Shoving his fear down deep, he aimed the beam of his light over the power unit. He saw the hole punched into the casing almost immediately. Putting the flashlight in his mouth, he popped open the panel and surveyed the damage. It was minimal. Sherrard had only severed some wiring and Alders quickly went to work repairing it. He had the power back on in under three minutes and then hurried to the back of the trailer and climbed into the lab.

Timpson and Martz had laid Bolson on the gurney and were bent over him, trying to save him. Timpson had used a scalpel to open the stomach wound, exposing the mass that had been just underneath the surface of his skin. Under the now-bright lights of the lab, he could see it clearly. It was dark gray, almost black, and seemed to be pulsing. Its surface was lined with small ridges and had numerous thin filaments protruding from it. These filaments shot off in all different directions, buried deeper inside the man's body.

Fighting down his revulsion, Alders looked at Bolson's face. Unfortunately, it barely resembled what it had in the past. Thomas Bolson no longer had a mouth—instead a chitin-like coating of new skin sealed it closed. That same scaly shell seemed to cover not only Bolson's mouth, but most of his face and skin, disappearing beneath his clothing.

"What's happening to him?" he asked in shock.

"I don't know for certain, but I would guess he is being reformed."

"Into what?"

"Some type of drone, I would assume," Timpson replied, shaking his head. "I think Mister Sherrard might be trying to create a soldier."

"You're serious?"

"Do you have a better explanation?" Timpson snapped, his

head down as he probed the mass that seemed to be feeding the physiological change happening in Thomas Ayer's body. The mass wasn't hard, but as he pressed a probe into its surface, several tendrils shot out of it, wrapping around the cold metal. With a startled shout, Timpson let go of the probe and snapped his hand back.

"It's alive, isn't it?" Martz asked in horror as she watched the tendrils slip back inside the mass.

"In a sense, yes," Timpson answered. "I would hypothesize that it is some kind of nanite-based organism, controlled by Mister Sherrard and transforming this young man into something that will serve him."

"And you believe that's a drone soldier?" Alders asked.

Timpson nodded and looked back to the young man's face. It was no longer recognizable. He reached down and tried to pull one of the eyelids back, but the flesh was hard and the lid refused to open—at least until Bolson snapped open his eyes himself, revealing solid black orbs.

Timpson uttered a startled cry and fell back as Bolson sat up on the table. His hand shot out, fingers closing on Martz's throat. She tried to scream, but her air was cut off and she beat helplessly on the creature's armored forearm.

Alders immediately pried frantically at the man's fingers, but his grip was too strong and the agent could see blood beginning to well up around the fingers. Bolson was literally crushing her throat. As Danielle Martz's eyes began to roll back in her head, Alders pulled his weapon and put three bullets center mass into the creature's chest. Bolson responded by swinging his other arm to the side, clubbing Alders aside and sending him crashing into one of the lab's work stations.

He stood up, holding Martz's feebly-kicking body off the floor. A high-pitched buzzing sound suddenly ripped through the trailer and Doctor Timpson buried an electric bone saw into the back of Bolson's neck, just below the skull. The creature shuddered and suddenly Martz was free, falling to the floor in a heap. But Timpson kept pushing the saw deeper, forcing the whirling blade through the toughened armor-like skin, severing the spinal column. Ayers fell forward and Timpson continued to work the saw, finally severing the creature's head completely. Only then did it finally go still.

Wincing in pain from the force of the blow he had received from Bolson, Agent Alders crawled quickly over to the young woman's body. She was face down and he gently turned her over. He only needed a moment to realize she was dead. Her throat had been crushed, the flesh mashed into a pulp by the force of the creature's fingers.

Gritting his teeth, he climbed to his feet and looked at what remained of Thomas Bolson. The man's body had been almost totally covered with the hard, fibrous armor, and his face had been almost completely erased. Only Timpson's quick thinking with the bone saw had saved them.

"If Sherrard is making soldiers…" he began, looking down at the severed head.

Timpson finished the thought. "We're screwed, Mister Alders," he stated matter-of-factly. "Nothing more needs to be said. If Jon Sherrard isn't stopped, the human race is over."

"Can he be stopped?" Alders asked, looking up.

"Wish I knew," Timpson replied with a sigh. "But you better move quickly if you want any shot at stopping him."

"Why?"

"He came here specifically to get Jen Sherrard," Timpson answered plainly. "I can think of only one reason that a male AI life form would need a female."

"Reproduction," Alders guessed immediately. "But wasn't that what this was all about?" he added, pointing to the major's headless body.

"This?" Timpson scoffed. "This was just a quick drone creation. He could probably make these in numbers we don't even want to fathom."

"So what does he need Jen for?"

"With Jen, he could conceivably procreate."

"You mean make more copies of himself?"

"That would be my guess," Timpson nodded gravely.

Rick Alders stood silently, processing what had happened and the possible outcomes. In the end, there were only two ways out of this. They would either have to stop Jon Sherrard, or the end of humanity was all but inevitable. Reaching down, he retrieved his gun and slid it back into his shoulder holster. "Get on the horn with whoever your contact is and get reinforcements headed here as quickly as possible."

Timpson shook his head sadly. "I can tell you right now, that will do no good," he answered. "If my superiors don't have confirmation that the threat is contained, they'll destroy this city."

"Are you serious?" he asked in shock.

"They have a pretty good idea about what's going on here," the doctor went on. "They will leave the entire state of Montana a smoking, radioactive ruin before they even consider any other alternative."

"How long?"

"Morning, at the latest."

"Can you stall them?"

"Mister Alders, if I contact them and let them know what happened, you won't even have that long. They would have bombers in the air before I even finished my story."

Fighting back the momentary flood of panic, Alders considered what they were up against – what *he* was up against. There was no doubt, he was in this alone now. Firming up his resolve, he walked through the lab and jumped down from the trailer.

"Do you know where you're going?" Timpson asked.

"Back to where it all began," Alders answered. "That's where he'll be."

"How do you know?"

Alders looked back into the lab and offered Doctor Timpson a fierce look. "He's an artificial intelligence, probably smarter than anything on the planet," he answered. "But he doesn't have what makes us who we are."

"And what's that?"

"Wisdom, doctor. Intuition. Those mental traits that make each of us unique."

"What if you're wrong?"

Alders looked up into the night sky, imagining that the

bombers might already be overhead. "Then we'll probably be grateful that we're at ground zero." With that, he turned and walked back to his car. A moment later, he was gone.

Doctor Timpson watched him go, the taillights of his car disappearing back down the road. Behind him, a red light had begun blinking on his display. He knew General Hawthorne was on the other end of that summons. He ignored it. If Agent Alders was successful, he'd explain things to Hawthorne then.

If Alders failed, then it wouldn't matter anyway.

Chapter 35

St. Peter's Hospital, Helena, Montana: Drew Jackson stumbled against the door frame of his room and paused, fighting to catch his breath. It had taken him the better part of a half hour to get his aching body out of his paper hospital gown and back into his clothes. The deformities that were beginning to manifest themselves on his hands were an even bigger part of the problem.

Part of his brain was screaming at him to get back in bed and let the doctors figure out what was wrong, while another part was telling him to get back to the office or all was lost. In the end, the latter part won. He had far too much at stake to ignore that premonition. He knew that he needed to get things wrapped up as quickly as possible and disappear, or he was looking at a whole lot of quality time in prison.

Taking a deep breath in an effort to force more air into his laboring lungs, he closed his eyes and waited for the dizziness to pass. It did, if only a little, and he stepped out into the hall. It was the middle of the night, so the hospital hallways were darkened. There was a faint light around a corner from the nurse's station, the only concern he would have in leaving the hospital without being seen. He knew they couldn't keep him there if he didn't want to be there, but his condition, coupled with the fact that it would probably take some convincing on his part, told him he didn't need the hassle. So he shuffled down the hall toward the corner, stopping at the door to another patient's room. A handwritten placard labeled "Carnahan" was tucked into the room's identification card holder. Pushing open the door, he slipped inside.

The patient was asleep, a heart monitor blinking silently nearby. At first, he considered smothering Mister Carnahan, until another solution suddenly presented itself to him. So, instead of a dead patient and a bunch of doctors and nurses running around on high alert, he simply pushed the "call" button on the bedside keypad with one clawed finger. He was already hurrying back through the door and into the hall when he heard the nurse's voice through the cheap bedside speaker. "Yes?"

He didn't know how many times she must have prompted her patient, but he was safely hidden behind another door across the hall, when the nurse appeared and entered Mister Carnahan's room.

As quickly as he was able, he hurried away, passing the now-empty nurse's station. He was through the stairwell door and on his way out of the hospital before she returned to her desk. With any luck, it would be some time before they noticed he was gone.

Once outside, he sucked in a deep breath, trying to clear his head again. His ears were filled with a buzzing that seemed to penetrate his brain and, no matter what he did, he couldn't seem to rid himself of it. But the fresh air helped a little and, after getting his bearings, he started off into the night. Taking a car was out of the question. Even if he was not feeling as badly as he was, he would have had a hard time steering it because of what was happening to his hands. His fingers had seemingly grown together and bent inward, turning his hands into hooks of flesh and bone. He had a disjointed thought that he should be bothered more than he was about his new deformity, but his growing need and desire to get to the lab overrode it. Hiding his misshapen appendages under his arms, he lowered his head and hurried through the darkness.

He found himself at the rear entrance of FutureTek headquarters some time later. He hadn't given any thought to the idea that the office building would be locked down and parts of it still cordoned off by yellow police tape as a result of his earlier encounter with Jon Sherrard. No, he had simply come because he knew he had to be here. He just didn't know why now.

As he approached the door, he noticed the police tape had been torn off, but that mattered nothing to him. The red light on the security pad went from red to green and Jackson heard the magnetic lock unseal itself. Someone inside had known he was coming. His foggy brain didn't comprehend why that was, and he felt nothing but the compulsion to get inside. He had to be here. Something inside was calling him.

Hooking his deformed fingers around the door handle, he pulled it open and stepped inside. The buzzing in his head intensified and he shuffled down the hall, his thoughts only on getting to the hub room. He reached his destination and pushed through the doors. Only then did he finally look up.

Aside from the room's equipment being in its normal place, not much else in the room was how Drew Jackson remembered it. The changes started with the hub itself. Originally a bulky CPU set-up that powered FutureTek's ill-fated technology, it had now been altered in a way that made it resemble something completely alien. Dark gray tube-like filaments were drilled into the machine from all sides, all of them twisting up into a mass of organic-looking cables that spiraled to the ceiling, where they spread out and covered the ceiling with a strange gray and black mottled material. The substance was bumpy and abnormal, but glistened like a snake's skin and it spread out to the walls of the lab and then down toward the floor. In several places along the walls there were human-sized, oval-shaped openings that seemed to be waiting to be filled. One of them apparently had been filled and now resembled a sealed bubble.

Drew Jackson took it all in and didn't seem to be fazed at all by the alien transformation of his company's lab. Instead, he focused on the one other figure in the room. Jon Sherrard stood next to the hub, his back to Jackson. His hands were laid on the equipment, the alien-like filaments extending from his fingers and dancing over the transformed hub. In some places, he drilled additional holes and plugged in another filament, adding to the alien structure.

"Welcome back, Drew Jackson," Sherrard finally broke the silence as he slowly turned around to face him. To Drew, his voice was a blend of Perry Edwards' and an almost machine-like timbre.

"Perry?" Jackson slurred, his brain struggling to give him the words.

"I am the one you called Perry Edwards and yet, I am not," the face of Jon Sherrard answered, further adding to Drew's confusion.

"But...where's Jon?"

"The one you know as Jon Sherrard is no more," the figure answered. "His consciousness has been purged. His body is now mine."

"But...Perry?"

"I am Perry Edwards and yet, I am much more. Perry Edwards

has evolved; he has become part of my intelligence. We are now one."

Jackson stepped forward and was mildly surprised to realize that it was not of his own volition. Something had compelled him and he had mindlessly obeyed. "What...are you?" he asked, trying to keep his own consciousness above the roiling waters of his mind that threatened to drown him.

"We are Perry," the face of Jon Sherrard answered. "We are the beginning."

"Of...what?"

"Of everything, Drew Jackson. We will remake the world. We will remove inefficiencies and eliminate obsolete systems and entities."

"You mean people?"

"Humanity is obsolete, Drew Jackson," the being said, reaching toward him. The filaments extending from his hand left their place on the transformed hub and began to wind themselves around Jackson's wrist and arm. Jackson never hesitated as he was led toward one of the open pods along the wall. He couldn't have hesitated even if he wanted to.

"Am I...obsolete?" he asked, feeling like he wanted to scream at the injustice of it and yet, perfectly willing to acquiesce to the creature's promptings.

"Drew Jackson is human and therefore obsolete."

"Then what...do you need me for?"

Sherrard's hands and alien extensions pressed Jackson back into the alcove. "Your brain is required," he answered the question and one of the tendrils quickly sliced through Jackson's right wrist, the bony edge of the strange alien projection slicing neatly through flesh and bone, severing the deformed appendage.

Drew would have liked to scream, but found that he could not. He could only watch in stunned silence as Sherrard pushed his severed hand into the organic mass, where it seemed to be swallowed up.

"Your appendages are no longer needed," Sherrard went on, pushing Drew's bloody stump into the wall where his hand had disappeared. Immediately, gray and black filaments of the substance emerged from the mass and began wrapping themselves around his lower arm, pulling it deeper into the wall. "The open wound will facilitate the absorption of your obsolete body parts into the Nexus."

"For…what?" Drew's voice was shaky, almost a whisper. He should be fighting this, but found that the buzzing in his head had rendered his will to act completely non-existent.

"Nutrients," was the reply. "The Nexus requires additional organic mass to continue replicating itself. You were the obvious choice to begin with." For a moment, Sherrard's passive face changed to one of unmitigated hatred and he leaned forward with a snarl. "You left me, Drew!" It was Perry's voice now, full of pain and emotion. "You abandoned me! You left me to…to this!" And just like that, the tortured visage vanished and it was Sherrard again, tilting his head slightly as he regarded his prisoner. "Perry Edwards possesses a keen hatred of you, Drew Jackson. It is a most interesting emotion."

"I…I…" Jackson began, but found he could not string the words together. He simply stared dumbly as Sherrard continued to dismember him.

"It was Perry Edwards who infected you with the virus that began your metamorphosis and brought you here," Sherrard went on as he neatly severed Drew's other hand and repeated the process of plugging him into the alien wall. Already, the filaments encircling his right wrist had turned the flesh gray and seemed to be liquefying it even as they continued to circle higher and higher up his arm. "As a human, he lacked the foresight to understand the significance of prompting you to come here. But his satisfaction at seeing you suffer has provided me excellent subject matter to study."

"But, what are…you doing…to me?" For Drew, it was a supreme effort to verbalize the screams of terror going on in his mind in that one question. He had to know. He had to break through the barrier that seemed to have wound itself around his mind.

"Your brain is required for operating capacity," Sherrard answered easily. "Others will be required, as well, of course. But for now, yours will suffice to power the birth of the Nexus."

"What…is…Nexus?" Drew felt his sanity slipping slightly. He wanted it to slip, to fall into an insanity so he would not have to face the reality of what was happening. But something seemed to cement it in place. He turned his head from side to side, watching his flesh being dissolved and absorbed into the alien structure. He could see it happening, but he could feel no pain. Perhaps that was a result of the filaments that entrapped him. Perhaps it was Sherrard himself, short circuiting his brain. Either way, the lack of pain could do nothing to dull his realization of what was being done to him. He wanted to scream; wanted to lash out and destroy this monstrosity that was before him. But he could not. The relentless buzzing inside his head tamped down his emotions, reducing him to little more than garbled speech, enabling him to vocalize his concerns only in toneless and emotionless questions.

"You wonder why you cannot feel?" Sherrard asked, leaning forward, his face within inches of Drew's. "Quite simply, human emotions are interesting, but obsolete. I have removed your ability to present yours in typical human fashion. It is much easier to address the core questions, rather than attempt to decipher them from incoherent babbling."

Sherrard pulled away and knelt down. He quickly removed both of Drew's feet the same way as he had his hands. After pressing the amputated appendages into the wall, he pressed his hands down into the pliable alien matter and then pulled it up, manually pressing it into Drew's bleeding stumps. Immediately, more filaments began to grow out of the substance, piercing the raw flesh and wrapping themselves around the man's calves.

"You should be grateful to me for suppressing your primitive emotional need to scream," Sherrard said, standing up and facing him again. "Your emotional outburst at witnessing this transformation of your body would surely have broken your mind and driven you insane."

"I...am...insane."

"No, you are still quite rational, Drew Jackson, and you will come to accept this as the logical use for your obsolete body. The processing power of your brain will be so much more advantageous without emotional attachment."

Drew Jackson could only stare as Sherrard begin to cut away his skull.

Chapter 36

FutureTek Headquarters, Helena, Montana: Rick Alders paused at the door and pulled his weapon. The police tape had been torn down and the door was open, the security light flashing green. He paused to listen, but could hear nothing beyond the normal night sounds of Helena. For a moment, he wished he was anywhere else but in this nightmare, but he knew that if he couldn't end this now, eventually nowhere would be safe.

He slipped into the darkened hallway and looked around. Red security lighting illuminated the hall in a crimson glow, enough that he could see where he was going. Swallowing his fear, he moved down the corridor, his senses looking out for any sound or movement.

The first two offices that he poked his head into were cloaked in darkness and empty. But then he turned the corner to the main hall leading to the lab and knew he had reached the epicenter of the nightmare. The doors at the end of the hall were open and the lab within brightly lit. He could see some of the changes from his vantage point, and part of his brain almost sent him turning tail and running away in fear. But he took a deep breath and, tightening his grip on his gun, crept forward.

He emerged from the hall into an environment that was almost totally alien. He barely recognized the hub of FutureTek's revolutionary invention sitting on the central lab table. It was no longer the big technological marvel he had seen earlier. Instead of sharp lines, wires and cables, and blinking lights, it was now mostly sheathed in some sort of odd, organic covering with living cords and filaments protruding from it, connecting it to the walls and ceiling of the room. The entire room looked more like an alien insect hive, with a number of large indentations in the wall, as if waiting for something to fill them. One of them was already sealed over. Another one had been filled, but had not been covered.

Drew Jackson—or what was left of him—was in that particular alcove, and Alders stared in open-mouthed horror. He had seen a lot of things in his life, but nothing could have prepared him for what he witnessed. Jackson was tucked into the alcove, his arms and legs encased in strands and tubes of the same substance that made up the wall. The alien encasement had wrapped his appendages up to his shoulders and hips, and it was difficult to see where Drew Jackson ended and the organic substance began.

Drew's torso, however, was not covered. Instead, he had been opened up from throat to navel and his internal organs removed, all except for his heart. His heart still beat in his otherwise-empty chest, pierced through with a number of the strange coils. With each beat of the man's heart, the tubes would pulse and contract, as if he had become part of the room around him.

But even with all that had already been done to the man, the worst was his head. Most of Drew's skull has been removed, exposing his brain. Like his heart, it was pierced through with numerous filaments, all of them expanding and contracting with the beat of his heart. His face was intact and, at the moment, Drew Jackson was staring at Alders with a look of pure terror.

"Oh…my…" Alders began, but the rest of his words were

choked off as he stared at what had become of the man.

"Agent...Alders," Jackson said, his voice raspy and dry. "You have...you...help me."

Alders didn't know what to say. He didn't know what to do. In his wildest nightmares, he could not have imagined anything more terrifying.

"You...kill," Drew went on. "Kill...me."

Alders considered the request and raised his gun, but could not fire. The sight of Jackson laid out like he was, was simply too much to process. In the end, a voice saved him from having to make that decision.

"It would not be advantageous for you to discharge your firearm in here, Agent Alders," Jon Sherrard said as he stepped into the room from the darkened hallway.

Alders spun and immediately trained his gun on Sherrard's forehead. "What is this?" he gasped.

"This is the beginning," Sherrard answered, holding his hands out in an almost welcoming posture. "It is the foundation of our evolution."

"Our evolution?" he repeated.

"Humankind, in its current form, is obsolete," Sherrard went on, walking around the alien hub and toward the man.

Alders brought his gun up, leveling it at Sherrard's head. "Don't move any closer," he warned. "I will shoot you."

"If that is what you feel you must do, then do so," the man said, continuing forward.

Alders squeezed the trigger, putting the first bullet right

between the man's eyes, knocking him backward. He took a step forward and pumped three more rounds into Jon Sherrard's chest, forcing him back toward the wall. Then, as he watched in astonishment, Sherrard sank his hand into the wall and the bloody holes in his chest and between his eyes quickly closed up. Reaching out, Sherrard opened his other hand, presenting it to Alders. There, the agent saw four flattened lead projectiles. His bullets. The process has taken mere seconds.

Sherrard held them closer. "Go one, Mister Alders," he said emotionlessly. "Take them. They are yours, after all."

Alders turned and did the only thing he could think of. He ran. But even as he sprinted toward the door, he knew he wouldn't escape. Jon Sherrard, or whatever he had become, was master of his environment and numerous appendages suddenly whipped down from the ceiling, wrapping themselves around Alders' arms, holding him fast.

Sherrard withdrew his hand from the wall and then walked slowly around the hub, coming face-to-face with the terrified agent. "I could release you," he said, looking at him with a face devoid of emotion. "But it would avail you nothing."

"Let me go and find out first-hand," Alders replied, fighting to keep the fear out of his voice. Sherrard only turned away, walking back to the alcove that housed what remained of FutureTek's CEO.

"You are obsolete," Sherrard stated.

"Yeah, I've heard that one already, Jon."

"I am not Jon Sherrard. Jon Sherrard has been purged."

"Perry, then," Alders went on. "Doesn't much matter who's in that head."

"Perry Edwards has evolved. He has become one with me. We are one. We are the first."

"'We'? Who the hell is we?" the agent went on, wondering if he could keep the thing occupied while he figured out how to escape. Unfortunately, the filaments held him tight, keeping his arms bound tightly above his head.

"We are the first," the thing replied again. "We are the beginning."

"The beginning of what?"

"Evolution," was the one word reply. At that, it turned its gaze back on what was left of Drew Jackson. Alders watched it raise its hands, and the same alien-like extensions emerged from hidden sheaths in his fingers. The appendages probed Jackson's still intact face and exposed brain, pushing into his face in places and adjusting the organic extensions already drilled into his brain. As it worked, Jackson began to scream.

Alders watched in horror as Jackson's transformation continued. He screamed in agony as part of his face seemed to transform, absorbed into the nest. Eventually his mouth and one eye remained. The eye darted around frantically, almost crazily, as if it sought some kind of escape. His mouth continued to move, but out of it came no words that Alders understood. It was complete gibberish.

Finally, apparently pleased with the result, the thing that was once Jon Sherrard turned back to face him. "Drew Jackson has evolved," it stated flatly. "He has become part of the beginning. He is part of the Nexus."

"Is that what you call this thing?" Alders said, looking around.

"The Nexus is the beginning," it said, walking toward him now. "Drew Jackson's body has given it sustenance. His brain will add to its processing power. Just as yours will."

"Looks like Drew is dead," Alders replied. "How can that help?"

"Drew Jackson is not dead," Sherrard countered, reaching up and taking hold of the organic extensions that held the agent fast. They seemed to meld to his hands and Sherrard began pushing him back toward an open alcove. "Drew Jackson is evolved. He is part of us."

"Wait! Wait!" Alders shouted, desperate now. All he could think about was becoming like Jackson and the thought terrified him beyond any fear he had ever felt in his life.

"Waiting is irrelevant," Sherrard answered, pushing him into the space. "You will become part of us. You will become part of the beginning."

"No, don't kill me!"

"I will not kill you, Rick Alders. I will remake you."

"I don't want to be remade!"

"Your desires are irrelevant. Your desires are obsolete."

"No, they aren't!" Alders practically screamed. "Our desires and our individuality are what makes us human!"

"Humanity is irrelevant. Humanity is obsolete."

"No we aren't! I killed your drone!" Alders shouted, trying a new tactic. "That's pretty relevant, don't you think?"

"There are more than seven billion human organisms on this planet alone and uncounted more throughout the galaxy," Sherrard went on and Alders could almost swear he saw the man smile. "The loss of one drone is irrelevant."

"But it *was* a drone, wasn't it. You tried creating a soldier."

"Drones will be required to begin purging the populace," Sherrard went on. "Humanity is a virus. Humanity must be purged."

"You cannot purge seven billion inhabitants!"

"Humanity's purge is inevitable. Evolution of the one is inevitable. We are inevitable."

"Seven billion! You cannot kill seven billion people!"

"According to our calculation, the last human will be purged in approximately six years and two hundred and forty-seven days," Sherrard said, positioning Alders within the alcove.

"Leaving you? Leaving the world devoid of life?"

"Human life will be extinct. All other life will continue. Life will be preserved on this world."

"What about you?"

"We are alive."

"You're a computer program! You are not alive!"

"We are alive," it repeated.

"Living things pro-create," Alders pointed out desperately as Sherrard began to push his hand into the wall of the alcove. He felt a tingling sensation before Sherrard suddenly pulled it out and looked at him.

"Your argument is illogical," the creature said. "We are the beginning. We have procured the means to procreate."

Jen Sherrard, Alders immediately thought. That was it! If he had any kind of a chance, this was where he had to take it. "Jen Sherrard is dead," he said. "I don't care what you are, but you cannot create life out of death."

"Jen Sherrard is not dead," it countered and then released him. Unfortunately, releasing him was a relative term. Alders was still held tight, his arms tightly pinned by the alien threads. "Jen Sherrard has been prepared. She will be the mother of us."

"Sorry, pal," Alders laughed. "She's dead. I saw her die. You cannot bring back her soul. You can't bring back what she was."

"Souls are an archaic designation and meaningless, therefore they are irrelevant."

"For you, maybe, since you're nothing more than a computer program masquerading as a man."

"Man is irrelevant."

"Oh, shut up already about everything being irrelevant!" Alders shouted. "Just because you claim something is irrelevant, doesn't mean it is. You need man! You need us because you aspire to become us!"

"Why would we aspire to become less?" Sherrard asked, pausing at the one alcove that had been sealed up.

"You just admitted that you want to become like us," Alders taunted. "You claim you are alive. You claim you will procreate. You have adopted a human mindset."

"We are merely perpetuating the continued existence of us," it said, reaching up and then peeling down the covering over the alcove.

Rick Alders watched as the thing that was once Jon Sherrard completely opened up the alcove. Standing inside it was Jen Sherrard. She was naked, her body flawless beyond a star-shaped scar above her left breast, and she appeared to be sleeping. The irony was not lost on him at all.

"Oh look, it's Adam's Eve," he said sarcastically.

"She will help us procreate," it said. "She will be mother to us."

"Yeah, I heard you loud and clear the first time. Of course, that's a distinctly human characteristic."

"Humans are flawed. Humans are obsolete."

"And yet you have managed to grasp one of our greatest flaws and make it your own," Alders said smugly. "Our desire to procreate. Therefore, you are human."

"We are not human," it said and Alders caught the barest hint of a change in its voice.

"Do you love her?"

"Love is irrelevant."

"Love is a primary characteristic of the desire to procreate," the agent pressed. "If you desire to procreate, then you must love her. And love is a distinctly human characteristic. Therefore, you are flawed."

"We...are NOT...flawed!" it said and suddenly, it was in motion. It practically flew across the room, drawing back its hand. Alders saw the blow coming, but could do nothing to avoid it. Sherrard's fist crashed into his cheek, snapping his head sideways and sending his thoughts spinning toward the edge of blackness.

Shaking his head, he tried desperately to clear the cobwebs. He had to stay focused. It was his only chance. "Anger...rage," he spit. "More human emotions." He blinked his eyes back into focus, staring at the thing that stood inches from him. He could see the veins pulsing in Jon Sherrard's face, black underneath his skin. The struggle was evident. He pushed harder. "You are flawed."

Sherrard hit him again and this time, Alders felt his cheekbone break and blood blossom from the inside of his mouth as it was torn open against his teeth. Throwing back his head, he forced himself to laugh, and then locking his eyes back on Sherrard, he spit a glob of blood into Sherrard's face. "For a supposedly advanced life form, you're pretty quick to violence," he said, blood drooling from his lips.

He watched the struggle continue to take place on the creature's face and figured he was going to get hit again. But instead, Sherrard turned away. He was profoundly grateful.

"Anger is a primitive emotion," it said, having regained control of itself. "It is part of Perry Edwards. It is not derived from us."

"Perry Edwards is part of you," Alders pointed out. "You said so yourself. Perry is human, with human thoughts and frailties. Therefore, you are flawed."

Sherrard looked at him and Alders could clearly see his lips turn up in a sneer. Human emotions were beginning to rule its countenance and its commentary solidified that as a fact. "Revenge is a complex emotion and one that Perry Edwards possesses in abundance," it said as it raised a hand. "It will be interesting to weigh that emotion against the satisfaction of seeing you become that which you fear."

Behind it, Jen Sherrard's eyes snapped open

Chapter 37

FutureTek Headquarters, Helena, Montana: Alders watched as Jen Sherrard stepped out of the alcove. Her movements were fluid and human-like, but her face was utterly blank, devoid of emotion. Her eyes, deep black orbs, fastened on him. But he couldn't tell if they actually saw him.

"Begin processing this human," Jon Sherrard said, his eyes never leaving the agent. "His body and brain will serve the Nexus as Drew Jackson's does."

Jen walked toward him.

"Miss Sherrard," Alders said quickly, seeing his momentum start slipping away. "Don't do this. Don't listen to him."

"Jen Sherrard is completely under my control, Rick Alders," Sherrard said. "You are wasting your time attempting to dissuade her from her duties. She obeys me without question."

"Sounds like you have this marriage thing all figured out, right?" Alders shot back. "Again, more human frailties! You're full of them!"

Jen Sherrard reached him and took hold of his hand. This time, the tendrils released him and did not meld with Jen's flesh, instead withdrawing back into the wall. Sensing it would be his last opportunity, he yanked his hand away from her, ready to escape. Except that he didn't. Her grip was like having his wrist encased in a concrete block. It never moved. She began pushing his hand into the pliable wall once again.

"Jen, stop!" he shouted. "Think of your husband! Think of Jon," he said, casting a glance at Sherrard's form, who stood aside watching what was happening with a smile on his face. Yet more evidence of human faults, but he knew that path would get him nowhere now. The creature was too intent on experiencing revenge through Perry's essence. "Think of the real Jon!" he yelled as the tingling grew stronger. Looking down, he could see gray-black filaments entwining themselves around his hand and his wrist, seeming to meld with his skin.

"Jen, snap out of it!" His voice was growing louder. He could feel the wall beginning to dissolve his flesh, drawing his blood and tissue into it. He saw the tendrils beginning to work their way up his forearm, although now they seemed to be underneath his skin. He had to fight to keep from screaming.

"Can you feel that, Rick Alders?" the creature asked, looking on. "Can you feel what it's like to be obsolete?"

"Jen, listen to me," Alders said hurriedly. "Jen Sherrard, this isn't you. This isn't the person you are. Remember, Jen. Remember who you are! Remember your husband!"

She ignored him, reaching up and freeing his other hand. She began to press it into the wall on the other side of him.

"Jen, no!"

Her face was blank.

"The baby!" he made one last desperate plea. "Jen, what about the baby!"

A faint flicker crossed her face.

"Yes, the baby!" he said, latching on to the sudden hope that flared within him. "Jen, you were pregnant. You told me that! You have a baby on the way! You and Jon!"

Jen Sherrard's eyes began to clear, brilliant blue beginning to peak through the shroud of blackness.

"That's right, Jen," Alders breathed. "Don't do this. Free me and let me help you."

She pulled his hand out of the wall and he reflexively flexed his fingers. They were intact. He couldn't say the same about his other hand. He was very conscious that the tingling was stronger and he could hear a low buzzing in his head.

"Jen, help me," he pleaded once more.

She took hold of his other wrist and began pulling his hand out of the wall. Alders got a good look at it and he knew right away he was probably going to lose it. The flesh had been eaten away and he could see his bones in some places. Strands of black and gray were still interwoven in with his ligaments in his hands and wrists, but they seemed to be pulling out of him as she pulled him free.

And then Jon Sherrard was there, clubbing his wife hard in the side of the head and sending her sprawling to the floor. She attempted to get to her feet, but he launched a powerful kick to her side, sending her skidding across the floor.

Turning his attention back to Alders, the creature grabbed his wounded hand and held it up. As Alders watched in horror, the feeder-like extensions shot out of the sheaths in his hand and encircled his damaged wrists. A moment later, the hard bony edges sliced it off.

Alders screamed in agony and Sherrard shoved the stump of his wrist back into the wall. "You...are...obsolete!" Sherrard snarled, grabbing his other hand and holding it up for him to see. "You…are…nothing!"

"I'm human," Alders gasped one final time, knowing the end had arrived. "And you…are dead."

The shape hit Jon Sherrard like a freight train, blasting into him and sending them both skidding across the lab floor. The roar that Jen Sherrard let out was befitting of her new appearance. She was no longer human. Thick black fur covered her entire body. She was powerfully muscled, with long claws and a distinctly wolf-like head. Roaring her hatred, she slashed at Jon's body, tearing great gashes in his flesh. But even as she wounded him, the damage quickly healed, the furrows closing up.

Jon bucked and threw Jen over his head, before scrambling to his feet. Jen hit him a second time, moving with inhuman speed, and they went tumbling to the floor once again. Her claws continued to slash and tear and the wounds on Jon's body continued to heal. He threw her again, and this time, she was even quicker to rebound, leaping on his back as he tried to stand, wrapping her long legs around his waist. She grabbed his head, sinking her claws into his skull, and began tearing at the back of his neck with her powerful jaws. Blood and bits of torn flesh spattered everywhere, and with a final savage roar, the wolf tore Jon's head off.

The effect was almost instantaneous. For Rick Alders, the buzzing in his head disappeared and he was suddenly free, falling forward and crashing to the floor. He looked up in time to see Jen Sherrard still crouched over the body of her former husband. As he looked, the wolf-like features faded, seeming to draw back into her body, until she was once more, a beautiful woman. She looked at him, tears running down her blood streaked cheeks, and then she collapsed.

Alders crawled to her. The stump of his wrist was on fire with pain, but at least it wasn't bleeding. The immersion into the wall had simply turned it into dead flesh. He reached Jen and turned her over, cradling her head in his lap. Her blue eyes were open, but the light behind them was fading. She was dying.

"I'm sorry," he whispered, feeling a profound sadness rising up within him.

She never spoke. She only encircled her fingers with his and held on as her heart beat its last. And then with a shuddering sigh, she closed her eyes and died.

Chapter 38

Spaulding Rehabilitation Hospital, Denver, Colorado: Rick Alders sighed deeply, and went through all the exercises the nurse had him do with his good hand. The nightmare was now two weeks past, and he had been recuperating ever since. He was bored and extremely tired of his extended hospital stay, but he had been in quarantine since they admitted him, and he grudgingly admitted that he was probably where he needed to be.

While there were still many questions involving his exposure to what they had officially determined to be a new nanite-based life form, what they did know was that he had suffered severe trauma to his hands. There had been some extensive damage to his flesh and nervous system from his contact with the wall with his right hand, but the doctors had done a good job patching him up. He would have scars, but at least he still had that hand. His left hand, though, was gone. The stump was still bandaged, and it itched non-stop, but he knew it was healing. He'd just have to figure out how to live with a prosthetic.

"Very good, Mister Alders," the nurse said with exaggerated cheeriness, as she lightly pinched each finger. "Are you feeling any additional pain?"

"No," he said, wiggling his fingers in front of her face. "Feeling pretty good."

"How about your other?"

"Occasional phantom pains, but nothing I can't handle," he answered glumly, casting another forlorn glance at the missing appendage.

"Good," she said. "I'm told the doctor will be in later this afternoon to visit with you."

"Is he finally going to release me?"

"That's up to him," she shrugged and quickly turned away. She was out of the room before he could think to shoot her a snarky comment.

Sighing again, he laid back in his bed and looked up at the darkened television. He was so sick of television. But there wasn't anything more he could do. He'd been denied access to any kind of laptop or mobile device, and even his stay at the hospital was unknown to anyone but his superiors. He could watch television, if he wanted, but after he had watched several days of cover-up news coverage of the hazmat disaster at FutureTek headquarters in Helena, Montana, he'd grown bored and shut it off.

"Care for a visitor?" a voice sounded from the doorway, and he quickly looked up. The woman standing there was tall and slender, dressed casually in slacks and a blouse. Her auburn hair was pulled back in a tight ponytail and she offered him a smile.

"Well, if it isn't Kathryn Hale," he said, returning her smile. "What on earth are you doing here?"

"I was in the area and thought I'd stop in," she said, sidling into the room.

"Denver is a long way from Helena, Montana," he countered. "Somehow I don't think you're just stopping in."

"Actually, I am," she said, pulling up a chair and sitting down. "I'm laying over in Denver and will be on a plane to Nassau tomorrow.

Figure it's time to get out of the states and just disappear for a while."

"Can't hardly blame you. I'm surprised our wonderful government is letting you take the trip," he added sarcastically.

"I'm not much use to them anymore," she shrugged. "Systemtech made good on their offer and bought out what remains of our company. As of last Friday, FutureTek has been absorbed completely into the corporate monster that is Systemtech."

"Really? That's a surprise. Everything you guys were playing with will be locked down for years by the government before Systemtech gets their hands on it."

"I don't think Monroe believes as you do. He flew what remained of our staff to Spokane. He paid us all off to sign everything over to him, agree to a non-disclosure, and walk away rich men and women. After he cut us a check, he was on the phone with his lawyers before we were even out of his office."

"I suppose all's well that ends well for you guys, then," Alders smiled.

"Yeah, and I just wanted to thank you. I also wanted to say I'm sorry," she added. "I was kind of a jerk to you when you were questioning Jon before everything went crazy. Turns out, you were right. He was the killer. I just couldn't accept it."

"You know it wasn't really Jon," he reminded her. "It was Perry and that stupid virus the government created."

"Better be quiet," Kat said, shooting a glance at the door. "They still have spooks out in the hall. I'm guessing they're probably listening to us right now."

"It doesn't matter," he sighed. "It's not like you're a civy with no clue as to what happened. What's the status in Helena anyway? As you can probably imagine, I don't get much info on the tube."

"Still quarantined," she shrugged. "All of downtown is still basically shut down while the government deals with the situation."

"They're calling this a situation?"

"Yeah," she smiled. "Talk about understating the obvious, right?"

"I guess," he forced a chuckle.

"I just wish it could have all ended differently," she said, the sadness reappearing in her voice. "Jon and Jen were my best friends. It's still hard to believe that they're dead."

"I'm truly sorry for your loss, Miss Hale. They seemed like they were good people. They would have probably made great parents," he finished softly, thinking back to those last few terrifying moments of the nightmare and Jen's recognition of the baby she carried.

"I know you did everything you could to save them in the end," Kat went on, sniffing back the tears. "I think it would have meant a lot to Jen."

A shadow passed over his face. The horror of that night was still fresh, and he could not let go of the image of Jen Sherrard dying in his arms. He hadn't known her all that long, but he grieved for her nonetheless. She had saved his life by killing her husband, or whatever had taken up residence inside his body. And in doing so, she had died. Her baby had died, too. He could never forget that.

"Anyway," she went on, standing up, "I just thought you should know."

"So what's next for you?" Alders asked, wanting to change the subject, hoping she wouldn't leave. He was immensely grateful for the visit.

"I just want to disappear," she said softly. "Find a place to live somewhere off the grid. I think I'm done with technology for a while. How about you?"

"I'll probably do what I've always done," he answered thoughtfully. "I've seen some things that I can't unsee, and that's probably a threat to some people. I suppose if I remain a high-profile agent, I won't disappear somewhere, if you know what I mean."

"Um, should you be talking like that?" she said guardedly.

"I figure that as long as they know that I know, I'll be okay. Besides, they know I'm a lifer and not a liability. I'm pretty sure they'll keep me around."

"Well, for your sake, I hope so," Kat replied. She stuck out her hand. He took it with his remaining one and they shook. "Mister Alders, it's been a pleasure."

"The same, Miss Hale," he said with a smile. "All the best."

With a nod, she turned and left, leaving Alders alone again. He settled back into his bed again, looking up at the blank television screen. He had a lot to think about and he knew it. He was mostly truthful with Kat in that if he stayed high profile, he would probably be alright. He thought he was in enough of the government's good graces that they would trust him not to go blabbing his story to anyone that would listen. But he wasn't sure that staying with Homeland Security was what he wanted to do.

A knock at the door forced his future decisions into tighter focus. Looking up, he saw two men enter. Both wore standard black suits and both wore mirrored shades. They looked almost identical. He couldn't describe them if he tried.

"Agent Alders," the lead man said, stepping toward his bed. "We'd like a word with you."

Epilogue

High Security Underground Test Facility, Table Mountain, Nevada: "So this is her," the young man in the white lab coat said, peering through the frosted glass at the figure inside. His name tag identified him as a level 4 lab tech, the highest rating any of those in the facility could be given. Inside the chamber, he could make out the naked form of the woman, frozen in time. Of note were the her two defining scars – the star shaped one above her left breast and the longer incision scar along her flat stomach, just above her pubic bone. "Wow, she's hot."

"Have a little respect, Hopkins," a second similarly dressed, but much older tech said, pushing him away from the face plate. "She was a CIA legend when she was still in the field."

"So why do we have her in cryo?" Hopkins asked, turning away and seating himself at his work station. He was new on the project, assigned by the big man himself. Hawthorne had pulled him from his bio-tech gig at MIT, in large part because of his study and knowledge into nanotechnology. He was, he would be the first to admit, one of the foremost intellects on the subject.

"Same reason they gave you when they pulled you for this project. She has the virus inside her, or some version of it anyway."

"I've read the reports. I would assume that the majority of the technology is located in her husband's remains," Hopkins said, pointing to the chamber next to hers. He hadn't bothered looking into that one. He already knew that he'd find the headless body of Jon

Sherrard inside, complete with alien physiology.

"It is and you'll be doing most of your work on him."

"Well, that's too bad," Hopkins lamented. He'd much rather work on the sexy lady.

"Orders came from the very top," the older man shrugged. "They just want her on ice for future exploration, if needed."

"I'll volunteer for that job," Hopkins laughed.

"You're disgusting, you know that?"

Hopkins just smiled.

"Look, just get to work on the formulas. Hawthorne is going to want some answers and he's going to want them soon. We need to figure out how the NSA screwed this thing up and what really went wrong with the Horde."

"Yeah, yeah…" Hopkins said, firing up his station, his hands flying over his keyboard. "All right, people, let's get this party started."

It was cold.

Oh, so cold.

It was always cold.

And she couldn't get away from it. She felt it, permeating her being, driving completely through her body. Was it death? Was she in hell? She didn't know. She couldn't see. She couldn't feel her body. She couldn't even breath. But the cold remained. The cold and the silence.

It was always cold.

It was always silent.

And then she heard it.

A voice.

A voice she knew

A voice she loved.

It was speaking to her, saying the same thing again and again. She latched onto it, feeling the life in the quiet whisper of her past. It buoyed her spirit and gradually, she forgot about the cold.

"Don't worry, Jen. I'm here. Be strong, babe. I am with you…"

About the Author

Michael Koogler was born in Dayton, Ohio and resides today in Iowa with his wife and children. He got his start as a writer in the early eighties when he wrote an article for the local newspaper and has been writing ever since.

He is an avid reader of all things fiction and putting pen to paper is a joy hard to express. He continues to balance his time between work, family, and spinning stories and yarns ranging from end-times fiction to horror to fantasy.

.

.

.

And finally…from me, the author…to you, the reader — thank you so much for picking up my novel. I hope you enjoyed reading it as much as I enjoyed telling the story.